The Nightfall Trials

Book 1 of The Elders' Hex series

THE CARAVAN	11
THE SECONDBORN	28
TAYNA	34
THE RED MOON SQUARE	40
CHOSEN BY THE ELDERS	48
THE GOVERNOR	54
A FEAST IN THE WASTELANDS	68
LAST MINUTES OF DAYLIGHT	86
TEÍR MEKHERET	90
THE TOWER	96
THE FALL	103
THE WARDED MANSION	115
THE KEEPER	123
THE GOLDEN CAGE	134
THE WELL	142
THE DARK WORLD	150
THE FOREST HUT	160
DEATH AT DAWN	171
NIGHTHAVEN	181
THE UNSEELIE COURT	197
THE ROOM OF REFLECTIONS	214
AEIDAS'S HAPPY PLACE	225
THE COTTAGE	233
A MIDNIGHT SNACK	245
DEATH IN THE MIST	256
THE MONSTER FROM THE DEPTHS	267
THE SANCTUARY	276
THE LAST SUNSET	292

THE HORDE	296
LONG LIVE THE KING	314
THE PITS	325
THE SCAFFOLD	330
ESCAPE	337
THE PROPHECY	339
EPILOGUE	344

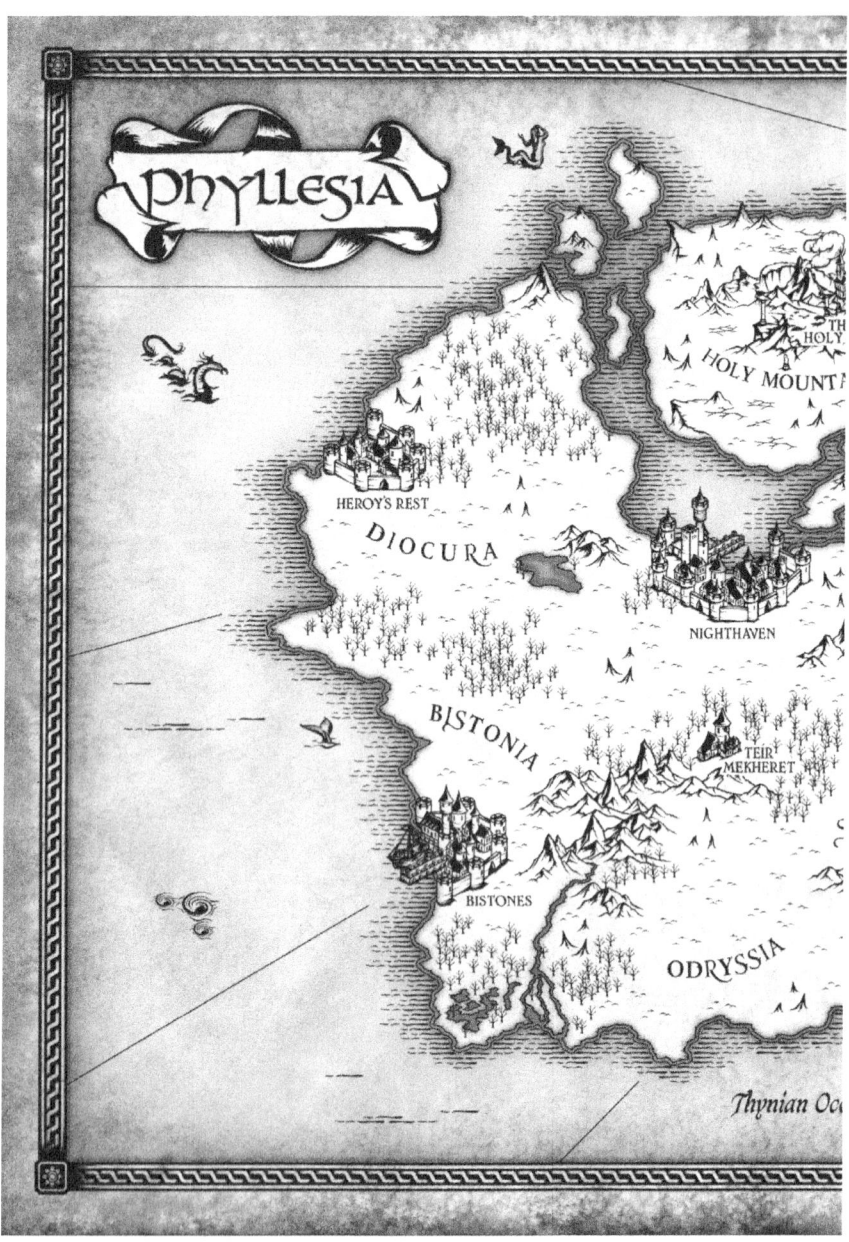

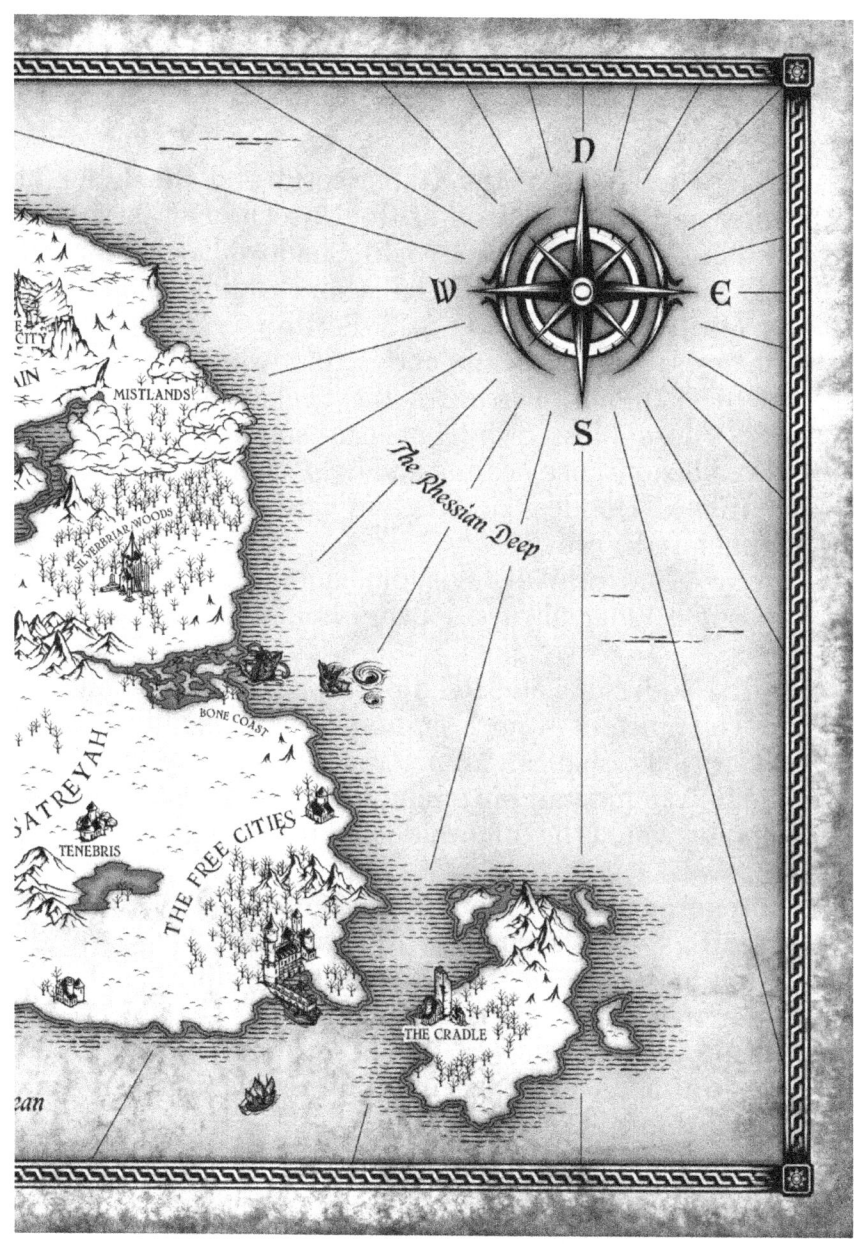

CHARACTERS

The Elders' Pantheon

Atos - The Ruler of the Underworld and the Elder of Winter and Night. Patron of the Unseelie Fae. A chosen few blessed by him can wield Shadowblades and use spells like kinetic blasts, fireballs, air bending, and more.

Cymmetra - Goddess of Fertility and Nature, protectress of hunters and agriculture, wine, the daylight, and the summer. Patron of the Seelie Fae, partner of Atos. Those blessed by her can summon Sunblades, weave illusions, use healing and light spells.

Raynisse - Goddess of Arts and Crafts, depicted with a hammer and a brush.

Heroy - God of War, Wisdom, and Debate. The most handsome Elder always appears holding a sword and a book.

Seuta - Elder of Fate, Relationships, Love, Community, and Tolerance. A shapeless, non-physical deity who can take various shapes: a maid, a child, or a domestic animal, watching and listening to people's conversations. Seuta instigated the other Elders to cast the Hex.

Characters (Alphabetical Order):

- **Aeidas** - The second-born son of the Unseelie King, heir to the throne after the death of his brother.
- **Aernysse Stargaze** - The court mage of the Unseelie King.
- **Aydalla** - A Fae participant in the Nightfall Trials, a court huntress.
- **Ayrene** - A human girl living in the Unseelie palace, Talysse's maid.
- **Chiron** - The high priest of the Five Elders in Nighthaven.
- **Desmond** - Aeidas's rat friend.

- **Eloysse** - The mage protector of Tenebris.
- **Ephraina** - A cousin of Tayna's adoptive parents.
- **Friar Ben Hasoth** - A caretaker and teacher in the Blessed Dawn orphanage.
- **Galeoth** - A contestant in the Trials who allies with Talysse.
- **Godey Goldtooth** - Innkeeper of the Bountiful Bosom Inn where Talysse helps as a serving maid sometimes.
- **Haeddyn** - A Fae courtier who attacks Talysse.
- **Lord Nyxie** - The kitchen cat in the Unseelie palace.
- **Magister Deepwell** - The highest-ranking human in the city of Tenebris, serving as a mayor and magistrate, reporting to the Unseelie Governor of the province.
- **Myrtle** - Talysse's best friend and business partner.
- **Ornatus** - An ancient mage and holy man from the dead city Teír Mekheret.
- **Raynar** - a stable boy in the Unseelie palace, Ayrene's brother.
- **Sorayah the Songstress** - Beloved of Ornatus.
- **Sorcia** - The fiancée of Aeidas's dead brother.
- **Squinting Ann** - A shady character from the back alleys of Tenebris.
- **Stebian** - Myrtle's son.
- **Talysse** - An orphaned human with a secret.
- **Tayna** - Talysse's sister.
- **The Child (or Lord Deirhaîm)** - An ancient vampire, appearing as a child, a contestant in the Nightfall Trials.
- **The Mercenary** - A human contestant in the Nightfall Trials.
- **The Warrior Pony Princess (Tomira)** - A female human contestant in the Trials, nicknamed WPP by Talysse.

- **Viridis** - An ancient Dryad, confidante, and tutor of Prince Aeidas, tending to the royal gardens.
- **Woodrick** - A Fae participant in the Nightfall Trials, a shifter.

PROLOGUE

Friar Ben Hasoth's history lecture for the children of the Blessed Light Orphanage:

"Gather around and listen closely now, for today, we delve into the history of our world. Even the gods who shaped this realm from starlight, stone, and pure magic—the Elders—cannot recall who first ignited the flames of the endless war. What we do know is that the only victors were those who feasted on flesh and bone, reveling in the bloodshed.

"Centuries of relentless conflict between the Seelie and Unseelie Fae have ravaged our world, leaving it in smoldering ruins. The once-sacred mountain, home of the Elders, is now but a shattered memory. Enraged by the Fae's ceaseless slaughter of innocents, the Elders split the mountain asunder and left this realm, cursing it. Fiery rivers erupted from the summit, consuming all life and transforming the lands around it into a poisoned wasteland. For years, black vapors shrouded the sun, and from this eternal twilight, the Shadowfeeders emerged. Their tainted touch turned every living being into mindless thralls, ravenous for the flesh of the living.

"The Elders' curse has hexed our world and all who inhabit it. Nights now stretch unnaturally long, sometimes enduring for weeks, bringing with them death and despair. The Shadowfeeders and their armies of thralls—the Tainted Ones—are the true rulers of our world, not the Unseelie Fae who falsely claim victory.

"The war is over, but we—the humans and all living souls—have lost everything.

"Now, I know what you're thinking: is there hope? Of course there is! Despite the nights growing longer and darker, and the Shadowfeeders creeping ever closer to the few remaining cities, the Elders, in their mercy, left us a tiny flicker of hope—the Blessed Light. A magic spell only the most skilled mages can cast, our only protection against the night and its horrors. These mages are our true heroes and protectors, not the armies of the Unseelie King who enter the human provinces only to collect taxes. Their Blessed Light spells shield our dwellings in the light of the Elders, protecting us during the long nights and helping our crops grow. But, as with all precious things in this tormented world, mages are incredibly rare…"

TALYSSE

THE CARAVAN

Sunsets are the most dreadful thing. The death of the light is even worse when you know what lurks in the dark, and you hope and pray that you will live to see the sunrise.

When the light starts fading, doors are locked, kids are called home, and animals are herded into the stalls. All eyes turn to the horizon, exploding with orange and pink, and many draw triangles in the dust at their doorsteps—the sacred symbol of the Holy Mountain, home of the Elders.

I scoff. As if any of this could stop those who come with the darkness.

The gilded palanquin glides through the streets like a vision from a lost, better world. The peeling gold leaf catches the last sun's rays, and the warm breeze billows the curtains like the sails of a ghostly ship. Townsfolk bow as it passes, but I keep my eyes fixed on the mage inside. Glossy black curls, eyes cold as a frozen lake, ruby lips a thin line—she is the most beautiful woman I've ever seen, though beauty is common among the Fae.

Her impassive features betray nothing. Will the Blessed Light spell hold until dawn? Will her spell be strong enough to protect the city and the fields? The Unseelie mage scolds her servants to hurry up without sparing us, the commoners, a glance.

"May your nights be short, Blessed One!"

"The Elders bless you!" Shouts ripple through the crowd, eyes darting to the sky, lips moving in prayers. More and more townsfolk murmur against the Unseelie oppressors, but mage Eloysse is our only protector and the closest thing to a hero we have in Tenebris. Concerned eyes follow the mage's procession as everyone tries to guess how long the night will be. The last one spanned over a week. And tonight, something is alarming in the angle the dying light hits the pavement on the market streets, in the way the pigeons grew quiet and disappeared from the roofs of the Temple of the Elders.

Mage Eloysse is running late. A merchant caravan, larger than any seen in Tenebris this year, has just arrived, and she was probably eager for news.

The nights are getting longer. Rumor has it Eloysse's powers are barely enough to hold our wards against the darkness and keep the Beacon alight. The city has grown too big, its outskirts barely touched by the halo of the Blessed Light, but the Unseelie Governor refuses to send one of his precious mages to help Eloysse. Or he's doing it on purpose—too many humans means too many eyes spotting the injustice we have suffered from the Unseelie for centuries. A rebellion in the human provinces is the last thing the king needs after the untimely death of his heir and his weakening grip on the crown.

The last crimson rays disappear behind the roofs. For one long moment, the city stands still, holding its breath.

Terror trickles down the crumbling walls, gathers in the street corners, and gains flesh in the back alleys. I ball my fists so hard that my nails dig into my flesh. Will the city go down with the last light?

A crackle of magic and golden light erupts from the Beacon, spilling over the city like a shimmering veil. I let out a breath with a hiss. The magical halo unfolds from the Beacon at the heart of Tenebris—the tallest tower—and ripples over the city all the way to the walls and the fields beyond. The sounds of life swiftly return to the streets. Street musicians start a merry tune down the Merchants' Alley, someone hums, children laugh, and the housewives start dinner.

I tuck a few stray strands into my crown braid and head down the road to the Bountiful Bosom Inn. Everyone loathes the darkness, but the night is the time to make money, and the Elders know that I need it.

Many seek comfort from the dread of the long nights in the company of others. Is there a better way to forget that death lurks beyond the fragile protection of the magical halo than some sweet wine, some loud music, and friendly faces?

Carrying a heavy tray loaded with roasted ribs, honey buns, poppy seed sconces, and chalices dripping with sticky mead, I swiftly meander between tables and patrons. The aroma of the fresh food and the spices makes me drool.

The caravan that has arrived today has lured many townspeople to the inn, and there are many tables to tend to. A caravan is always a reason to celebrate, as Tenebris is too far away from the big cities and the trading routes of Phyllesia. Traveling the Wastelands is becoming increasingly difficult lately. Caravans have their own mages to protect them from the Shadowfeeders and armed to-the-teeth mercenaries to keep the Tainted Ones at bay, as many lose their way in the dark, never to be seen again. Since I was able to walk to the fence of my father's mansion and peek outside, I've wondered how the world beyond the city walls is and was a little jealous of those brave enough to travel. Father has told me of his travels, about the caravan mages taking turns to cast the Blessed Light spell, their portable crystals shrouding the camp tents in a shimmering veil of magic, of terrifying sounds in the night, and clashes with hordes of Tainted Ones. There is a whole world out there, dead, gruesome, and cruel, but also full of marvels like starry skies, oceans, and abandoned cities waiting to be discovered. The itch for the unknown had settled in since my childhood.

"Charred woods, burnt lands, desolated cities, and monsters, lots of monsters," is all my best friend Myrtle says when I talk about my plan to flee to the Free Cities. She is probably right that there is not much left of the world out there, just the bustling Unseelie metropolises, fattened up by the wealth of the whole realm, but the legendary Free Cities at the shores of the Thynian Ocean have become my only hope. A human autonomy where everyone is free to be what they desire.

Slamming the mead on the table, I startle the newcomers, who utter their thanks with a strange accent. The locals are already buying them drinks, trying to untie their tongues. Everyone craves news from the outside world, as messengers rarely reach us. There's nothing precious we can offer the Unseelie overlords, so they seem to have forgotten about our existence.

Experience has taught me to instantly recognize different types of travelers. The artists and bards are dressed in colorful and expensive clothes; they tend to splurge on extravagant meals and give generous tips. The merchants are the opposite; they're wearing inconspicuous but fine garments and keep to themselves. Mercenaries and mages are quite obvious, and I prefer to avoid them. But there are other types of customers tonight, and their presence gives me chills: the Unseelie.

Their too-beautiful faces and the way they look at us are just creepy—as if stripping us of our flesh and staring directly into our minds. Something is stirring in the Unseelie kingdom, but all Fae can rot for all I care. Unseelie and their wretched politics are problems of Magister Deepwell, not of the common townsfolk. From me, Fae have already taken everything they could—my parents and my old life.

I quickly collect the greasy, empty plates and head back to the kitchens, hoping to find Myrtle.

The inn is alive with music—the sounds of flutes, drums, and violins fill the air, making feet tap and smiles bloom. Couples twirl in dance, cheered on by the clapping patrons around them.

Darting among the tables, I serve drinks and steaming plates with food and bat away a few naughty hands. It's close to midnight when Myrtle finally appears. Elders, she has really made an effort tonight. Her unruly curls are gathered up in an intricate hairdo, and the deep neckline of her dress invites everyone to take a longer look. But the way she scans the men around is purely professional. Just like me, she is here on business. A child out of wedlock has put Myrtle on the streets. Forced to sell her flesh to strangers, she quickly accepted my suggestion for a partnership. If the evening is good, we will meet dawn with a decent amount of coin in our pockets.

Godey Goldtooth flashes his radiant smile behind the bar, pouring drinks and keeping a close eye on us, serving maids. He makes sure that the Bountiful Bosom provides everything a traveler craves after the soul-draining nights in the Wastelands but does not trade with flesh. So, Myrtle and the other girls take their customers to the dark alleys outside, where anything might happen.

The air is thick with the smell of booze, unwashed bodies, and tobacco. The travelers have attracted the usual crowd, starved for news and a good bargain: prostitutes, musicians, beggars, and all kinds of shady opportunists.

The next time I pass by Myrtle, the hands of a skinny stranger are wrapped tightly around her waist, and she winks at me as she stomps her new red slippers in the fiery rhythm of the drums. The candlelight gilds her brown curls, and her dark eyes sparkle with delight. My arms strain from the weight of the mead chalices, but I nod and smile, responding to her signal while navigating the crowd.

The man she dances with is the perfect target. He's dressed in silvery brocade and probably has just arrived with the merchants' caravan. The way he gropes Myrtle would have made my blood boil, but I know that Myrtle intends to be groped. It is part of our plan. She's like those colorful blossoms Friar Ben has told us about, who lure the lost insects to their death. The merchant's eyes are glazed from the mead, yet I place another chalice in his hand. The more drunk, the better.

Myrtle would exhaust him with dancing and invite him to a more private place later. She always takes our targets to the stables—the place where I've been spending my nights since I ran away from the Blessed Dawn orphanage. Depending on their state, she offers them her company, or if they are too sober—I'd join and suggest a game of dice or cards and more drinks. The goal is always simple—getting whatever is in their pockets. Judging by the heavy silver chain with rubies around the man's neck, this will be one very profitable evening.

The crowd thins after dinner as many patrons take to the streets. There are always artists and musicians traveling with caravans, and there are people already gathering on Red Moon Square. A rare treat has been announced tonight: a puppet spectacle, and the whole city is crackling with anticipation. Each distraction in the dull life in Tenebris is more than welcome.

Myrtle and her companion are still dancing, but she nods at me when I pass by them. Her partner is barely standing on his feet. It is time. After wiping off the last table in my section, I untie my apron and hand it over to Godey.

"I am going to dress up and go to see the show, Godey," I say while dropping the five copper pieces he gave me in my pocket. What he's paying for helping out at the inn is enough to buy a piece of bread and some sour apples once a week but not to make a living. He took pity on me years ago and has been turning a blind eye to me sleeping in his stables ever since, but if he knew of my side business, he would hand me straight to the City Guard. Blessed be the Elders; he is not suspecting of my odd partnership with Myrtle.

"Go have your fun, lass," he rumbles behind the bar as I head to the door.

The familiar smell of hay, laced with manure and horse sweat, welcomes me as I push open the tall plank doors. The stable boys have left already, probably eager to see the show or spend their scant wages at the merchant stalls on the Red Moon square.

The stables are nearly full, caravan horses are deeper in the longhouse, the animals' breathing and shuffling echoing in the warm air. I throw myself on the hay-strewn floor in my corner next to the door, snuggling in my old blanket.

Elders, I'm tired. And the night is just beginning.

Resting my back against an old saddle, I dim the flame of the lantern. My hand finds the loose floorboard easily and slips underneath. I sigh in relief when my fingers touch my sparse belongings. Some clothes, a lock of my mother's hair, Tayna's old doll, a letter my father sent me from one of his many business trips that I know by heart, and most importantly—my purse. Since my sister got adopted by that horrible noble family, and I ran away from the Blessed Dawn orphanage, every coin I came across lands in it. It is our only hope, our way out, our escape. Soon, there will be enough money there to buy us a caravan passage to the Free Cities, where I can find a job, and Tayna can go back to school like a twelve-year-old girl should. By the hell pits of Atos, the night is so promising that it could be tonight!

A cackle makes the horses prick up their ears and snort. Myrtle is finally coming.

Slamming the loose plank down, I cover it with straw just when the door flies open, and she stumbles in, supporting the stranger she was dancing with. His hands are all over her tight bodice as they walk past me, my friend whispering something in his ear. They stumble deeper into the stables, and when the merchant leans into her neck and grabs her ass, Myrtle throws me a look over her shoulder. It is one of those looks we women use to communicate with other women only. He is totally drunk, her black eyes tell me. He will pass out soon. I give her a thumbs up, and they leave the light circle of the only lantern here.

Soon, it will be my turn.

I snuggle in my blanket, blending in with the straw and the grooming tools scattered around, the straw poking my skin under my worn-out cotton dress. I pretend to be asleep but watch carefully what's happening under my half-closed eyelids.

The weight of the man is pulling her to the floor. Good. The sooner he passes out the easier for me and Myrtle. It will be over fast, and hopefully, we'll get to see the puppet show and make some more money. There are two possible scenarios for this situation: if he passes out, we will just relieve him of his possessions and let him sleep it off. The other option is he stays awake and gets frisky. Then I'd pretend to wake up, startled by the noise, and offer them a game of dice or cards while he ingests the amount of alcohol needed to pass out. Then we're going to check the contents of his pockets.

It has always worked so far. We have targeted travelers and rarely local men. All of them were too drunk to remember anything and assumed they lost their coin gambling. The business has been going great for two years, and Myrtle was able to rent a small room across the inn and take good care of her baby boy.

Should we take the heavy silver chain off his neck? There's a pawn shop in the back alleys, and its owner never asks questions. Worth considering. An alarming thud from the shadows where Myrtle and the man went startles the horses. A grunt, some shuffling, and a muffled moan confirm my suspicion that something is not right.

Knowing every plank in these stables, makes it easy to sneak around the murky light from the lantern hanging high on the beams to the dark outline of two intertwined bodies on the floor.

The brocade tunic of the merchant is ruffled as he is struggling to stay on top of Myrtle. His white, bony fingers are rolling her skirt up. He looks far more sober than before, but the really alarming thing is the silvery glimmer of something pressed against her neck.

Elders.

He's holding a knife.

Myrtle spots me over his shoulders, and we have another wordless conversation.

"I am fine," her dark eyes say, "go ahead and do your part while he is busy."

I believe her. Women in her line of work can protect themselves. A well-aimed kick in the groin always works, especially when they expect you to be helpless.

Proceed with the plan, she winks.

I drop and crawl nearer, soundless as a shadow. The man grunts, his blade not so close to her neck now. We all know that type. They like it rough and need an extra kick to do the deed. His pants slip down his thighs, and Myrtle's eyes urge me to get closer.

My fingers crawl closer to his pants, and she points her chin to the left. So, this is where he keeps his money. When I landed on the streets, pickpocketing was the first available career option for someone that young, but I never took to it. After completing the training of some older kids with moderate success, it became obvious that I am lacking something essential to be a good thief: inconspicuous looks. People always noticed and remembered the odd white strand in my raven black hair and my unusually bright eyes, so different than the blonde and hazel-eyed Satreyans like Tayna. So, years ago, I dropped pickpocketing for far more lucrative and complex schemes.

My hand snakes into his pocket, and I grin at Myrtle when I feel the cool, hard touch of silver. It's Free Cities' money, easy to tell by the relief of the coins, but silver is silver anyway, even if it is not Unseelie money. Half of the dozen coins should suffice, slip my wrist out, and prepare to crawl back into the shadows. That was easy.

Myrtle's legs, sprawled around the merchant's bare ass, are suddenly stiff. That cannot be good. Peeking over his brocade jerkin, my breath hitches. The blade is leaving a bloody trail over the olive skin of my friend. Panic creeps into her wide-opened eyes.

My plan to crawl away and then pretend to enter the stables, faking a loud surprise, is immediately abandoned.

I react without thinking and regret it instantly. Acting on impulse, I grab the man's legs, attempting to yank him off Myrtle. Startled, he drags the blade down between her breasts, cutting deeper before he realizes what's happening. Then he swiftly rolls over and slashes the air just inches away from my bodice, his eyes mad but sober.

"Are you trying to rob me, you stupid whore?" he snarls, unclear if he means Myrtle or me.

I am on my feet, considering whether to run and call for help—the inn is just a hundred feet away, and the merry music spills into the night. But a bloodied, confused Myrtle, her face twisted by pain, struggles to stand up, and a tide of primal rage floods my common sense.

No way she stays alone with this madman. He is up and slashes the air with his blade, and I almost stumble backward, stunned by his ferocity. "Atos take you," I curse, and just like that, what was a normal evening turns into a fight for our lives.

He slashes again, a mad smile curling his thin lips. Leaping back, I raise my fists defensively, and he snorts. As if they would protect me against the ten-inch razor-sharp blade.

"I bet you didn't expect that, right?" He leaps forward, the knife slicing my sleeve open and nearly cutting the flesh beneath. "You think I haven't figured out the little game you two are playing?" I let him talk and drop to the floor to avoid another swing, delivering a well-aimed punch in his thigh. The man gasps, and for one brief moment, I nearly burst out

22

in cackle. If it weren't a life-and-death brawl with a madman, it would have looked ridiculous, as the man is naked from the waist down and trips frequently in his pants.

Then he makes an odd gurgling sound and stumbles back.

Myrtle hangs for her dear life on his back, her bloodied forearm pressed against his throat. He recovers fast and throws himself with all his weight to the floor, crushing her under his weight. He swiftly turns around, facing the now unconscious Myrtle, and raises his blade.

This could end so badly.

"I will cut you open now, then your friend. And rest assured, nobody would miss two thieving whores; even if they do, I will pay my way out, just like I always do—" He hisses through clenched teeth, pure hatred lacing his voice.

There has to be a way to clean up that mess, as there are certainly people who'd miss us. Myrtle's young son, who has just started walking and is the main reason she's agreed to that little scheme of ours, and my gentle, golden-haired young sister, who would be married off to the highest bidder if I don't find a way to get her out of the greedy claws of her adoptive family. If only this rabid dog could see this; if he could understand that the brutal life out there has shaped us into what we are, that without money, we are all doomed, stuck and waiting here for the Fae to summon their mage back and leave us unprotected in these long, hopeless nights.

Yet, I decide to save my breath. Men like him have preyed on women like us since the dawn of time. He thinks himself superior, a predator, stalking the nameless and voiceless people like us. If we die, the City Guard won't waste time investigating. One wrong step, and we will be just two corpses carted to the Gallows Hills' pits—the mass grave for poor sods like us.

Death comes quietly and swiftly for the commoners of Tenebris. And in some cases, it is even welcomed by the deceased one's family and neighbors. One less mouth to feed, less precious space to occupy under the magical halo.

Well, if he's a predator, he's a weasel, not the lion he thinks he is, and it is time to teach him a lesson. The streets are a hard teacher, a brutal lover; they beat into all of us the simple lesson to never show vulnerability. There are too many like this bastard who get drunk on the feeling of being in charge. Myrtle knows that very well, too; that's why she didn't fret when the weasel held the blade to her throat.

It's time to show him that he has picked the wrong nameless women to mess with.

Fists against a knife are bad odds, so it's time to fight dirty, too. Time ceases to exist when I close my eyes. The stables dissolve into nothingness. Ancient power thrums from the depths of the silvery lake in my mind. Its still, heavy waters reflect strange constellations, spelling my name. The magic within calls to me, tempts me, stirring a visceral hunger for something indescribable—like the cryptic message of a dream that seeks one out every night, elusive, yet persistent.

This magic simmering beneath the heavy waters is a tantalizing promise of power that I have struggled to resist since childhood. Mother and Father, aware of the danger it poses, had taught me to conceal my gift.

When you're born with the rarest commodity on Phyllesia, you have a bullseye painted on your back. Not all mages end on gilded palanquins like Eloysse.

But right now, a blade hovers over Myrtle's heaving chest, so I let the deep hum of the waters resonate with my bones, down to my marrow. Answering its siren's call is easy, and its power crawls along my veins, fills my insides, and blurs my mind.

The world quickly gains its shape back; its contours are sharper than ever. My fingers flash shimmering claws as I unleash the scorching power thrumming within me. The merchant is hurled across the stables and lands against a wooden beam, snapping it like a toothpick. His knife is lost somewhere in the straw. He lets out a pained gasp and then lies sprawled like a rag doll.

By the Elders, is he dead?

Silver sparks still shower in the stale air like specks of dust in the sunlight, and the horses have grown unnaturally still.

"Talysse," Myrtle calls me softly, struggling to stand up. I kneel next to her, pressing my sleeve to the cut on her chest. "Did you kill him?" she asks, shaking just a little. Terror surfaces in her last words, visions of gallows and nameless graves, of our loved ones tossed into cruel fates.

Overcoming my natural instinct to run is not easy. Helping Myrtle up, we drag ourselves to the motionless man. She disgustedly pokes his pale thigh with her red slipper.

"The bastard is still alive, Talysse." She spits on the floor and points at his evenly rising chest. She drags a bloodied hand over her face and brushes the straw off her skirt.

"Let's pray he won't remember a thing. He can twist the story and tell that we have attacked him, and the City Guard would rather favor his version than ours. Did you," her voice drops to a whisper, "use your gift?"

A gift, she calls it, as the word "magic" is dangerous, even this deep into the provinces of the Unseelie Kingdom. Though curse is a more fitting name for that silver lake that lets me borrow its spells when things get tight.

Mages are nearly extinct since the Elders unleashed the Hex upon our world and left us all to fend for ourselves. As soon as one is identified, it's reported straight to the Unseelie Governor. Their fate after is unclear—they are either tossed into the deadly Nightfall Trials or taken to the Unseelie court for "training," never to be seen again. At least the humans. Lost are the powerful spells of the old days when mages could split mountains, summon armies of spirits, move oceans, and create objects out of thin air. Fae and humans alike are left with some defensive and weapon-conjuring spells and the Blessed Light, the cruel gods' only mercy. The couple of spells I wield are at the level of a village fair magician, but they grant me the element of surprise and have saved me more than once.

"Don't worry, Myrtle. I bet his ego is too fragile, and he won't tell anybody that he got beaten up by—how did he call us? Whoring thieves?"

Laughter is the best medicine, and we cackle like two mad witches over the unconscious merchant at our feet. If someone sees us right now, we'd certainly end up at the Gallows Hills.

"Come to my room, Talysse," Myrtle pleas as we prepare to head out. "Then we will see."

"The night is still young." I peek out of the stable doors. The crescent of the moon is still high beyond the golden veil of protective light cupping the city. The warm breeze carries music and laughter from the Red Moon square. "The caravan is still here; think of all the possibilities. But you need to get back home, Myrtle. Clean that wound up."

She tosses me a long, silent look, wiping the blood off her neck and cleavage with the hem of her skirt. "You're right. I am done for tonight. Be careful, Talysse," she says and slips into the night.

"You too. See you later," I whisper back and retreat to the dark corner where I keep my belongings. Cold sweat trickles down my brow as I hurriedly change into my best clothes. The last thing I need now is for that psychopath to come back to his senses. The Elders are merciful because he is still out when I throw one last look from the door, and the planks around him are slightly charred—the telling sign of magic.

After splashing my face with cool water from the barrel left for the horses at the stables' entrance, I braid my hair again. The need to see Tayna guides my steps in the opposite direction of Red Moon Square. Just one more hit—one big one—and we will be taking the next caravan to the Free Cities. Then this weasel can whine to the City Guard as much as he wants, and her calculating adoptive parents can find another kid to groom into the perfect bride to sell.

THE PRINCE

THE SECONDBORN

The serene golden face of my brother glitters in the light of the wax candles. The burial mask has recreated his features up to the smallest detail and matches his golden locks, draping the red silk of his coffin.

The Golden Prince. The throne heir. My older brother.

I reproach myself for not feeling anything but a terrifying void inside me. The heavy incense and the scent of the embalmed body sting my nose, and my eyes well up. A lonely tear drips over his golden mask, but I quickly get myself together. An Unseelie ruler is expected to be ruthless and have a heart of stone. Mourning is for those below me.

Some nobles faint and had to be carried to their chambers; others drop on their knees and pull their hair in perfectly faked mourning. Terror and despair have been sweeping the Unseelie court for weeks. The heir to the throne was poisoned at his coronation ceremony before the eyes of his family and his entire court.

Murders by poisoning are quite a common way to trigger shifts of power in the Unseelie Kingdom. And I know very well that too many fingers are pointing at me: the Captain of the Shadowblades, the elite spies and assassins legion taking orders only from me, the future king's right hand. The court sees my men for what they are and fears them: powerful and loyal warriors able to summon blades of pure magic and dismiss them at will.

Slipping a poison into the prince's drink is the easiest thing to do.

Good. Let them fear us.

My mother's sobbing still lingers in the vast hall, but my father is strangely quiet. His eyes—narrowed, cruel, challenging—wanders the room and rests on me.

"Are you prepared to step into his shoes, secondborn?"

Secondborn. His cold words thunder under the lacy arches of the domes above. The crowd of courtiers freezes, like creatures sensing an approaching storm. Some cower, others ruffle their feathers and place their bets.

"I have asked you a question, secondborn." His icy blue gaze penetrates my flesh, and I feel his grip on my mind. He hasn't used my name since the rightful heir dropped his chalice, his face turned purple, and his last breath left his body with a painful hiss. Like the rest of the court, he probably thinks the throne heir's death is my doing.

I emerge from the incense haze, shrouding my brother's body, and stride to the throne. My steps echo over the polished black marble floor, each one growing heavier.

"You do understand that the burden to rule is now yours after the untimely passing of the true heir."

The true heir.

He repeats all the messages he branded into my mind since I was a babe. Swallowing the humiliation, I halt at the feet of the throne, shaped from a crystal that fell from the stars. The wailing of the courtiers has ceased, and the crowd is watching us, claws drawn, teeth bared, like a beast waiting to pounce. Now, blades are secretly drawn, poison vials are opened, and loyalties are being tested.

The power shifts in the court of the Unseelie King happen fast and unannounced. The weak and kind ones are weeded out, and millennia of backstabbing and lust for more power have turned us into a race of ruthless murderers.

Subconsciously, I shift my weight, assuming an offensive stance. Years of ruthless military training have beaten it into my muscles. The silk and velvet carpets covering the steps to the throne swallow the sound of my move. The palace guards' hands reach to the hilts of their swords, and their postures tense up. I can guess what's on everyone's minds right now. Will the arrogant, murdering prince go the last mile and kill his father in his lust for the crown?

The nobles let out a collective breath of relief as I drop to one knee and lower my chin. Those who placed their bets on me might not be happy, but a bloodbath between the palace guard and my Shadowblades with the whole court caught in the middle is not something I desire. Not right now.

"I understand, Father. And I am ready." The words ring loud and clear. They're true. There's nothing I have desired more. I'm prepared.

I will be a king.

The king that would change everything in this wretched world.

The king and the queen will withdraw to their summer palace after my coronation. The long centuries of rule have taken their toll on my father, and his enemies whisper that he's softened lately.

A mistake I would never make.

But how do I rule over a court of vipers and backstabbers? How do I keep the countless cousins, uncles, and nobles with great ambitions and large armies in their place?

By making them reveal their intentions. By forcing them to take the first step and strike.

Pushing to my feet, I turn around to face the court crowd. Turning your back to the king and the queen is already an offense punishable by death. Still, everyone knows very well that my father, my old, angry, and wary father, his frame already distorted by the weight of his long life, would never follow through and kill his only heir.

I stalk the herd of nobles, and a thin smile curls my lips when I notice how they flinch. Fearful gazes drop to my empty right hand. They know that I can summon my Shadowblade in the blink of an eye. And no usual weapon is a match for it.

The Wildling they call me behind my back, referring to my many ventures into the Wastelands beyond the protective halo and the thick walls of the capital.

My steel studded boots are still crusted with the black soil of the desolate lands, and my travel clothes bear the faint scent of the wild, of tainted blood and ashes. Relishing in their fear, I ignore the old king's angry calling.

Nobody would risk challenging me openly; that much is clear. And it is not a duel invitation or an army at our gates that I worry about. It is the drops of poison in my food; the dagger slipped into the hand of someone I trust.

I open my arms in a dramatic gesture and let them take in my tall frame, the crimson stains on my leather armor, and the speckles of black blood over my face and hair. Let them see who they will be challenging should they decide to take over what is mine.

"Father, Mother, I am ready to rule." I pace along the line of courtiers and halt before Aernysse Stargaze, the court mage, then dip my chin in a sign of respect. She straightens her bony shoulders and bows, sensing that I am speaking the truth. "And as you seem to be having doubts, I would like to prove myself worthy of the crown. I ask for permission to participate in the coming Nightfall Trials."

How do you make those who plot against you in secret reveal themselves?

By giving them the perfect opportunity to strike.

The courtiers hold their breath, and I clearly hear my mother gasp behind my back. The ancient black eyes of the court mage narrow and dart to the throne dais. I resist the urge to turn around and see my parents' reaction. My mother's eyes are probably wide in terror that she will lose another son, and my father's knuckles are white from clutching the armrests of the star crystal throne.

If he refuses to let me participate, he will show weakness and admit that his last living son, the Captain of the Shadowblades, is not strong enough to handle the deadly Trials.

"Prince Aeidas, you are granted permission to participate in the Nightfall Trials. May your deeds please the Elders!" the king finally declares.

A deafening cheer erupts beneath the arched vaults of the throne hall, contrasting oddly with the stillness of my brother's cold body and the mourning priestesses at his side. My gaze sweeps over the crowd and I spot some of my Shadowblades scattered among the courtiers, all blending in, dressed in mourning red. They carefully watch the reaction of the crowd: some of the nobles are already plotting my demise.

Perfect.

Since the Seelie Fae are gone, the Nightfall Trials are all about hunting humans and keeping their magic in check. Humans breed like pests, and if we allow every human mage to survive, soon hundreds of magic-protected human settlements will sprout across the Wastelands, triggering rebellions and wars for resources. The Nightfall Trials are a great chance for young Fae nobles to hunt and thin their numbers; it is cruel but necessary.

But this year, they will be hunting a prince.

TALYSSE

TAYNA

I have never seen the stars. Only a few have—travelers and adventurers who dared to venture deep into the Wastelands, far beyond the safety of the Beacons. I've devoured every story about the outside world in the Temple library, but my mind still struggles to imagine how a sky filled with countless flickering lights would look. The shapes they create—the constellations—are said to have once guided the priests of old, allowing them to foretell the future by the movements of these celestial wonders. It's a concept so fascinating and alien in a world perpetually bathed in a golden magical shimmer.

  The soft light of the Beacon veils the city and its fields in its gentle halo. Dozens of crystals, strategically placed throughout the city, reflect and amplify the spell. Magic is life. Light is life. Beyond the city walls and the protected fields, everything has succumbed to the Taint. Shadowfeeders prowl the darkness, their howls echoing over the walls, haunting the townsfolk's dreams during the long nights. Everything living in their path is either torn apart and consumed or corrupted, doomed to become one of their thralls—the Tainted Ones.

The narrow back-alley reeks of urine and cheap sour wine. A couple of rats scurry behind the moldy crates lined along the walls. There is no living soul on the streets anymore, and the lights in the windows go out one by one. Those who are not at Red Moon Square are saying their prayers, hoping that the sun will rise in the morning. The Beacon glows like a golden torch at the heart of Tenebris. Light burns in the narrow window beneath the amplifying crystals on top. Mage Eloysse will stay awake all night with the help of some potions, she'll be working her spells, sending magic words into the crystals, and keeping the city safe. Elders help us all if she falls asleep or exhausts her gift. Rumor has it that the Unseelie Governor has rejected Magister Deepwell's pleas for another mage. The old man in charge of Tenebris is a fool. Even the children know that you can't expect mercy from a Fae.

The growl of two brawling stray cats startles me, and I wipe the sweat off my brow, hastening my step. The night is hot and young, and the festivities will continue for a few more hours until everyone drops, exhausted. There'll be enough time to browse the merchants' stalls and make some money after seeing Tayna.

The streets are getting broader, the pavement beneath the thin soles of my worn-out slippers—smoother. The houses on both sides of the road are painted bright, cheerful garnet red. They are so tall that they pierce the golden haze of the halo. Some roofs sport miniature star crystals, which capture and amplify the light of the Beacon—extra protection for the wealthy inhabitants.

The light is getting thicker—it looks like a glittering net of magic that is nearly palpable. Flowers in pots and even trees—a luxury in a world where nights might last weeks, are on every street corner. I love this neighborhood not only because it reminds me of my parents' mansion but because of all the colors—blots of happiness in a world of gray and white.

Just a couple of blocks away from Tayna's adoptive family's house, heavy steps and clanking of weapons disturb the night silence.

The Night take you! City Guards. The last thing I need now is someone asking questions. Hastily, I open the upper buttons of my shirt, pinch my cheeks, flare my skirt, and let my long black braid snake between the mounts of my high breasts.

"Good evening, honorable guards!" A saccharine smile stretches my lips. The streets have taught me that everyone tries to put you in a certain box. And if you're good at acting, you can steer them toward the box you wish them to put you in. "A pretty young thing, probably earning some coppers from the gentlemen of this respectable neighborhood." This is the box I fit perfectly now, winking at the younger guard, who blushes like a maiden and quickly looks away.

"By Atos!" The older one grunts and rolls his eyes, and they continue on their way. Maybe the men are annoyed they cannot go to Red Moon Square, but it went better than expected.

The garden crickets grow quiet as I jump over the low stone fence and land in the grass. Sneaking between the manicured bushes of the two-story mansion, I curse when I see that the light in my sister's room is off.

Tayna is already asleep, but something urges me to wake her up. Some dark, ill feeling that's been there since that mad merchant went flying across the stables. I scoop some gravel from the alley and toss the tiny rocks at her window. After three clicks, the sleepy face of my sister appears in the gap between the white starched curtains and beams when she spots me peeking behind the thick cypress. Her tiny face, framed by the heavy blonde braids, disappears, and a minute later, she is in my arms.

"Talysse, so happy you came to see me! It's been such a terrible day—" She sobs, her face buried in the curve of my neck. My chest tightens, and I wipe off her tears with my thumbs.

"Another suitor?" I softly ask, cupping her narrow face. She has inherited my father's straw-blond hair and warm hazel eyes, so common for Satreyah. But this dreamy smile comes from my mother. At twelve, my sister is already a beauty and too young to marry, but her adopters disagree. Eager to cash out her looks and innocence for money and a title, they're actively looking for suitors since she started bleeding last summer. Rumor has it that all the luxury they're living in is coming from marrying off their beautiful adoptive daughter to rich older men.

Yet another reason for me to do anything within my power to get us out of here.

"I am scared, Talysse. He is enormous. And the women are whispering that he is already twice widowed—both his wives dead at fourteen...Cousin Ephraina told me that his last wife had a tiny pet goat. He got jealous that she was spending time with it and made her slaughter it, cook it, and eat it...what if we have a baby, and he gets jealous, Talysse?" Her wide hazel eyes meet mine. Blood is thumping in my temples, and my jaw locks. If that bastard tries to hurt her, I will flay him alive. Yet, I am not planning to linger around and let this wedding happen. If all goes well, we'll be on our way to the Free Cities with the next caravan.

"I think that Cousin Ephraina is a fool. Besides, we're leaving for the Free Cities soon—" I even manage a smile and a wink, but deep inside, dark claws are ripping my heart apart. Cousin Ephraina is not a fool, and the haughty adoptive parents of Tayna would sell her like cattle to the first murderer if he is willing to pay the price.

I need to act soon.

Tonight.

I'll make some coin, just a little more to buy us safe passage. Then I'll get Tayna and we'll until the next caravan to the South agrees to take us.

"Tell me about it, Talysse!" Her teary eyes lift to meet mine, and I tell her the story of our imaginary trip, a story that always calms her, and send a feverish prayer to the Elders that it happens soon.

"The caravans cross the Wastelands, protected by mages. Father has done it often and told me everything about it! When night falls, the mages place star crystals around the camp and cast their spells so the travelers remain safe in their tents. Then they all sit by the campfires and tell each other stories or sing songs to mock the darkness...but you know that mages are scarce, and traveling with a caravan is expensive, and the Free Cities and the shores of the sea are far, far away. Of course, some poor souls have tried crossing the Wastelands alone, without the protection of the Blessed Light magic—"

"What happened with them, Talysse?"

I smoothen the loose strands of hair over her forehead and whisper, "They were never seen again. But fret not. Tomorrow, I will have enough money to get us on the safest caravan. And you will get to ride a pony, just like the one you had at home—"

The weight of the memories breaks my voice, and I force my gaze up, squinting against the golden light, once again trying to see the stars. If only I could read our future in the constellations, like the ancients!

Hurried steps and shouts startle us. Judging by the noise, a large group of men are approaching.

Guards.

They come around the street corner, carrying torches, their blades drawn. Seems like a search party. Probably, a robbery or a murder happened somewhere nearby. Lights appear in the windows of the stone mansion behind us.

"Get back to bed, Tayna! I will come to get you tomorrow." One last hug, one traitorous tear, and I leap over the fence, away from the guards.

TALYSSE

THE RED MOON SQUARE

I was right. Everyone who's not asleep is here. A bard with a blond mustache sings the Ballad of the Sun Queen, winking at the blushing girls in the audience. Loud swarms of kids dart between the quickly put-together stands, where merchants praise their wares. The whole town is bustling with life and colors, everyone wearing their best clothes.

At the heart of the square, next to the old well decorated with decaying statues of the five Elders, remnants of Tenebris's past glory, is the highlight of the night. The puppeteers have erected a colorful structure set ablaze by the light of many cleverly placed lanterns. The crowd is really dense there, and vendors make their way among the townsfolk, offering refreshments. As much as I'm curious about the world before the Hex, I don't let the cardboard trees and silk flowers on the makeshift stage distract me; I am here for business. My eyes wander from face to face, searching for my partners.

"Help a poor blind woman," a familiar voice warns me just before Squinting Ann crashes into me. Seems like the Elders are merciful tonight. Ann is generous, and her schemes always work flawlessly. She has never cheated me before and has the largest network of sinister acquaintances. She looks around to see if anyone is watching before leaning in closer.

"The tall one over there," Squinting Ann winks at me with her dark eyes, "seems rich. Take him to Wet Dog Alley. Got four of me best boys waiting there."

I quickly spot the tall, hooded frame, sticking out of the crowd like a sore thumb. He's watching the play. There's something odd about him, and as if the townsfolk sense it, there's a wide empty circle around him. People are avoiding him as if he were a Shadowfeeder.

"Are you sure, Ann?" Doubt strangles my voice. "He looks…dangerous."

"You don't get to pick the targets, girl. You do it, or I'll find someone else." She shrugs. "Wet Dog Alley. Now," she says before diving into the crowd, shaking her tin cup with coins and feeling her way with a stick. "Help a poor blind woman, good people."

I frown. It's just another job, so what is this ominous feeling clenching my gut? The man surely looks rich. One more job, and Tayna and I will be on the next caravan, away from this shit hole. I conjure the image of the tiny house with a garden we have always dreamed about. Just as usual, it works like magic. Cold, focused determination replaces the insecurity. There's some dark allure about this stranger. The fine fabric of his cloak and his polished boots studded with steel are already drawing many eyes. Some sinister individuals, lingering in the shadows behind the merchants' stands, have a muffled discussion, throwing him dirty looks.

Time to get to business before someone else snatches my prize. Tonight, I am wearing my best silk off-shoulder blouse. The white is not that crisp anymore, and a more observant eye would spot the telling signs of wearing off on the elbows, but it complements my sun-kissed complexion and makes my eyes stand out. Pulling the neckline even lower, I make sure my collarbones and the arch of my shoulders are on display. An emerald-green velvet shawl is draped over my right shoulder to conceal my burn scar, not out of vanity but because I don't want to imprint myself in the memory of the rich stranger. The plan is simple: attract his attention just enough to bring him to the place where Squinting Ann's boys will be waiting, but not leave any durable memories so that he can describe my appearance to the City Guard.

Puppets with brightly painted faces present the Final Standoff between Seelie and Unseelie—when the Unseelie vanquish the army of the Seelie Queen and win the war, triggering the Elders' Hex. It is supposed to be a tragic event, leaving tens of thousands dead and destroying our world. Still, the misfitting merry music and the witty comments of the puppeteers cause ripples of roaring laughter among the crowd around the booth. It is one of these rare moments when Tenebris does not appear as the cruel, gods-forsaken place it is. Lifting the gray woolen skirt borrowed from Myrtle last week, I flash some ankle and make my way through the audience. An oblivious bystander would see a young woman trying to get to the front row to see better, but I am moving purposefully to the tall man, hoping that he is a rich and naive merchant, romantic and desperate for a flirt with a stranger from this Elders-forgotten place and not some experienced mercenary who'd see my game right through.

Deliberately stepping on some feet and pushing people with my elbows, I make it to the stranger Squinting Ann has chosen. Too tall and broad-shouldered, his cowl is pulled low over his face but doesn't cover the black and gold jerkin beneath his cape or the expensive deer-leather riding boots with onyx spurs. There is something alien, dreadful, and enticing about this man, something that makes butterflies flutter in my gut and urges me to run at the same time. Unsure if it is his powerful warrior frame or the shimmer of a concealed blade at his thigh, I have to make an effort to silence the alarming bells in my head. Squinting Ann's boys will manage to overpower the foreigner and relieve him of his purse; they've managed to handle bigger men than him.

Routine kicks in, and I assume my role as bait. We are so close that the unusual heat of his body penetrates my thin blouse, and I flip my thick, dark braid away from my unscarred side, displaying the long line of my neck. "You are a shameless flirt, Talysse; if it wasn't for your scruples, you could have made it great in my line of work," Myrtle has always said.

Casting a casual look back, I make sure that he had noticed me and nearly let out a gasp.

Elders help me; I've never seen a man like this. Thick black eyelashes cast shadows over blue-green eyes, which faintly glow in the shadow of his cowl. In Tenebris, sparkling colors like this exist only in the murals in the Temple of the

Elders, their nuances so deep and pure that they seem to glow. The bards would call this shade "dreamy," and for all the damsels in their ballads, it spells TROUBLE.

There is an odd iridescence in his irises, similar to that of the back-alley cats when they stalk their prey in the gloom—something not entirely human. His head cocks, and the light of the stage lanterns falls on his full lips, curling into a barely-there smile as if he doesn't want to admit his amusement.

His attention shifts back to the stage, where a life-sized puppet with bright red cheeks and long hair made of yellow yarn descends from a cardboard-cut Holy Mountain. The Sun Queen has failed her mission to beg the Elders to lift the Hex. The show will be over soon.

Long fingers hold the intricately embroidered fabric of his cowl, ensuring it stays in place. The stranger seems to want to remain anonymous. Hmm, that might be useful. His hand is graceful, but the callouses on his fingers betray a warrior. As much as I try to remain professional and not get curious about the man who'd be beaten to a pulp by Ann's boys soon, I cannot help it. What is he doing with the merchants' caravan? Maybe he is really one of the mercenaries from the Free Cities hired to protect the travelers?

Something is disturbing in the way he pulls his hood down and wraps himself in the gray cape as if trying to blend in, to pass for someone poorer and more insignificant than he is. Very odd. Usually, it is the other way around—men try to look richer and more important than they are. Despite his efforts to remain hidden, I catch myself glaring at the swell of a strong neck and a defined jawline.

Trouble.

There is that hint of a smile again in the shadow of his hood. A white line of even teeth flashes between his lips, and again, there is something alarming, something worrying enough to make me frown and almost abandon the plan. His incisors are too long to be human. They dig into the flesh of his lip as if to suppress a laugh. And something inside me tightens up like a bowstring.

The opportunity to set the plan in motion arises when some kids run past me, shoving me lightly. Flailing my arms around, I land in the stranger's arms and melt in the warm, tight grip of lean muscle.

"Thank you for catching me, dear sir," I mumble, doing my best to blush and appear really mortified by the situation. His nostrils flare as if he's taking in my scent while I timidly untangle myself from his arms.

"You are from somewhere far, right, sir?" I ask, trying to start a conversation. His smile widens, displaying dimples on his cheeks. I still cannot see his entire face, but I can bet that these eyes left a trail of broken hearts. He just watches me silently, another odd thing. Usually, men are very responsive, but this one seems to require another approach. The play is finished and the artists scatter to the crowd with their hats, and everyone throws some coins in them. When they reach me, I slip a hand in my pocket, and my face pales.

"Oh no! Damned children! They stole my purse!" I curse loud enough for the stranger to hear. "I'll get them and show them—"

Without looking back, I storm off the crowded market square, heading to the scarce lights of the back alleys. This is a daring move; it's too late for a new plan in case he doesn't follow me. Then, my only option would be to find another job. Halfway to the Wet Dog Alley, I throw a look over my shoulder and grin—the tall man is following me. It's unclear if he's doing it out of chivalry or with some sinister plan of his own. I don't care. Ann's boys will be there. They'd do their job clean and fast and give me a fair share, just like they've always done.

The Wet Dog Alley reeks of urine and dog poop, and rats the size of cats scatter to the dark corners. His steps echo behind me, and, just as planned, five massive silhouettes peel from the shadows at the walls, holding thick bats.

"Well, look what the cat dragged in tonight, boys! Some fine pussy it is!" Sam drawls and whistles through his missing front teeth. Two of them grab my arms, twisting them behind me, and I do my best to look like a damsel in distress. "And the knight is coming to her rescue," he adds darkly and stalks to the tall man.

"A knight? All I can hear is the jingle of gold in his purse," Sturdy Tadeus adds, already swinging his bat at the stranger.

Elders help me because what unfolds before me is unreal. With a move so fast no mortal can master, the stranger has Sturdy Tad and Bloated Tammy on the floor, howling in agony, their arms twisted at odd angles, and draws the blade hanging on his side. He tenses up for a lunge at the other two boys. A lunge that would end badly for them, as no bat can stop a seasoned warrior wielding a blade.

No way I'm letting this happen. Slow Unkas's wife is sick on the child's bed, and he's the only one who provides for her and their newborn daughter. Unkas and his friend release me immediately, preparing to parry. They look ridiculous compared to the battle-hardened stranger.

Atos take that greedy bitch Ann. This was a miscalculation of epic proportions. Frantically, I'm preparing to cast a spell—probably create an illusion of a city guard asking what is going on there. Illusions siphon my arcane energy within the blink of an eye, and they're far from perfect but could create a good diversion. The mysterious man beats me to it. The walls framing the ally crack from the unleashed force, and Unkas and the other boy are hurled against the masonry.

Squinting Ann needs to compensate me handsomely for what she got me into.

Once again, on this Elders-cursed night, I fear for my life.

This is no ordinary rich man we've decided to rob tonight. This is a mage.

Just when I think that things cannot get worse, fate laughs into my face and...makes things worse. The stranger approaches me, his blade sheathed but his hand raised in a hard-to-decipher gesture. His cowl has slipped, and his face is fully revealed now. His lips are turned up, revealing those dimples, as if the whole thing is damned entertainment for him.

Seems like Death is finally catching up with me tonight. I turn on my heel and run into the depths of the alley, pulling down crates and kicking rubble to find the concealed tunnel—the only way out of here.

For that is no man.

The stranger is an Unseelie.

TALYSSE

CHOSEN BY THE ELDERS

I jump over hedges and avoid angry dogs and vigilant townsfolk. Completely out of breath, I make it to the boarding house, where Myrtle is renting a narrow, humid room.

She is dozing off over a bottle of white wine and two empty cups, the single candle on the table nearly burned out. She has washed away the blood and cleaned her wound; only a red line across her skin reminds her of her ordeal. She wakes up with a start when I gently touch her shoulder.

"Talysse," she whispers, her dark eyes darting to her son. He's sleeping peacefully on the narrow bed in the corner, clutching the rag dragon I made for him. "I was worried sick! Ran to Red Moon, but you weren't there! They are looking for you everywhere. That bastard called the guards and now they are combing the city, searching for an unlicensed mage. What should we do?"

It takes me some time to realize which bastard she means. The Fae or the merchant at the stables?

Cold sweat rolls down my spine despite the summer heat. This must be some bad dream. To be hunted when I'm so close to my goal. I drop into the unstable chair and try to steady my trembling fingers when I pour myself some wine.

Taking a generous swig of sour wine, I glare at her. "I'm leaving, Myrtle. I cannot put you and Stebian at risk. Practicing magic without permission from the Unseelie is punishable. Just as harboring an unlicensed mage." Another swig and the desperation is slowly replaced by cold, sharp determination. "I am getting Tayna out of that cursed house tonight, and we'll hide until things settle down. Then we leave with the first caravan heading out."

It all sounds too simple, but all my belongings—and my money—are beneath that loose plank in the stables. The first place they'd look. To the hell pits of Atos with all Fae, guards and merchants! I rub my neck, feeling the noose around it tighten.

"Or—" Myrtle clears her throat and lowers her voice, leaning closer, "you could volunteer for the Trials. They're looking for mages in all of Satreyah. Did you see the posters? How you sent that prick flying! It was glorious! Your magic is strong, Talysse. You will win! And then you can save this whole gods-forsaken place. Tayna, me, and Stebian included."

Shaking my head, I down another glass of cheap wine. We've been through this so many times before. The issue here is that Myrtle's opinion of me is too high. I am not the fair maiden with a selfless heart the bards are singing about. Breaking curses, slaying dragons, saving cities—those are things I'm not even remotely interested in. In fact, I try to avoid them as the plague. Like everyone in this backwater town, I just want—for once—the juicy part of the meat pie. I want Tayna to go back to school instead of marrying and becoming a toy to some lunatic; I want to have a job where I can look people in the eye without fearing that they would get the city guards. After everything this life has taken from me, it's fair.

"You know that I just want to get away from this place, Myrtle. There is nothing but bad memories here for me. No future. And as soon we're settled in the Free Cities and I am earning some coin, I'll send for you and Stebian. But don't make me feel like I'm responsible for this gods-forsaken shit hole."

She shakes her head, throwing a look at the door. "But you are, Talysse. Magic is rare, and you've been chosen. So don't talk to me about responsibility—someone else has made this choice for you. This ship has sailed. The Elders think that you're good enough. And I do, too. If I know a person who can do this, it is you. You are not a pampered mage from some fancy castle or some nobleman who can swing a blade. You are resourceful; you have survived out there, and it hasn't broken you or stained you. It has made you stronger—"

"Oh, but it did, Myrtle. My dead parents are still with me; they speak to me every night, accusing me of being unable to protect Tayna." These words come out too loud, and we both look around nervously.

"You have done your best to keep her safe." Myrtle slams the table with a fist then immediately regrets it.

"I have not done enough. With every single minute she remains in that cursed house, her doom is coming closer."

"You are wasting the blessing the Elders have bestowed upon you—" she hisses.

"And you don't know what you are talking about," I snap. "Do you think that weaving some illusions or throwing someone against a wall can help me defeat Unseelie-trained mages? Do you know what kills most contestants in the Trials? It's not the Wastelands or the Shadowfeeders. It's the other contestants."

We sit in silence, reining our emotions in, drinking more than we should. My eyes rest on Stebian, so small and vulnerable and so unaware of it. Watching a child wander the Dreamlands is the most calming thing. How many nights back in the Blessed Dawn orphanage have I curled up against the tiny body of Tayna, her quiet breath and the scent of innocence drying my tears?

"Winning the Trials means money and fame. You and Tayna will never have a worry in your life. You will become a Protector just like mage Eloysse. Think of all the possibilities, Talysse!" Her hoarse whisper fades, and the shadows in the room grow thicker. There's a desperate, unspoken plea in her words—one by one, the Unseelie are calling off the Protectors of the neighboring cities, leaving them unprotected. Without their spells to power the Beacons and keep the Shadowfeeders at bay, the cities were overrun and corrupted. Waves of refugees flooded Tenebris, and many didn't live to see the dawn.

I respond with a question, and the conversation takes its usual dark turn. "Have you heard of any humans winning the Trials, Myrtle? Any humans surviving? You realize only the winner gets to live, right?"

"There is one in the Free Cities. They say that she is taking a bath in a tub of gold—"

"You're better than believing this nonsense, Myrtle." I throw my hands in the air and immediately regret my too-harsh tone. It's been a hell of a night. "You know how these Unseelie are—" we both look around because speaking ill of our masters is a crime punishable by exile in the Wastelands, "—they are murderers. They killed all Seelie, their brethren, and now they're looking for ways to thin our numbers out. Why do you think there's no new mage coming to Tenebris? They want to see the city fall. And you know what they did to my parents. They are tricky, and they do everything for their own gain."

She looks around, as if the thin wooden walls have ears. This sort of talk is dangerous, though most of the townsfolk have similar thoughts.

"You should stop seeing death and evil in everything, Talysse. You have the rarest commodity in Phyllesia. You are gifted by the Elders, and you can help many. You just need to believe in yourself, for once. Then you can change all our lives."

Our usual bickering is draining me. How to convince her that the orphan rejected by all adoptive families for being a troublemaker, the one who saw her parents hang, the one who was not good enough for anything, cannot save anyone? Not even her loved ones.

"Tayna had another suitor today. It's the worst one yet."

Myrtle's face softens immediately, and she takes my hand, squeezing my fingers. "Yet another reason for you to sign up for the Trials. I heard some important Fae have arrived with the caravan—"

I lock my jaw, realizing that my decision has been made. "I am leaving, Myrtle."

Enough of this. I push my chair back and head to the door. Exhaustion is already dulling my senses, but I cannot risk being discovered here.

"May your night be short."

She opens her mouth to say something when mayhem erupts, and our little world comes crashing down.

TALYSSE

THE GOVERNOR

The rough floor planks scrape painfully against my face, and hard knees dig into my back, pinning me down while my arms are twisted backward. Stebian's piercing falsetto slices through the night. "Mommy, Mommy, Mommy, Mommy—"

Crashing objects and overturned furniture signal Myrtle's fierce struggle. "Leave my child alone, you monsters!"

A cold male voice cuts through the chaos, "You're all coming with us, by order of Magister Deepwell!"

Steps of steel-plated boots thunder in the tiny room. I catch a glimpse of Stebian, kicking and writhing as an older guard hauls him out. Two others wrestle down a hysterical Myrtle.

"Chain the mage with warded shackles, quickly!" The brute's order fills the room. More hands grab me, and a gauntlet swings at my face. Pain explodes in my temple, and everything goes black.

*

Just like any other night, the nightmare swallows the reality around me, dragging me into the suffocating, agonizing, immersive experience of the most dreadful day of my life.

"For harboring Seelie Fae refugees, a crime and treason against the crown, Governor Aeidas sentences you to hang." The words of the Unseelie clerk hang in the hot air at Gallows Hills. Public executions usually draw a large crowd, but not on that summer day.

A two-wheel cart is parked behind the gallows, and bloodied blonde locks hang through the gaps between the planks. Some dark liquid trickles from its bottom. I recognize these locks—the Seelie they have found hiding in our barn. Dead and ready to be carted off into the mass grave behind the gallows.

It's over fast, and I start crying again because I've missed the final moment of my parents while trying to guess what gruesome death has befallen the Seelie.

Their feet dangle unnaturally at the height of my eyes. Mother's golden brocade slipper is lost somewhere, and her left foot is dirty and bloodied, the hem of her pearl studded gown covered in mud. I remember that dress—my father brought it for her from his last trip to the East, and she clapped her hands in joy and gave him a loud kiss on the forehead. Father's polished riding boots hang behind the shiny armor of the Unseelie soldiers, lined before the gallows.

"Child, you should not see this," someone says with empathy. I open my mouth and close it, unable to form words, unable to scream anymore. How to explain to my four-year-old sister that she will never see Mommy again?

That our house is torn inside out, most of our possessions burned, and we're never to set foot in our home anymore?

I wake up gasping for air, choking a scream, struggling to put in words something elusive and incredibly painful, but just like any other night, I simply can't.

And what would that change?

Would it give me back the years in the orphanage and living on the streets?

Would it erase the memory of Tayna being assessed and prodded like cattle, her sleazy adoptive parents feeling her joints, checking her teeth, and making her sing before leaving with her? Her screams and pleas when she realized I was not coming with her?

That day at the Gallows Hills changed everything and I just stood there, numb, unable to do anything. Seeing it in my dreams is my punishment.

I slowly shake off the nightmare. Where am I?

Something sticky clings to my eyelids, making it hard to open them. A headache of cataclysmic proportions blooms inside my skull like a bloody, fiery flower. I finally manage to crack an eye open. Humid, stale air floods my senses, triggering a coughing fit. Sprawled on a cold, wet floor, uneven stones cut into my flesh. A lone wall sconce struggles to pierce the darkness, and the solid metal bars confirm my suspicion—they've dragged me to the city's dungeon. Muffled moans and whispers echo from the darkness beyond the narrow cell.

I wonder if the rumors are true—that they are keeping people infected with the Taint to observe the stages they go through before they completely lose their humanity and become blood-thirsty, brainless beasts, craving the flesh of every living being. Rumor has it that Magister Deepwell's family was Tainted, and he keeps them locked in the dungeons, as he couldn't bring himself to grant them a merciful death.

"First, the infection taints the eyes—all parts of them gradually darken in the first hours after the bite or scratch of a Tainted or a touch of a Shadowfeeder. The blood and the life juices of the freshly Tainted turn black, and their skin and hair—pale, while their nails and teeth grow unnaturally, and their bones expand in unseen ways. When their transformation is complete, there is nothing even remotely human to them, and they are not able to recognize even their loved ones. They roam the Wastelands thirsting for flesh..." Friar Ben was telling us in his class and his words gave us all nightmares for weeks.

A shrill shriek pierces me to the marrow, and I sit up, rattling the chains around my wrists.

This was no human voice.

Have the city walls been breached?

Are Myrtle and her baby also in this Elders-forsaken dungeon, and Tayna—

Rolling my shoulders and twisting my hands, I struggle against the chains until sweat drips into my eyes. I have to get out of here. It's clearly pointless. Magic or physical strength won't get me out of here.

Mine and Tayna's lives are literally depending on what's between my ears. And so far, it has always managed to get me out of the tightest situations.

Rule number one: always keep a cool head.

When the Stormbird brothers waited for me every day after Friar Ben's classes to beat me up because I'd refused to share my apples with them?

Kept a cool head, formed some risky alliances, and came up with a new plan every day, which made those fire-haired demons give up in the end.

That time when Corporal Darron from the City Guard thought I'd cheated him on dice? Well, maybe I did just a little. Darron—people believe that he has giants somewhere down his ancestral tree. The man was twice my size, and yet I managed to escape his wrath.

Those and countless more stories—every night of my life has been a story of survival, and I'm not planning to give up yet.

Not when Tayna's life and happiness are at stake and when Myrtle and her son are somewhere in this dreadful place.

Heavy steps rumble in the corridor, clearly heading my way, and the other prisoners grow suddenly quiet. Even the monstrous howling has stopped.

Limbs shaking, I push myself up and press my face against the rusty bars, trying to see who's coming.

When the pale face of the merchant Myrtle lured to the stables appears, I take a sharp breath and struggle not to stumble back.

Get your shit together, Talysse. It's time for rule number one.

"That's her, constable! This is the woman who tried to kill me with magic!"

He points at me, and I cannot help but feel a sting of pride when spotting the bandage around his head.

The constable's cold gaze studies me through the bars. This mountain of a man has a spotless reputation and has put a great deal of my kind behind bars. Or worse. Another streak of bad luck. Bribing my way out with sweet promises or seduction is out of the question.

"Are you sure?" the constable asks, his tone betraying no emotion. This man is an iceberg.

"I swear it on my honor." The merchant touches his white bandage. "It is her who assaulted me, and as the Free Cities Trading Ambassador, I want to see her punished."

For the sake of fucking Atos.

From all the men we could've picked, we decided to rob the bloody Trading Ambassador!

The constable shrugs and leaves without saying a word. That's all the information he needs to seal my fate. I rub my eyes with the heels of my hands, tempted to punch myself in the stupid face. This is all very, very bad news.

The ambassador lingers before my cell and glares at me with red, hatred-filled eyes as if I am some kind of bug he contemplates how to crush.

"I'll be laughing when you hang, bitch." He spits on the dirty stone floor. "And your whore friend, too."

Taunting me when I'm cornered is a bad idea. Threatening me with the unjust fate of my parents is worse. But involving my friend? I summon a tiny flicker of magic around my fingers, pretending I'm about to hurl it at him, cackling like mad. The warded shackles suppress most magic, but he doesn't know that. I laugh like a demon when he runs down the corridor, but as soon as his footsteps die out, I throw myself on the floor, trying to steady my shaky hands.

Things cannot get worse on this cursed night. I quickly shake off this blasphemous thought, as fate has always proved to me that things can always get worse. It's our limited mortal imagination that cannot picture anything worse.

*

The hours stretch, and my headache makes me retch again. In some delusional flashes of hope, I try to slip my hands from the tight, cold grasp of the shackles, then bang against the cell bars or pace around endlessly, rehearsing speeches in my defense.

Which are utterly useless. Everyone knows what happens to poor, nameless women when they stand up against men in power.

Especially women from a family of traitors.

I will hang.

And Tayna will marry a monster.

I cannot tell how much time has passed, but my feet are sore from all the pacing, and my wrists are bleeding. The rusty lock clicks, and two guards in full armor march in.

"You're coming with us," the shorter one says in a tone not used to objections. My feet nearly give in when they roughly shove me forward.

The Governor's Palace is an ancient, sad place. Tenebris hasn't had a real governor for centuries, as the city is too small to be relevant for the Unseelie. Even mage Eloysse left the once grand halls and haunted stairwells and settled for a smaller, comfortable mansion near the Beacon.

Decay eats at the tapestries spun over the crumbling masonry, and mold covers the exquisitely carved marble statues, making them appear like decaying corpses. The waft of death lingers in the dark passageways, and dust muffles our footsteps. The palace is old, built by the Seelie long before the Elders' Hex to rule over what was once a prosperous province. It's occupied by the City Guard and the meagre city administration now. Yet when we climb up the wide staircase leading to better-maintained parts of the palace, the place is bustling with unusual activity. There are too many guards, their armors so polished they reflect the flicker of the many wax candles, their postures straight—as if they're preparing to march into battle. Two of them stand before a tall, ornate door and push it open when we approach.

When I see the crowd in the audience hall, my fists ball so hard that my nails dig into my flesh. Seems like half of the city is here, but three figures at the center stand out. Surrounded by guards, there's Myrtle, cradling her baby, and Tayna, still wearing her nightgown.

My stomach plummets when the guard shoves me roughly, and I stumble forward, nearly grabbing Magister Deepwell's crimson robe to steady myself. He has materialized out of nowhere, raising his hands to quiet the murmur of the crowd. The people around us are nobles and rich citizens of Tenebris. No commoners. The way everyone glares at me doesn't mean anything good. So, it will be a public execution then. What a befitting end for a daughter of traitors.

"Magister Deepwell," my voice nearly betrays the panic making its way to the surface, "I am ready to face the consequences of my actions, but I ask you to free the innocents in this room—Tayna and Myrtle."

Murmurs ripple through the crowd. Obviously, everyone is outraged that a prisoner is speaking first.

"You confess without knowing what you are accused of?" Magister Deepwell raises a bushy white brow, and the wrinkles on his forehead deepen. The man has been famous for his gluttony but never for his cruelty, so this whole display is puzzling.

"I confess that I tried to rob a merchant, who arrived with the caravan—"

A murmur, "Liar, she tried to kill me," confirms that the ambassador is here, too.

The wrinkles on Magister Deepwell's face smoothen. "This is not why you are brought here, child. If that were your crime, you'd be whipped and sent to the fields for a year. You've been brought here before the good people of Tenebris to celebrate a unique opportunity."

Maybe Seuta has finally, mercifully, decided to let me go mad. What in the name of Atos's hell pits does this all mean?

Slowly, my tired brain starts bringing the pieces of the puzzle together.

The secret that my parents so carefully guarded has been revealed. I have magic, and everyone who has magic has no choice—

"Now, kneel before his Excellency and thank him for this opportunity." Magister Deepwell's tiny eyes glitter with delight. Swallowing hard, I look around to see who he means. I kneel on the cracked marble floor. The survival of my loved ones is more important than any remnants of pride I have. I'd crawl on my belly if this means Tayna and Myrtle are leaving this tomb free.

A tall, silver-haired man steps out of the shadows of the gallery. There's something hauntingly familiar about the straight line of his wide shoulders, and the restrained smile on his lips, displaying the edges of needle-sharp fangs; about the way his hair falls over his richly decorated armor. Elders, only his breastplate must cost a fortune. The hall grows still when his heavy steps halt behind the lithe frame of Tayna, and his cold emerald gaze locks with mine.

No.

This cannot be.

"Thank Governor Aeidas for this opportunity, Talysse."

A raging blizzard of emotions clouds my mind and snuffs out my common sense.

Was he wearing the same smile when he signed the death sentence of my parents? Were his eyes shimmering with sheer amusement when he had ordered the poor Seelie hiding in our barn tortured and killed? I struggle against my restraints, succumbing to pure, mindless lust for murder. For a brief moment, violent fantasies of me flaying this beautiful, cold smile from his face and clawing the light out of these iridescent eyes take the best of me.

Just like at the puppet show and in Wet Dog Alley, he is studying me with interest. I take deep, ragged breaths to control my trembling limbs. I might be impulsive, but not mad. Not yet. Terrifying as it is, we are all at his mercy.

Mercy and Unseelie are two words one cannot put together in a sentence. All cities of Satreyah ravaged by Shadowfeeders are witness to their wickedness.

They have been preying on us humans for millennia, and with the Seelie gone, they keep us around only because they need labor to produce the goods for their cities and the food for their tables. To them, we are nothing but cattle.

The hairs on my nape stand up, and my ears start ringing when the governor crosses the hall and looms over me, his smile still on his lips but his gaze cold and dark as a winter night.

"Remove her shackles," he orders, and the guards rush to do his bidding. Finally free, the temptation to seek my magic out is too tempting, but the lithe frame of Tayna in the background makes me reconsider. He suddenly picks up my hand, the brush of his calloused fingers unexpectedly soft, and lifts it to his eyes.

"Interesting jewelry. Seelie made, if I am not mistaken." His cold tone is in stark contrast with his warm touch. This is the voice of a skilled interrogator, laced with threats.

"It's a gift from my mother—" I say, yanking my hand away. His touch still lingers on my skin.

"It's magical," he notes thoughtfully and cocks his head. There is no question in his words, but I feel the necessity to explain.

"It is casting a minor glamour. Concealing a burn mark I have—" My mouth is suddenly so dry that talking is a challenge. His gaze slides down my collarbone and shoulder and he studies my scar, now fully on display after my green scarf was lost somewhere. I do not fret under his scrutiny. The scar is a part of my story, a precious memory of my life before the Fae messed it up, and I don't care if someone finds it unpleasant to look at.

"Why didn't you take it off? Seelie artifacts are to be reported and handed over to the authorities," he states, his pupils turning sharp as needles. Icy sweat trickles down my spine. It'd be better if this bastard decides my fate faster and sends me away.

"I can't, it's too tight."

He laughs. The sound is cold and humorless, like the rattle of weapons on a moonless night, the hissing of a snake unfurling.

"Oh, of course you can; you'll have to lose a hand."

Even Magister Deepwell pales at these words. "Which would be a pity, as you are just about to volunteer for the Nightfall Trials," he says impassively, his gaze still pinning me. The corner of his lip curls up. This monster looks amused.

The heavy silver waters of the magical lake inside me roar and chant my name, seducing me to use their power.

"I am what?" I ask, naively hoping that he means something else.

"You are about to volunteer as a tribute for the Nightfall Trials. As your province still hasn't presented a participant, I believe it is divine timing that we found you just during my visit here."

He crosses his hands behind his back, turns around, and strolls toward Myrtle and Tayna. The hall has grown quiet, the crowd holding its breath.

I raise to my feet and take a step to follow him, but Magister Deepwell stops me. A warning is written all over his round face before he steps aside and lets me pass.

Elders help me. The governor looms over my little sister, his hands casually resting on her shoulders as he's looking straight at me. Cruelty flickers in his eyes when he asks,

"Are you going to pledge yourself now before these honorable townsfolk, Talysse, or would you prefer to do it before me and Magister Deepwell?" I ignore the way he hissed my name and focus on my sister. Her innocent hazel eyes are wide with marvel, her blonde crown braid messy. She's oblivious that she is in the hands of a murderer.

"Or do you need some convincing—" He doesn't finish the threat, but his fingers dig deep into the soft skin of Tayna's shoulders, and she winces, looking up at him in surprise.

"Talysse," the magister is next to me in a swift move, unexpected from his plump body, "consider your choice wisely."

"And what choices do I have, Magister?"

"Volunteer for the Trials and represent Satreyah, earn respect and the chance for riches and a better life, or face charges for an attempted murder of a diplomat," Deepwell announces sternly.

"And witnessing your co-conspirators face charges for harboring a criminal and not reporting a mage to the Magistrate," the Unseelie Governor declares in his cold, non-human voice.

I bite my tongue to stop myself from screaming. Once again, I get to relive this terrible feeling of powerlessness, just like the time when the City Guard kicked down our door and arrested my parents.

But this time, I'm not a frightened child anymore. Life on the back alleys of Tenebris has taught me how to stand my ground, sprout claws, and bite.

When fate hasn't granted you any advantage others have in this life, you can rely solely on your mind. It is the one thing they cannot take away from you.

"I volunteer for the Nightfall Trials." The words roll loud and clear. The hall shakes with applause.

"Very well. You leave at dawn." With these words, he withdraws to the shadows.

When life gives you sour apples, you should brew some sour apple cider, they say. When life gives you sour apples, steal some milk, flour, and eggs and bake a fucking pie is the motto I live by.

I haven't chosen this path, yet it is a consequence of a strain of poor decisions. And here I am, ready to bake some pie.

TALYSSE

A FEAST IN THE WASTELANDS

Volunteering for the Trials hasn't changed my prisoner's status; I'm still in my cell deep in the Governor's Palace dungeons. Still, it has just brought me some luxuries, like blankets, a bucket of fresh water and food delivered every couple of hours. Another luxury appreciated above all was Myrtle's visit. She reassured me that Tayna was safe, delivered back to her adoptive family and that the magister cleared them both of all charges. She thoughtfully packed a pair of soft velvet pants, a clean cotton shirt whose color was barely recognizable, and a leather doublet that looked nearly new and probably expensive. A lump got stuck in my throat when she tried to distract me with stories from the inn and Stebian's antics. We blinked away tears and laughed like children, and just like that, the guards announced that the visit was over.

We stayed in each other's arms until they pulled us apart. There were no solemn farewell words, just a silent nod, an acknowledgment that this might be our last meeting.

*

The familiar streets of Tenebris fly by behind the curtained window of the carriage, each corner and alley a chapter of my life. We pass the old bakery; sneaking glazed bagels from the bakery was a childhood thrill, their sweet aroma unforgettable. Next to it is the fashion tailor's shop, its tall windows displaying dreamlike dresses, where me and Tayna would spend hours admiring the gowns we could never afford; the crumbling Temple of the Five with its dusty library, which has seen better times... And just before the tall city gates—the Gallows Hills and the countless unmarked graves behind them. Somewhere there lay my parents, among numerous others, and a couple of Seelie who happened to be in the wrong place at the wrong time.

Is it the euphoria of the sun-drenched open road, the warm summer air holding promises of long sunny days and short nights, but it all fills me with an unexpected sense of freedom as soon as the carriage passes through the city gates. For the first time in a long while, there's hope. I stretch out on the worn velvet seat, the soft new clothes hugging my skin, and hum a melody. Everything is as it should be, for now.

The carriage is tossing me left and right the further we get from the city. The road is in miserable condition. The Unseelie don't invest much in infrastructure; the remnants of roads in Satreyah were built by the Seelie centuries ago. The fields around Tenebris stretch like a sea on both sides of the road, the wind rippling their green surface. Crops and the workers are protected by magical crystals and Eloysse's magic during the long nights, even if they're outside the city walls. Peasants look up when they hear hoofs on the uneven pavement, and some of them wave at us with their straw hats.

Tall pillars stand out among the lush verdant, like the masts of a sunk fleet, their dark sails rolled up neatly: it's one of the inventions that followed the Hex and helped us survive in a world altered by the cruel gods. When the nights started getting long centuries ago, humans quickly realized that their crops needed light to grow, but too much light can be equally deadly. The golden glow of the magical crystals protecting the cities damaged the plants, so scientists from the past created those large foldable tents of dark fabric. In the long nights, they're pulled by dozens of workers and draft animals in carefully calculated hours to shield some plants from the excessive magical light. Working in the fields is a job for convicted criminals, who sleep outside the city walls and often fall prey to the Tainted Ones. It's where most of the kids from the Blessed Dawn orphanage end up, unless they don't have a sweet smile and golden locks like Tayna, or an affinity to bend the rules like me.

The vegetation soon turns gray and scarce, weeds mingle with the wheat, and the bird songs die out. All remnants of the ancient pavement are swallowed by the dark and barren soil.

We are in the Wastelands.

Centennial woods, bustling with life, stretched here before the Hex. Forests teeming with wolves, bears, foxes and smaller beasts, skies charted by eagles, birdsongs and the aroma of flowers in the air.

Now, every breath crushes the lungs with the distant stench of death and fire. Sun rays barely break through the sticky haze, tinting everything gray and muffling the sounds of voices and hooves. Soot dances around like morbid snowflakes.

The governor's soldiers have regrouped. They ride close to the carriage now, peering into the dead forest surrounding us. Unseen threats reach out to our caravan from the dead branches, and I shuffle nervously. It's the first-time traveler syndrome, probably, though the soldiers also look all tensed up. Now, back in Tenebris, the sun has warmed up the crystalline waters of the Fountain of the Five on Temple Square, and all street urchins are diving into its clear waters before the priests come out, chasing them to the streets. My chest tightens as the rows of black charred trunks around blur my vision. We ride as if a Tainted horde is at our heels.

My stomach growls, drawing my eyes to the picnic basket on the opposite bench. I reach for a wafer, the sweet taste a brief solace. Outside, the tainted sunlight shifts. Atos's hairy armpits, it is getting dark! Terror solidifies in my gut when the soldiers spur their horses and gallop ahead. What Fae trickery is this? Have they brought me here just to abandon me at Nightfall?

A glow, much stronger than the thinning sunlight, filters through the lacy curtains of the carriage window.

Have they somehow led us through a portal? The dead forest is transformed into another world. Hundreds of torches stand on both sides of the road. The forest floor beneath the wheels is draped with golden cloth, just like the old tales describe the Sacred City of the Elders.

With one final shudder, the carriage halts, and the door flies open. I hop down, nearly losing my balance after hours of sitting. A loud crackle of magic and a bright flash above startles me, and I whip my head up. Elders! A thick, blinding protective halo unfolds over a wide clearing crowded with colorful tents. At its center, surrounded by dozens of Fae soldiers in steel armor, stands a grand, domed tent of fine fabric.

Soft music and the clank of glasses spill out of its entrance.

"Welcome, Talysse of No Name," a masculine voice startles me. The Fae male is dressed like a prince and greets me with a polite bow. A refined courtier, without a doubt. "You are late; forgive us for starting the feast without you."

"A feast?" I say, voice trembling. It is not what I've expected from brutal Trials with a survival chance of around zero.

"Please follow me." The courtier glides over the cloth of gold, giving me no choice but to follow.

The hairs on my nape stand up as we pass by the dozens of Unseelie soldiers, their polished armor shining in the golden light of the halo. Atos take them; there are so many of them! Sitting around their campfires or patrolling in smaller groups in the space between the tents, they ignore us. The unease of their presence still lingers as we slip into the large tent. So, this is what a lamb among wolves feels.

The air under the tall dome of thin fabric is surprisingly cooler and—are these snowflakes? Just below the draped ceiling rages a tiny snowstorm. If it is a clever illusion or some unknown spell, I cannot tell, as I'm busy staring at the crowd in the wide space. More than a dozen humans and Fae are sitting at a long table loaded with steaming roasted meats, pastries, mountains of fruits, and sparkling wine in tall golden-rimmed glasses. My mind cannot fathom all the abundance, but my stomach does, and to my embarrassment, it rumbles loudly.

"Lords and ladies, here comes Talysse of No Name from Tenebris, Satreyah Province. May she please the Elders in these Nightfall Trials!"

I wince at the wave of attention crushing on me, curious eyes staring at my clothes, evaluating my posture, glaring at my scar. I take a step forward, straighten my shoulders, and plaster a grin on my face.

Everyone quickly returns to what they were doing: eating and talking in hushed tones.

The courtier shows me to a seat at the head of the table. On my left sits a strong-built man with a bronze complexion and blond hair so typical for Odryssia. His bright eyes linger on my clothes and my scratched face. His lips curl into a thin smile, and he leans back, crossing his arms over a velvet jerkin threaded with gold. He looks like the man I'd wished to marry if everything had gone as planned in my life. If I had grown up as a refined, fancy-educated lady in my parents' mansion, not as a daughter of traitors, an orphan, and a criminal.

I nervously tuck in some loose strands back into my crown braid and study the rows of unfamiliar cutlery, terrifying as siege weapons lined up before the city walls. Well, that should do. I pick the largest spoon and start scooping steamed vegetables into my plate. A cackle makes my hand freeze mid-air. The Odryssian man whispers something in the ear of a statuesque blonde human woman sitting next to him, and she's laughing, her eyes pinned on me. Obviously, my cutlery choice was amusing. Her long, flaxen hair drapes her back, and she's leaning on his shoulder, quite an intimate gesture. When our eyes meet, hers flicker with disgust, and she quickly leans closer to the blond man and whispers something in his ear. Something that makes them both burst into laughter at my expense.

I raise a glass to them, looking the princess-y woman straight in the eye. This makes her uncomfortable, and she looks away. I shrug and shovel buttery vegetables in my mouth, refusing to feel self-conscious about my worn-out velour pants, faded shirt, and the doublet, which has had its share of owners before me. The contrast to what she is wearing is striking; the light leather armor that hugs her curves looks specifically crafted for her, embellished with a golden coat of arms. The crowd from the back alleys of Tenebris eats princesses like this for breakfast. Responding with a grin, flashing too many teeth, I let them laugh and shift my attention to the rest of the group.

Thank the Elders for this seat! The chair on my right is empty, and it gives me the opportunity to study the others without the annoyance of small talk.

A short and bulky man with a shaved skull and bare, muscled arms, focused entirely on the food, sits next to the woman in the fancy armor I've already nicknamed Warrior Pony Princess. He's wearing shimmering chainmail and is chewing so intensely that thick veins are bulging on his temples. Droplets of fat glisten on his bejeweled vambraces.

Every time he looks up from the spiced drumsticks and creamy potato puree, he watches the other guests. Especially the Fae. We obviously share the same disdain.

I know his kind; I have seen them on caravans passing Tenebris. He is a mercenary, a ruthless man tempered in the Wastelands, aware of all the dangers lurking in this dead world. And a damned good one, judging by the myriad of gold rings on his short, sturdy fingers. Well, this is someone I'd love to have on my side, yet mercenaries are selfish and unpredictable. He cocks his head when he regards me, his low, sun-scorched forehead wrinkling. Almost immediately, his dark eyes turn cold, and he looks away. Seems like he's just classified me as harmless, not strong enough to be trouble.

I wonder if the man wields any magic or if all he has is just brutal force. Magic is rare, and very often, some of the five provinces send regular humans when they cannot find any mages for the tournament. If he relies only on his muscles and battle experience, he might be in for a surprise.

I pile some more food on the silver plate inlaid with gold flowers, ignoring the snarky comment of the WPP that I've probably never seen that much food in my life. Atos's hell pits, she's right; at least not food like this: a juicy mushroom-stuffed starling with a spicy radish purée on the side. Cutting the meat into small pieces, I resume my observation.

A brutish Fae female with shaved sides of her skull and gruesome tattoos is quietly sipping on her wine, watching everyone with half-lidded eyes. She's wearing a moss-green tinted leather armor. Odd jewelry made of bones pierces her nose and the high tips of her ears.

"This is Aydalla, court huntress. Beware of her. She is brutal, and she detests us," a warm male voice makes me drop my fork. A broad-shouldered man with messy brown curls and a blinding smile pulls the vacant chair on my right. Now I know what he means by *us*. He is also human. Judging by his sun-kissed skin probably from the Free Cities. My eyes are drawn immediately to his heavy golden earrings engraved with arcane symbols. "Protective runes," he clarifies, misinterpreting my greedy gaze. Those earrings can fetch a handsome price at Mute Gorb's pawn shop. "Small magical talismans are allowed in the Trials." His fingers tap on my bracelet, and for a moment, all color drains from his face, but he quickly recovers.

"Same here, protection," I mumble, pulling the ragged lace of my sleeve to cover the bracelet, reluctant to share the story of my accident and the trinket, which Mother believed would make my ugly scar less obvious. I'm not sure if it works, as the red, angry skin is still there, but I guess it would've been much worse without it.

"Well, Talysse of No Name, you look like you're in desperate need of a drink. And some company." He fills my crystal flute with faintly shimmering Fae wine and piles a tiny iceberg of cheese on his plate. "Too bad you've missed the introductions, but I can see that you're observant enough. I am Galeoth, by the way. People call me Gale." He throws a piece of juicy ham in his mouth, watching me. His almond-shaped eyes have a warm, honey color; their unusual shape makes him look as if he's smiling all the time. A furrow appears between his dark brows as if he's struggling to process something.

"Well, you already know my name, and yes, I'm in dire need of a drink." I continue slicing my starling, wondering what the real reason behind his friendliness is. Men are never friendly to women like me without an agenda.

"Is it true you were living in a stable?" Gale asks, twirling his glass casually, and the Warrior Pony Princess snorts loudly. I take a long look at him while chewing on my starling. Surprisingly, there's no trace of mockery behind that smile, which seems to be able to melt the snow caps of the Holy Mountain. Just genuine curiosity.

"You mean after my parents were executed by the Fae, my sister was sold to the highest bidder, and I was forced to fend for myself when I was seventeen? Yes, it was hard to find shelter, so after weeks of being bitten by rats, nearly raped, and stabbed a couple of times, I managed to find refuge in a stable. It appeared to me grander than a palace." I chew on my piece with delight, looking him straight in the eye.

His amber eyes soften. "Apologies. I didn't mean to sound snobbish, Talysse, and I have respect for a fellow survivor," he lowers his voice. "Anyways, we've disclosed that Aydalla is to be avoided, but so is this one." He points with his knife without bothering to conceal who he is talking about at a very unusual Fae.

"What is she?" I whisper, glaring. A tall and slender female sits behind a glass of plain water, her frame almost ethereal yet menacing. Her skin, a deep, bark-like hue, is veined with pulsating dark green lines that hint at the power coursing through her. Her hair cascades like twisted vines, a tangled mass of deep green and black tendrils, some of which move and slither with a life of their own. Her eyes, glowing an eerie emerald, are fixed somewhere ahead in a quite unsettling way. Dark, leaf-like patterns adorn her limbs. Foreboding energy buzzes around her, and the seats on both sides of her are empty.

"Is she—"

"A Dark Dryad? Yes. Dark Dryads never speak, so nobody knows her name or why she has volunteered for the Trials. No need to tell you to steer clear of this one. Dark Dryads—"

"—can summon roots and vines and crush their foe or poison them as they have powers over venomous plants." Gale nods, and his lips stretch in an approving smile, displaying the even row of his teeth.

"I see you know your Fae. Unexpected for someone living in stables," Gale says softly, ensuring the WPP and her friend don't overhear.

I raise an eyebrow and reply with a smirk. "What can I say? The horses have excellent taste in bedtime stories."

We both chuckle, and I lean closer to him. "Why are you telling me all this, Gale? Why are you so kind?" I ask, shoving a spoonful of purée into my mouth. Friar Ben always said I was too direct, but it has served me well so far.

"It doesn't hurt to have allies in the hell we're about to enter, right? And the other humans look…not so trustworthy," he says, gesturing subtly at the blond nobles and the mercenary sitting nearby.

I chew thoughtfully, then nod. "You've got a point there. Plus, I hear mercenaries have a habit of vanishing when things get messy."

Gale chuckles. "Exactly. And I'd rather not rely on someone too afraid not to mess up their hair or stain their clothes." He points his chin at WPP and her friend, who are too focused on their food to notice.

"Smart move," I say, grinning. "So, what's your story? Did you volunteer, tempted by their promises of riches and power?"

"Of course. Who wouldn't be? And let's just say the Trials would give me a chance to settle an old debt," he replies with a wink, but there is a darker nuance to his words. He remains silent for a moment, the clanking of cutlery and the voices of the others filling the awkward silence, then lifts his glass and downs it in one go, crimson droplets staining his richly embroidered cotton shirt.

"So, Talysse of the Stables, back to our Fae. You've already met the Dryad and the Huntress. Now behold Lord Woodrick, busy with this enormous piece of raw meat—"

I nearly choke on a mushroom when I spot the enormous Fae male across the table and the ferocity with which he's tearing at the meat. Sweet Cymmetra, he's even growling and gnawing on the bone! His spiky black hair is stained with blood, and so is his leather vest. Every now and then, he quickly scans the tent, his eyes the color of old gold. His vertically slit pupils dilate when he catches me glaring. He lets go of the meat, then nods and smiles, his lips revealing blood-stained and unnervingly sharp fangs.

"And you've caught the attention of the lord, the one thing you were supposed not to!" Gale throws his hands in the air dramatically.

"Great, just what I needed," I mutter, unbothered, continuing to study the Fae. An amulet carved from dark wood hangs around his neck. Unusual, as Fae prefer more complex and luxurious pieces. It is a rough wolf head. The hairs on my neck stand up when I realize what it means.

"Is he—"

"Yes, he is," Gale confirms. "A shifter. No need to warn you to stay away from him, right? Stay away from all of them, Talysse. They're here to hunt humans. And they don't fear death. Let me tell you, after you've lived for some centuries, the halls of Atos seem like a good alternative to all this."

"Note taken. My father used to say that the longevity of Fae messes up their heads, and some take their own lives, but many go mad and decide to go out in a blaze of glory. Surely, some of them are at this point right now."

"Bingo. And speaking of insanity, is this—" I strain my eyes to make sure that I'm seeing right, "is this a child?"

Sitting deeper into the tent, where the light is more scarce, sits a boy no older than eleven. He's clad in black, and the shadows around him thicken. Something is disturbing behind this look of innocence as if something old and foul is trapped underneath this pristine skin. The boy's irises glow bright red under the chestnut locks draping his forehead, and his playful smile cannot conceal the aura of danger his whole being emanates.

"It is anything but a child, Talysse, and something tells me he's the most dangerous of them all. Stay—"

"I know, Gale. I'll stay away from him." The boy snaps his head in our direction, his deep crimson eyes anything but childlike. There's sadness there, collected over centuries, and hot, barely-leashed frenzy. Praised be Atos, some servants swarm the tent bringing trays with more food and hiding the odd child.

"Yep, just keep to your lemony cake and leave the ancient horror alone," Gale says, leaning back and sipping on his wine as if he's at a friend's gathering, not about to enter the deadliest Trials on Phyllesia.

"You know," I say, stretching over the table to help myself to some lemony cake with gold leaf on top, "for a guy about to face certain death, you're remarkably chill."

"Gotta enjoy the little things, Talysse. Like cake. And not being eaten by a wolf-man or a demon child."

"Well, here's to surviving the night then." I raise my fork, offering a mock toast.

"To surviving the night," Gale echoes, clinking his wine glass against my fork with a grin.

"Wait," I say, licking my fingers covered in glaze. "Something's not right. Five Elders, five provinces, five humans." I point my sticky fork at us both, the blonde WPP and her chevalier, and the mercenary. "There should also be five Fae, right?" A creepy child, Lord Woodrick and his bone, the tattooed Huntress, and the silent Dryad. Four. The Fae wine hasn't messed with my senses. "Where—"

A crowd of Fae courtiers spills into the tent. The silky fabric shakes with a sudden explosion of cheer, and the air thickens with the scent of perfumes.

"Oh, great," Gale mutters, rolling his eyes. "Here comes the circus."

Someone important is coming.

All eyes are glued to the entrance, and I nearly spit out my last piece of cake when, at the center of the crowd, sharp, beautiful, and deadly as a sword, stands Governor Aeidas.

"What threads of fate is Seuta weaving right now, and for what purpose? Why is this prick here?" I whisper, my voice tinged with both dread and curiosity.

A Fae female who appears frail and ancient—if you can judge age with their kind—leads the group. She steps forward and spreads her arms in a dramatic gesture. The wide split sleeves of her white silk gown sweep the floor like the wings of an odd, old bird. Sacred symbols are tattooed on her forehead, in even rows down her cheeks and neck. A thick golden disk hangs on a massive chain on her sunken chest, bearing the sacred stamp of the Elders; this must be a mage of the highest rank. Her long white hair shimmers like gossamer, and her eerie eyes, entirely black, surrounded by long white lashes, seem to reflect the lights like a dark lake. Her pale lips draw into a smile that doesn't reach her eyes. Silence reigns before she starts speaking. Even Gale is glaring at her, his fingers nervously playing with his massive golden earrings.

"Welcome, honored ones, and blessed be the sacrifice you make in the name of the Elders! Welcome to the Nightfall Trials," she announces in a sweet, serene tone, sweeping those too-long sleeves in a well-practiced gesture. This Fae seems to be quite the performer.

"Now, welcome the last Fae contestant, Prince Aeidas of House Nightbriar, the heir to the Unseelie Throne!"

Deafening applause shakes the tent and rolls over the Unseelie camp. If Atos opened the ground beneath my feet and I plunged into the darkness of his halls, that would be far more preferable to the nightmare unfolding before my eyes.

The murderer of my parents is the fucking crown prince?

"He was serving as Governor of Satreyah when his brother perished. Now he's the heir to the Unseelie throne," Gale informs me coldly, making an effort to appear unimpressed by this display of power and excess.

"You mean when he poisoned his brother," I correct him, my eyes glued to the Fae who single-handedly destroyed my life. The jealous younger brother, raised in the shadow of the throne heir, decided he had enough and poisoned him on his coronation day.

"And this one, Talysse," Gale cocks his head pointedly at the Unseelie Prince, who looms over the crowd of courtiers, "this one you should avoid at all costs. If you have to choose between this cold-blooded killer and a Shadowfeeder, you'd better take the Shadowfeeder. At least you know what to expect."

I nod in silent agreement, still trying to untangle my feelings. Oh, isn't it ironic that Seuta has brought us together in this deadly contest, where I could slit his throat while he's sleeping and not hang for it? My lips curl up in a mad, anticipating smile, and right at this moment, the prince's intense gaze crashes into mine. Recognition ripples across his ridiculously handsome features. The Elders were too cruel, creating the cursed Unseelie so beautiful. And this murderer shines like the first sun rays after a long night, like a green shore before the eyes of a drowning man.

"A predator designed to trick and exploit," Gale mutters, echoing my thoughts.

Yet I cannot help the fluttering of timid butterflies in my stomach, so I drown them in wine. The realization that the murderer of my family will sit on that cursed throne, wielding unlimited power over the fates of all humans in the five provinces, disturbs me in ways I cannot even fathom.

When he leans back in his tall chair, his eyes seek mine again, and for a fleeting moment, something passes between us. I cannot put my finger on it, but I feel the pull, the undeniable allure of danger and darkness that has brought so many to an early grave. It's a velvety smirk in the dark, long fingers ending with sharp claws, able to caress or murder, depending on the mood of their owner.

"Talysse, are you drooling?" Gale teases, snapping me out of my reverie.

"Shut up, Gale." I toss a piece of cake at him. He deftly dodges and responds by throwing a grape, which I manage to catch with my mouth. We laugh, but the sound feels hollow against the undercurrent of tension that hangs over us.

Despite our playful banter, the reality of our situation presses in. The festive air in the tent is a fragile facade, barely concealing the gravity of what's to come. Around us, Fae courtiers move with a sense of anticipation, their eyes gleaming.

As the mage's dramatic announcement fades, it's clear that we are on the brink of something. The delicate balance of power and the intricate webs of alliances and enmities all seem poised for a drastic shift. The Trials are not just a test of survival; they are a stage for a much larger, darker play.

Gale's fingers toy nervously with his golden earrings. At this moment, it feels as if the very fabric of the world is being rewoven, each thread pulling us inexorably toward an unknown fate. The gears of some ancient, unfathomable mechanism are grinding forward, set to alter the course of all our lives.

And there we stand, at the heart of it all, caught between laughter and fear, ready to face whatever the Trials have in store.

TALYSSE

LAST MINUTES OF DAYLIGHT

"**Y**ou all know the rules of this sacred tournament, given to us by the Elders themselves, as many of you have been raised for this moment." The voice of the white-haired hag with the creepy all-black eyes drags me back to reality. WPP and her admirer look around proudly, and I roll my eyes.

"The rules are quite simple, Talysse," Gale whispers in my ear. "We have to retrieve some magical artifacts from deadly locations or perform some dangerous task. Everything is allowed to recover the magical artifacts, so expect many to come after you if you happen to find them first."

I scoff. "Wouldn't expect anything less. So killing is encouraged."

"Killing is encouraged and celebrated, indeed." He giggles.

"Of course. They're Fae."

"Silence," the Odryssian man shushes us, and we all look back at the mage.

"You will walk with only the faith in our Elders in your heart, may it be your greatest weapon," she continues.

"She means we'll be searched for weapons before we leave," Gale translates. "But once out there, in the night, you can use whatever it takes to win."

I remain silent, weighing all the possibilities. I'm confident I'll find something out there, even if it's just a simple club.

"To prove your valor, you, honorable contestants, are going to search for the magical objects only at night. And a long night is coming." She waves a pale, bony hand at the entrance of the tent.

"How does she know that?" I ask Gale in dismay. Just a handful of mages were able to foretell the duration of the night.

"This is Aernysse Stargaze," he whispers back, and silence reigns in the tent, disturbed only by the crackling of the candles and the crystalline vibration of the tiny snowstorm above us. My jaw drops. The ancient court mage, older than the Hex! By Atos, tonight, I am seeing legends come to life.

"I wonder what her game is," Gale leans closer to whisper in my ear and draws the cold gaze of the Unseelie Prince. His dark brows, beautifully contrasting with his long silver hair, pull together as he watches us from across the table. He's probably annoyed that I am already forging alliances. I shrug and shift my attention back to Aernysse. She spreads her arms in another dramatic gesture, her long white sleeves sweeping the carpet-covered floor of the tent.

"Join me for a prayer, children of the Elders, and you, lateborn!"

Crossing my arms, I spit on the floor at the condescending term she used for us humans. The WPP raises a fine blonde brow at my not-so-lady-like reaction and elbows her friend. If those two behave like this in the night out there, they'll be dead within an hour. The "lateborn" tag is a theological theory feeding the Fae philosophy of supremacy. Their holy books state (though no human has ever seen them) that the Elders created the Seelie and Unseelie first, and because the two kinds were quarreling all the time, they shaped the humans to give the Fae someone to watch over, to care for, and distract them from their squabbling. No wonder all their egos are hyper-inflated. They're probably fed this bullshit since the cradle. Human priests tell a different story: of us, created together with the Seelie and the Unseelie, each kind blessed by a different Elder with different abilities.

I'd rather enter the hell pits of Atos's rift than pray with these bigots. Moving my lips as if I am praying, my eyes inexplicably drift to the prince, who has leaned back into his chair, his face hidden in the shadows, his eyes flashing in a predatory way. My heart takes a small leap when I realize he's probably looking at me. What is this maniac's obsession with me?

The last words of the prayer swirl heavily in the air and Aernysse opens her strange eyes, scrutinizing each one of us. Both human and Fae shuffle in their seats, probably wondering what follows.

"You will be blindfolded and taken to Teír Mekheret now." Her voice has changed as if it comes from depths unknown, not out of the frail ancient body. "You will all be released not far from the city walls."

Murmurs ripple among the contestants.

"Teír Mekheret!" Gale drawls and whistles. "Elders know what lingers in the ruins of the cursed city!"

I shush him as the mage continues.

"There, one of you should retrieve a flint." The hag pauses, and we all look at each other, wondering if we heard right. "Not just any flint, but a piece of the Heart of the Sacred Mountain. With the right skill, it can start a fire that would keep Shadowfeeders at bay."

Everyone gasps. If this is not just another Fae lie, such an artifact would be priceless.

The mercenary clears his throat, and all eyes land on him. "If someone else finds this flint first, can we take it from them?" The sinister smile on his lips hints at what he means by "take." The Fae Huntress cackles. Gale was right; these really are a bunch of murderous freaks.

"Anything is allowed. Valor and piety shall prevail. When the night ends, you are not to harm any other contestant until the next trial begins. And before you think of it," she adds, "if you run away or abandon the Trials, your next of kin will be punished in a way Elders see fit."

The hairs on my nape stand up just thinking of the countless ways these monsters could hurt my sister. Not that I plan on backing down. I will do my best to wipe all their smug smiles off.

"It's a battle of talent and magic, so get ready to be thoroughly searched for weapons and blindfolded. Pray and prove yourself worthy of the Elders' blessing. May only the best see the dawn."

TALYSSE

TEÍR MEKHERET

Blindfolded, I stumble for a third time. My curse lands in the silence, interrupted only by the steps of my guards, like a rock in a lake. The camp is far behind us, the last remnants of smoke in the warm evening air gone a while ago. The Fae female walking next to me snorts. "You need to learn to move in silence if you want to last longer than ten minutes, human. The Tainted Ones have excellent hearing," she mocks.

"You try it with a blindfold, Unseelie!" I hiss back. The other soldiers accompanying us in the arduous march through the night forest cackle. I've lost track of time, and my legs are surely bruised from all the branches and rocks I've walked into. The guides let me do that on purpose to get their share of fun.

Technically, she's right. Humans don't have the Unseelie's sharp night vision, nor their speed and weapon skills, honed by centuries of warfare. What I have is the courage of desperation: the strength of the condemned fighting to flee the scaffold before the ax falls, the strength of a mother dragging her family out of a burning house.

Rough fingers yank my blindfold off, messing up my crown braid. I blink and tuck the loose strands back in while the world around me comes into focus.

A shove in my back sends me flying forward, and just like that, the Unseelie are gone.

I am alone in the Wastelands.

Before me, the tall walls of Teír Mekheret, silvered by the moonlight, gnaw at the night sky.

Massaging my knee, I look up and gasp. It's the first time I see the moon and stars without the veil of the Blessed Light Spell. The night sky, an indigo canvas, is studded with shimmering diamonds, each star a testament to the divine. The moon, a solid disk with mysterious symbols engraved on its surface, hangs over the ruins like a magical lantern.

The chill of the night slowly settles over the ancient pavement like a shroud. My heart pounds as I approach the jagged walls of the deserted city. Teír Mekheret was once the jewel of the continent before the war between Seelie and Unseelie drowned the world in darkness. Nobody remembers how the city fell, but legends of wraiths and vengeful spirits dwelling among the ruins persist. Adventurers, tempted by the promise of treasures, ventured into the city and never returned.

I scan my surroundings, eyes straining to penetrate the thick darkness beyond the crumbling arch of the city gates. The dead trees loom behind me like skeletal sentinels, their twisted branches reaching out like clawed fingers. Shadows lurk among the trunks. I shudder and hastily take my first step toward the city, the ancient pavement crunching beneath the worn-out heels of my boots. Each step feels like approaching the edge of an abyss, my breath hitching with every creak and groan of the ruins ahead.

The way to my new life in the Free Cities goes through this broad, paved street. Silence wraps everything, but it is not complete. The Wastelands and the old town might be long dead, yet the distant croaking of frogs, the song of the crickets, and the lonely call of a nightbird remind me that little souls survived the devastation of the Hex. The Shadowfeeders and their thralls devour all living, human, Fae, and beasts alike, yet life seems to find a way.

In the Bountiful Bosom, stories were told of animals, fast and smart enough to find food in the Wastelands and survive. Townsfolk talked about a herd of deer—majestic wild animals that haven't been seen in centuries—wandering around. Yet other rumors persist about creatures twisted and changed by the vile magic of the Shadowfeeders: bears, wolves, and dogs, thirsty for blood and flesh, eager to spread the Taint.

As my steps echo down the road, the shadows grow longer and darker, twisting and writhing as if alive. My imagination conjures images of Shadowfeeders lurking just out of sight, their hungry eyes watching my every move. The buildings loom over me, their once grand facades now crumbling and covered with dark, creeping vines. I shake my head. It's only in my head. I am alone.

The street takes me to a small square dominated by a marble fountain. The water within it is dark and still, a mirror reflecting the twisted ruins around. I swallow drily, my throat parched. The stories of careless travelers who drank from tainted streams and lost their minds resurface in my mind. In the Wastelands, water is a deadly gamble. Only a few rivers and streams remain untainted, and I must be careful.

Nothing to find here. No weapons, no water. I hasten my step and stretch all my senses, like the long fingers of an invisible hand, trying to feel some anomaly. Something magical. Magic has a specific vibration; it even has a taste. It's like a tender melody of wind chimes, like the memory of an exquisite dish on the palate of a starving person.

Each step is a risk, especially when walking the open street, brightly lit by the moonlight. The other contestants are as dangerous as the Shadowfeeders and their thralls. My plan is to keep my distance from everyone except for Gale. There's something trustworthy about him, as if he's a long-lost childhood friend or a favorite cousin who came back into my life.

A barely perceptible move ahead startles me, and I quickly step away from the street, bathed in moonlight. My heart beats against the ribcage so loud that every enemy a mile around might hear it.

What sorcery is this?

To the Atos's hell pits with my curiosity! My feet carry me forward against my will, mesmerized by the dance of tiny flickering lights in the thorny weeds sprouting from the walls.

Fireflies! A rare sight in this desolate world.

Fireflies are believed to be messengers of Elder Cymmetra, the protector of nature and beasts. Perhaps she's offering her blessing? I stand for several minutes, searching their dance for a hidden pattern, a divine sign.

This is no sign, just some bugs flying.

No Elder will help me. Only I can save my ass, and Tayna's future is in my hands, just like Myrtle and Stebian's.

The gods have abandoned this cursed realm after destroying it themselves.

And I have an artifact to find.

The deeper I go, the more this city reminds me of a tomb. Tall houses with collapsed roofs decorated with bas-reliefs and flower friezes stare at me with black windows. In the battle between decadence and decay, the latter is winning. I have to make my way around rubble and collapsed walls. Statues covered in dust follow me with wide-open white eyes. The sound of rocks falling from great heights rumbles deeper into the heart of this cemetery. No weapons in sight so far; nothing but rubble lies on the streets, and entering the gloom beyond the gaping windows is too risky. I fill the pockets of my pants with rocks. Rocks have saved me from tight situations more than once on the streets of Tenebris, and my aim is great. But what would these do against a horde of Shadowfeeders and their thralls? Or some frenzied Fae?

The street is climbing steeply, and I dig into my memories for any information about this city. All human capitals of old had magical academies, back when magic was not that scarce. Maybe if I find a higher ground, I can take a look around and locate the academy. It is a vague plan, but it is better than nothing. The only problem is that the others might be doing just the same.

Some parts of the Teír Mekheret are almost intact. It seems like a devastating wave of something gruesome swept through it centuries ago, but some areas were spared. The tower looming at the end of the uphill street is halfway torn by some grand force. Yet most of it still stands, and with some luck, there might be a way to climb it.

The moonlight drips over the ruins like quicksilver. The frozen sea of marble and decay presses on my senses. Searching for a small artifact here is worse than searching for a needle in a haystack.

Out of breath, I reach the top of the slope. The colossal bone-colored tower looms ahead, piercing the starry sky. Sections of the walls are in ruins, revealing spiral staircases within.

Wait a minute.

I curse softly when I notice the light burning in the arched ground-floor window.

Atos take me with my damned fireflies and cautious dancing around the ruins. Someone was faster and set up a camp on the ground floor. Shadowfeeders and Tainted ones despise fire and light—so this is for sure another contestant. Or is the ancient city not as abandoned as believed?

And because fate always likes to make things worse, a tender, otherworldly melody spills out of the door and reaches me with the night breeze. It lingers over the ruins and drips down the dead streets like the sweet scent of blossoms, like the fresh air after a summer rain.

Tempting and powerful, the flute seduces my senses and makes me abandon all reason. Is there any mysterious spell in the tune, or is it my hexed curiosity? I need to see who is playing this flute as if it were Elder Raynisse herself.

THE PRINCE

THE TOWER

The city is ancient, haunted by memories that cling to crumbling walls like shadows. Death lingers here, ever-present, watching from the darkened windows like hollow eyes.

Yet, in this desolation, there are tiny pockets of life, defying the decay. Bindweed has taken root in the cracks of the masonry, its slender vines reaching upward, blooming with small, white trumpet-shaped flowers. Praise Cymmetra! Nature always finds a way to remind us that there is still beauty in this cruel world. Cicadas and crickets have found a refuge between the leaves and are singing the oldest hymn of the night, a reminder of times when the gloom was a time for peace and rest.

My fingers close around a blossom stem, but an old memory holds me back.

The day I tried to pluck a flower from the royal gardens, driven by the desire to have something beautiful that was mine, Viridis stopped me, his deep green eyes flashing with disapproval. "Leave them for the bees and the tiny creatures whose lives depend on them!" he had said.

There had been another time, a darker memory that still stings. I was just a boy then, full of frustration and anger at the world that seemed to demand so much from me. While tending to the fragrant black roses, I spotted a stubborn weed choking one of the delicate stems. I grabbed the weed and yanked it out of the ground with all the strength I could muster.

"What are you doing, Princeling?" Viridis had appeared out of nowhere, his face a mask of anger that I had never seen before. The sight of it froze me in place; the weed still clutched in my hand. "I thought you came to my gardens because you valued life, not because you loathed it."

"But it's just a weed, Viridis." My voice trembled with confusion and a childish sense of justice. "It was strangling the roses!"

His anger had not abated. "Just a weed? And does that make it unworthy of life? Do we destroy what we do not find beautiful or useful? Is that what you believe?"

I had no answer for him then, only the burning shame of a child caught doing something wrong.

"And yet the Elders condemned them all to die, just like the rest of this world," I murmured.

"Maybe, maybe not. Maybe they have just laid them to rest until better times come and someone worthy finds a way to end this suffering. Like bulbs deep in the soil, maybe the life in the Wastelands waits for the spring. For the war to end."

"I thought the war had ended," I responded with a condescending smirk. The old gardener tended to get confused sometimes, the long centuries of his life clouding his mind. He often muddled memories with reality.

"Oh, is it? Then tell me, Princeling, when was the last time you slept without a dagger under your pillow? When was the last time your father didn't spend the morning signing death sentences to those aiding Seelie refugees?"

I swallowed my remark that he might lose his head over comments like that. Because even that young, I'd realized how right he was.

Yet his words settled in my heart and made their home there, sprouting roots and growing, just like the bulbs he mentioned.

I lower my hand, leaving the tender bindweed blossom.

A firefly lands on a waxy leaf. An omen of Cymmetra, I chuckle.

Time to press on.

Stomping my feet, throwing stones, trying to make as much noise as possible, I head deeper into the city.

Come and find me.

And yet there is no sign of anything living when I reach the tower in the heart of the town. This is a great place to linger—all fools will come this way sooner or later.

The echoes of those who dwelled here are still perceivable in the inky void beyond the torn-out gates. Dusty skeletons litter the floor, some of them covered in rusty armor, others are so heartbreakingly tiny. It seems the townspeople had their last stand here before the doors got breached by whatever ended them. Was it the Hex? Or my ancestors? I rub my collarbone, the Ancestral Mark burning, stinging my flesh, a constant reminder that my bloodline was one of those who started the war and triggered the Hex.

Scavenging through the ruins, I gather pieces of ancient furniture and tattered rags. With a whispered incantation, a fire spell ignites the pile, flames leaping hungrily to consume the remnants of those who once called this place home. Like moths to the flame, my enemies will flock here. Rolling a dusty carpet, I rest my head on it, then pull out the flute from my pocket.

In case they miss the light, the music will bring them here. The melody consumes me, and I feel smug like a spider at the center of its net.

The pale eyes of human kings and nobles, long dead, watch from the peeling portraits on the walls. But then, something unusual stirs—a delicate magic, faint but persistent. The magic feels fragile yet intriguing, like the tender white blossoms outside, holding within it a veiled power. I lower my flute. Elders, this will be far more entertaining than playing for the paintings.

"You may come out, human," the loud command disturbs the dusty silence.

To my surprise, she steps into the light instead of running. It's disappointing; I've anticipated a chase. The woman's dark hair is twisted in braids like a flower wreath around her head, and that unusual white strand over her forehead captures my attention. Her irises—clear as a mountain lake but framed with amber—are so uncommon for a human of Satreyah.

By what whim did the Elders grant her this magic? The thought gnaws, and for a moment, there's a temptation to summon the Shadowblade. But she steps closer, oblivious to the fact that I've just decided to let her live a little longer.

There's something in her defiance that amuses me, that rouses something deep within the darkness that has become my constant companion.

I remember the first time we met, how she lured me into a trap to be robbed by street thugs. It was a delightful evening, and the memory of her panic when she saw what I am still brings a twisted pleasure.

"What's that scar on your shoulder?" The question slips out before I can stop it, making me nearly drop the flute, surprised by my own curiosity.

She shrugs and tucks some strands back into her thick braid. It looks like something she's doing when she's nervous. "Got burned as a child. My mother left milk on the stove, and it was boiling over. I tried to help, and it spilled."

Elders, this must've been quite the torment for a small human child. She pulls the lacy collar of her worn-out shirt up, hiding the deep pink spot larger than my hand.

Once again, I wrestle with that wretched need to know more. "Was your mother careless? Or too busy working to watch you?"

"My mother," she responds, her voice is firm, defensive, "was the best one could hope for. She was a lady. And she was never careless. She just left—once—the Atos-cursed milk."

My eyebrows climb up. Is this human casting a spell over me, as now there are even more questions buzzing in my head like a swarm of impatient bees. How did the daughter of a loving mother, a lady, end up on the streets robbing people?

"I just want to climb up and take a look around. No quarrel intended. I won't hurt you." Her tone is steady, yet something lingers in her words.

And she takes another step.

"You won't hurt me now," I add what she has left out. We both realize how ridiculous this promise sounds, how odd this whole situation is, and a tiny miracle happens.

We laugh.

It sounds like the bark of two rabid dogs, but it brightens the morbid room. Even the skulls seem to grin in the flickering firelight.

She makes another step, and instinct takes control. My Shadowblade slips into my hand, heavy and deadly. For some reason, I hide it behind my back.

What should I do with her? Biting my lip, suddenly conflicted, I realize that it is better to end her now. At least it will not be the long, agonizing death that certainly awaits her if Aydalla or that Atos-cursed child finds her. The vision of her dead body on this dusty floor, among the centuries-old bones, stirs something inside me. Something raw and vulnerable that I don't want to acknowledge.

A weakness.

Weakness will be your undoing. Father's favorite saying.

While I struggle to rein in all these new, unbidden emotions, the human is already at the stairs, her steps quick and determined. There's tension in the line of shoulders, but she does not hesitate. A couple of steps and the gloom of the upper floor swallows her.

I lean back on my rolled carpet, raise the flute to my lips, and let the melody fill the air once more, though my thoughts are far from the music. They circle around the enigma that just climbed the stairs.

As the flames crackle and the music echoes through the ruins, I find myself wondering what kind of life could have shaped her into what she is now. What kind of pain could have left her with that same haunted look I see in my own reflection?

TALYSSE

THE FALL

Climbing the spiraling stairs, I leap over gaps; my shoulder pressed tightly against the cold stone wall. The prince's gaze is a weight on my back, following my every move. Any moment now, he could strike.

My trembling hand searches for support in the crumbling masonry. I have never felt so vulnerable in my life. My fingers close around a stone in my pocket—a small, pitiful defense against the full-blooded Fae with terrifying magic. The absurdity of it almost makes me laugh. What hope do I have? He's honed his powers into lethal precision over decades, while I can only manage a few unclear illusions or shove someone off balance.

Yet no lightning sears my flesh. No blast hurls me into the walls. The faint glow of flames fades with each turn of the stairs, and the darkness ahead thickens like a living thing.

This would be a perfect breeding ground for Shadowfeeders. Gluttonous to devour life, they can spawn in any shadow beyond the reach of the Blessed Light spell. Reluctantly, I summon a small light, creating a faint, shimmering cloud above my head. It casts just enough light to reveal the rubble and cracks, making the shadows entwine into monstrous shapes. The spell is too weak to keep the

Shadowfeeders at bay, and it will only last a few minutes. But that's all the time I need to find a vantage point.

The first level is blocked off—rocks and debris barricade the entrance. A desperate defense, perhaps, but it clearly didn't save the people who once lived here. Whatever swept through this city left nothing alive.

My steps sink into a thick layer of dust on the way to the second floor, untouched for centuries. Has no one else made it this far? Or did others try, only to meet their end at the hands of the prince? My breath catches at the thought; I am already dreading the idea of my way back. Maybe that cruel monster is just sitting there, waiting. The last notes of the haunting melody have died out a while ago. Maybe he's gone?

Small steps, Talysse.

The light spell starts to drain me, but I've reached the landing of the second floor. The faint glow of the spell reveals delicate filigree leaves and flowers carved into the stone, with traces of paint still clinging to the carvings—roses that were once a vivid red, leaves a deep emerald green. For a moment, I pause, imagining the beauty this place must have once held.

The human kingdoms rivaled the Fae ones before the Hex. Art, magic, and science competed to create the perfect society. So much lost to the greed for more power...

My fingers follow the faded paint. Colors have always captivated me—they are so rare in this gray world. I've often tried to picture a world drenched in color: vast green forests, meadows dotted with flowers in every hue, birds splashed with the paints of Raynisse's palette, clear lakes with golden fish…No decay, no death lurking in the shadows, no long nights.

Moonlight filters through the arched door, and I dismiss my weak spell.

My steps disturb the thick, rotten carpet, raising clouds of dust that shimmer like snowflakes in the light of my spell. Dark outlines of overturned furniture emerge as I cautiously approach an arched window, the night sky framed by intricate stone tracery. I glance over my shoulder, half-expecting to see the prince stalking me. But there's no one there. Whatever twisted game he's playing, he's letting me be—for now. The knot in my stomach loosens and I turn to the window.

The city sprawls endlessly beneath the moonlight, an ocean of marble frozen in time. It looks peaceful, but the darkness is too thick in the shadows of a tall ruin not far from the tower. It seems alive, expanding, its tendrils slowly snaking down the narrow alleys.

Atos's hairy armpits!

Shadowfeeders!

Nobody who has seen them lives to tell. Yet, some travelers speak of ten-foot-tall cloaked figures with malevolent eyes, clawed limbs, and unfathomable speed. Only the magical Shadowblades can harm them, legendary weapons wielded by a few powerful Fae, yet nobody has ever boasted about killing one. If you can't hurt it or outrun it, avoid it—simple wisdom from the streets of Tenebris. I carefully mark the spot on the mental map I'm drawing, vowing to avoid it at any cost. Then I continue scanning the ruins for something worth investigating.

There is a building that looks like an arcane academy. It's pentagonal, each wing devoted to one of the Elders. The courtyard is littered with rubble and overgrown with weeds. My heart drums in my chest. Finally, something that gives me hope! I prepare for the dreaded way out of this tower, when something else draws my attention. Someone was faster than me. Like a lost soul, flickering light creeps among the bushes while another one—a simple torch—climbs the grand staircase of the main entrance of the building. Another contestant must have started their search there. A tiny, excited yelp escapes me. Seems like the first clash of these Trials is just minutes away. And to make the stakes even higher, more Shadowfeeders appear in the dark alleys below, gliding through the gloom to the academy.

Time is running out. Soon, the city will be crawling with them, and wherever they go, their thralls—the Tainted Ones—will follow.

And then we're all screwed.

Sharpening that sense with no name, I try to find any source of magic.

And there it is. An oddity.

A mansion of white stone, untouched by decay or whatever destroyed the city. It sticks out like a sore thumb. The rays of the moon around it flicker with odd iridescence, reflected by its sparkling surface. It's just half a mile from the pentagonal building, and, praised be the Elders, no lights wander around it. The ruins stretch for many miles, and noticing it from the ground is probably impossible. I'm absorbed in memorizing the safest route through the maze of the streets when a loud thud and footsteps above startle me.

Someone is walking on the level above me.

Did the prince climb up unnoticed? That's simply impossible. I press my back against the wall, blending with the shadows next to the window. The heavy steps above head toward the stairwell. Whoever is upstairs is most likely coming my way.

Just great. I am caught between the intruder above and the murderous prince below. Best to hide and let them take each other out.

A deafening thunder shakes the building. Dust and tiny rocks shower from the ceiling, powdering my leather doublet. An agonizing female shriek slices through the night, piercing me to the marrow.

And drawing all Shadowfeeders in the town our way.

This was unmistakably the last sound someone did in this world. Someone perishing in great pain. And it came from downstairs, where the prince was playing his melody of death. The thunder, without any doubt, was a powerful spell.

My breaths come fast and shallow. The steps above resume, rumbling down the stairs. Whoever is upstairs is now in a hurry.

Shadowfeeders outside? Checked.

A murderous Unseelie Prince on my only way out? Checked.

Is some unknown horror from above heading my way? Checked.

Can it get any worse?

Atos take me; here I did it again. Challenged Seuta. And she loves proving to us, mortals, THAT IT COULD ALWAYS GET WORSE.

A tall, lithe male figure stands in the arched doorway. Completely still, I try to breathe as quietly as possible and lower my lashes to obscure the whites of my eyes.

The steps slow down when he reaches the square of moonlight in the center of the room.

"Talysse, praised be the Elders; it's really you!"

Those unruly brown curls, the firm jawline, the glimmer of massive golden earrings—"Gale?" I breathe and want to punch myself immediately; it came out too loud. "How did you get past the murderous bastard downstairs? Or were you hiding upstairs?"

"There's another way in, Talysse. Upstairs. Wait, what did you say? You walked past Aeidas, and he let you live?" His forehead scrunches a bit as if he's struggling to believe it.

"Yes, he was playing that cursed flute, and then there was that spell…don't come any closer; I am armed," the lie glides effortlessly off my tongue. "What do you want from me?"

"Really, Talysse? What do I want from you?" He spreads his arms, showing me his empty hands. "I am unarmed. And unlike the other one," his finger points downstairs, "sitting at the exit of this tower and slaying everyone who comes around, I have no deadly magic that can fry you in an instant."

"What do you want?" I insist, my voice hoarse with tension.

"I think we've been through that during dinner, Talysse." He takes another step toward me, the moonlight sharpening his handsome features. His ever-smiling eyes glow like amber. "We're both humans. Cattle among

111

predators. We can use each other's help." He takes another step, that disarming smile tugging the corner of his lip up. His too-perfect teeth flash in a not-so-human way in the moonlight.

"I'll cast a spell, Gale. Stay where you are." My magic is weak, and my chances against a man of his size are laughable. But to trust anyone in these Trials, where only one can emerge victorious, is plain stupid.

"Look, Talysse, Shadowfeeders are gathering outside as we speak, and there is a murderous Unseelie downstairs. Are you really having any doubts about whom to trust?"

An explosion thunders somewhere in the city, shaking the old tower. The floorboards beneath our feet screech and twist. The cracking of beams reverberates through the old structure long after the echo of the explosion has died out.

Tall blue flames consume the pentagonal building outside. It seems that the two contestants have found each other, or someone triggered a magical trap. And to make matters worse, the shadows in the ruins stretch and deepen. Tendrils of darkness feel their way around the ancient stones.

More Sahdowfeeders.

When I look back at Gale, it is already too late. He is at me. His fingers capture my wrists, and he pulls me in against his hard body, pressing a palm against my mouth, silencing a scream and a spell. There's something in the way he holds me—he's strong enough to crush me, yet he keeps himself in check. He restrains me firmly but tenderly like a mother holding an angry child.

112

"If I wanted to kill you, you'd be dead already," he whispers. Well, he has a point. The slow, steady beating of his heart and his embrace calm my wiggling, and I surrender.

He's the only human in these Trials that I'd trust. Maybe having someone around is not that bad—

"Look, Talysse, we are surrounded," Gale says in my ear, so close that his hot breath brushes the strands that escaped my braid. "And you have a decision to make. Trust me now, or go down these stairs into the monster who's killing everyone who enters. Find out for yourself if he'd let you pass...again. Or leave with me. You have my word that I will not harm you."

With these words, he releases me, and I stumble backward, my body protesting against the night chill. It's been a while since a man has held me like this. Gale stands in the square of moonlight, tall and broad-shouldered, his whole posture holding the promise of safety. There's something else in his gold-sprinkled amber eyes; something flashes and disappears like the back fins of a sea monster briefly rising above the surface and disappearing into the unknown depths.

Atos's warty backside. I hate choosing the lesser evil.

"Think fast, Talysse." His voice is hoarse, rushed. The white of his eyes flashes as he looks at the thickening shadows in the ruins beyond the filigree window.

Funny. He's worried about the Shadowfeeders outside but not about that cold-blooded murderer downstairs, who has just ended someone? For a brief moment, I wonder if he'd be able to stand against the Unseelie Prince. They're both huge men, roughly at the same height, their bodies honed by years of rigorous training. And there's something ruthless and rugged about Gale, something elusive, that doesn't fit the narrative of a Free Cities mage who's tempted by money and fame. There's more to this story, and I take a mental note to find out about it.

Tucking loose hairs into my braid, I straighten my doublet and take a deep breath.

"Where is that other way out you mentioned, Gale?"

When fate forces you to make impossible decisions, always go with your gut feeling.

Gale nods and peeks into the moon-silvered ruins outside.

"Atos take them! Shadowfeeders everywhere! They're coming our way, Talysse," he hisses.

With swift, silent steps, he disappears into the inky gloom of the stairwell. I summon my timid light back and follow.

We climb fast, leaping over rubble and old bones. Elders, what has happened here? What kind of terror was unleashed upon these people? How did they die?

The flight of stairs ends on a landing identical to the one below. The carved arched door opens up to another empty room, and Gale rushes in. Probably all chambers in the tower are similar, but this one is more damaged by the elements—holes gape in the floor planks, pieces of the outside wall are torn down, and the pinpricks of stars are clearly visible.

"Here, Talysse, I came in from here." He runs to a gape in the outside wall, overgrown with thick, centennial ivy. It's large enough for a man to squeeze through. "We climb down from here, Talysse."

Atos's warty ass.

I look down, and chills crawl down my spine like angry ants. It's a nearly forty-feet drop. There are cracks in the masonry and sturdy branches of ivy that could offer some support when climbing down the uneven walls.

But me and heights?

Those are two things that don't mix well.

My father tried to cure my childhood fear by encouraging me to climb all the trees in our garden. Certain spots in my body still ache when I remember it.

My fingers desperately dig into the masonry as I struggle to steady my breath.

"Are you sure it's…safe?" I swallow drily, fighting a wave of nausea.

Gale looks at me as if I've just lost my mind. "There is no safe here, Talysse. We're in the Nightfall Trials. There's no safe here. But let me tell you, it's far safer than getting anywhere closer to Prince Asshole. You either climb down or run downstairs to that murderer and a pack of Shadowfeeders." Seeing my throat bob, his tone softens. "It's easier than it looks, Talysse. The holes and the plants make it as easy as climbing a staircase," he finishes reassuringly.

I nod, trying to steady the shaking in my limbs. "You go first." I bargain, still suspicious that there might be some trick and he can push me to my death. Without saying a word, he swings his legs over the edge, grabs the thick ivy branches and starts his descent. He surely makes it look easy.

I watch him for a couple of minutes, but the unnatural silence from downstairs is more frightening than the abyss beyond the wall.

Trying to calm my breath, I get on my knees and slowly straddle the wall. My right foot dangles over the chasm, and my teeth are chattering.

My feet search for support and find it easily in the damaged stonework. Thank the Elders Myrtle gave me soft boots with flexible soles, so finding a purchase is not that difficult. The ivy branches are sturdy, and my fingers are strong enough to hold onto the rocks in the wall.

Gale was right. It's easier than it looks.

The crack in the wall is becoming a black ulcer in the tower body of the ancient tower. Gale must be further down, as I don't hear his ragged breathing anymore. It's just the cool night wind howling through the gaps in the masonry as if those trapped inside have regained their voice.

Don't look down.

One step after the other.

Don't look down.

Elders hate it when things are easy for me. A noise from below breaks my concentration. It's a soft, inhuman, guttural growl, and I react without thinking.

I look down.

And it is all it takes.

The gloom at the feet of the tower is taking monstrous shapes. Gray skin, scales, claws, and feral fangs merge together, forming grotesque figures. I recognize immediately what it is. A Shadowfeeder, right beneath us, its eyes—portals to a dark world full of suffering. Its dagger-sharp claws promise agony, and its teeth—a long death. The temperature around me drops immediately, and I can see the vapor of my breath leaving my lips, just like my calmness leaves my body. More shadows melt, and I realize that the Tainted Ones—the feral thralls of the Shadowfeeders, starved for living flesh, are not far. The last fragments of control over my body shatter. Tainted Ones can climb well.

"Talysse!" Gale hisses from the depths, desperately trying to get to me, but it is too late. "Talysse, let me help—"

Terrified and shaking, my fingers grab the wrong ivy branch. Too thin, too young, too loosely attached to the wall.

With a tiny, terrible noise, it rips off the masonry.

"Talysse—"

I am falling.

THE PRINCE

THE WARDED MANSION

I toss into the fire another unreadable book, rotten by time and the elements, and watch the dance of the flames. The blood of Aydalla the Huntress has already clotted on the ancient floor. Her black, empty eye sockets stare at the vaulted ceiling. She's sprawled next to me, her skin charred, already attracting the bugs. One more dead to haunt this tomb. But unlike the others who left their bones here, this one deserved it.

Fifty gold coins and probably some vague promise—that's all it took to sell her loyalty.

Sorcia is behind all this.

Just as my spies have reported, but I refused to listen.

I bark a bitter laugh.

How many males has Sorcia's poisonous beauty ensnarled and dragged to an untimely death? My brother's bride-to-be has always used her looks and family status for gain. Heartless and power-starved, that's what she is. But to send an assassin after me? This is a whole new level of stupidity.

The corpse of my brother was still not embalmed and prepared for the funeral ceremony when she tried to seduce me. To secure her place on the throne. I pushed her away, and it seemed she took it too personally.

Well, it looks like the tender neck of Sorcia would rather be kissed by the executioner's ax than by me. Because that cold, calculating seductress has made a mistake.

And mistakes in the Unseelie court end only in one way.

She's chosen her assassin poorly. Aydalla is skilled in killing and has been boasting about entering the Trials for months. However, the Huntress was a brute. A silly, arrogant brute. Emboldened by the rusty sword she found somewhere in the ruins, Aydalla sneaked upon me sleeping. Her confidence made her attack me without thinking. She chose not to ponder over the strange fact that a seasoned warrior had let his guard down and decided to take a nap during the deadly Trial. Next to the fire, in a city crawling with enemies.

All it took was one well-aimed spell, and her blood boiled.

Bring me the Heir's ring and get your reward.

This is the only sentence in the letter the assassin kept in her purse. Enough to recognize the elegant handwriting of Sorcia. Enough to lose a head, especially combined with the golden coins with Sorcia's family crest.

The plan seems to be working. My enemies are already making their moves, revealing themselves.

Time to move on. Time to continue my hunt. I step over the assassin's body and head to the door.

The cool night air brushes over my skin. Solid darkness creeps from the northern side of the tower, its long tentacles cold and relentless as death itself.

Shadowfeeders.

Elders, this will be a long, exciting night.

The thought of the human with strange magic upstairs makes me hesitate. She hasn't left the tower yet, probably cowering upstairs after she heard Aydalla's scream. For a moment, I stand in the empty street, watching the shadows lengthen. This area will be crawling with Shadowfeeders in no time. Tainted Ones will follow soon. Her magic is intriguing but weak, and they will tear her apart in the blink of an eye. Or worse.

This thought is somewhat...disturbing. Before realizing what I'm doing, I spin on my heel and rush back into the tower.

"Hey, human from Tenebris," I shout while climbing the stairs, "you'd better leave this tower; Shadowfeeders are heading this way!"

Odd. All rooms above are empty, as if the woman has disappeared into thin air. Or escaped through the crack in the wall. No corpse is splattered on the pavement two floors below, so she made it to safety.

There's no time to ponder over her fate as more Shadowfeeders crowd the streets around the tower.

I rush down the stairs, taking two steps at once.

Summoning my Shadowblade, I melt into the night and head to that warded white building I've spotted before.

*

When the Elders decided to unleash the Hex, Atos released the Shadowfeeders from the bowels of his

Underworld. Demons starved for life in all its forms; they are remnants of some long-forgotten war among the gods. Just like everything not belonging to our world, their presence triggers certain alarms. It always gets cold when they're near, and somehow all living creatures sense them.

The calls of the nightbirds over the ruins have died out, the songs of the crickets—muted. My hurried steps thunder down the desolate streets and draw the attention of the demons. The weight of my magical blade, its iridescent dark surface, and the pure arcane energy leashed inside it calm me.

Shadowfeeders don't like my sword. They've attacked me reluctantly before, just to test out its power, but quickly gave up after I've wounded one of them. The creatures are smart and self-aware. They value their lives or whatever twisted form of existence they have and prefer to exhaust Shadowblade wielders with hordes of Tainted Ones. I bet their thralls will show up at any minute.

The city is big, and the ruins offer many hideouts, even from demons spawned by the night.

By Heroy's spear! What was that? Have they taken to the skies now?

Something massive obscures the moon disc for a brief moment. It casts a winged shadow on the pavement, gone in the blink of an eye. Is it some new monstrosity sent by the Elders to torment us? Or some forgotten creature we've just awakened from its slumber?

This city seems to hide more dangers than a handful of Shadowfeeders.

The breeze carries the stench of Tainted Ones. They're near. The creatures are mindless and easy to trick, but once they catch the scent of a living thing, they don't give up the chase. They don't tire; they don't stop until they get whatever poor creature they're after. I've seen what Tainted Ones do to their victims: the trails of blood and intestines stretch more than a mile sometimes.

Is the human with the Seelie bracelet safe?

There she is, slipping uninvited into my thoughts once again.

Just like the city around me, she's a mystery. The woman gave me the impression of someone who can manage a tough situation, and here it is—another question to ask her next time we cross paths. Who or what taught her to be like this?

The humming of the ancient wards ahead interrupts those distractive thoughts. The white building ahead vibrates so intensely it would attract all remaining contestants sooner or later.

Smells linger in the night air, untainted by the stench of the horde. At least three passed here.

It's her.

I halt in the narrow street, crowded with debris, and sniff the air like a beast.

She's alive.

She does not smell like stables and manure like the jealous blonde female at the feast has accused her. Her scent is that of a hyacinth early in the morning—when the warmth of the day still hasn't lured out its full aroma. But there's something else. I throw my head to the side, take deep breaths, and frown. The human is not alone. Another far more intense smell swirls around her. A male. What does he want from her?

I let out a low growl and hasten my step.

It seems that these Trials just got a lot more entertaining than I have thought.

But the real fun will begin after. When I appear before my parents and the court, victorious and ready to take what is mine.

Long and patiently, I've been waiting and preparing for this opportunity.

We were so young when I first doubted if my brother would be a good king.

We were playing in Viridis's gardens. Just like all kids, we were fascinated by all the colors and scents and by the way living things grow. Fencing with our wooden swords, we soon got bored and wandered off into the tunnels of lush foliage, exploring this little world. While I helped bees out of the stream, my brother was busy killing the blue caterpillars hiding under the thick leaves.

"Why are you killing them?" I asked, watching him turn them into blue stains with his wooden blade.

"They eat the pretty flowers!" he answered without interrupting his sinister work.

"But they turn into beautiful butterflies!" I countered, angered for reasons beyond my young mind. My brother didn't listen to me. Only when I swung my wooden sword at him did he fight back.

It started with caterpillars, but his dark obsession with death grew over time. I knew it was the gloom inside him, the one everyone in my bloodline shares. Our burden since the Hex had been unleashed onto this tormented world. The void in his heart was simply too big, expanding and eating up the remnants of the joyful, smart boy he was.

"All living beings matter. Everyone, big or small, serves a purpose. You cannot discard some just because they appear too insignificant for you. You don't see the whole picture. None of us does. To the Elders, they are all musicians in the orchestra of life."

The songs of the crickets around me return as if to confirm Viridis's words.

The tender hyacinth scent guides me to the wards-protected one-story house I've noticed before.

It's surrounded by an overgrown garden. The crushed bluebells and stomped grass indicate they are headed to the black door of the abandoned mansion.

The foul magic of this place nearly knocks me off my feet when I get closer. Taking another step forward feels like entering another reality—the night colors around me change and distort; the sounds are muted, as if a thick membrane wraps this place, protecting it from the outside world. Yet the hyacinth scent lingers, luring me into an obvious trap with its gentle, seductive fingers.

My steps echo down a surprisingly well-preserved atrium. The checkered tiles are nearly intact, and the silvery paint of the murals reflects my light spell. There is a pile of debris to my left—so odd and out of place. Tiny rocks still cascade down the heap.

Someone was here recently.

A loud rumble followed by an avalanche of rocks crushes me, and the floor cracks. I instantly summon a magical shield to protect myself from the tons of stone burying me. Shrouded by dust and utter darkness, the last thing I hear before the tiles beneath my feet collapse and the chasm swallows me is a hateful: "Die, you Fae bastard."

TALYSSE

THE KEEPER

"**T**alysse, wake up!"

A rough shake forces my eyes open. The first thing I see is the moon hanging low in the sky like a ripe fruit.

Gale's face slowly drifts into focus. His dark brows are locked with worry, and loose curls stick to his sweaty brow. He looks exhausted.

My muscles ache, but I'm alive. How, in the name of the Elders, did I survive this? The memory of the fall and the blackness choking my senses hits me, and I nearly vomit.

"What—what happened?" I mumble, wiggling my fingers and toes. Nothing is broken. "How did I make it here? Alive?"

Gale's almond-shaped eyes lock onto mine as if considering something. "Thank the Elders, the drop was not too deep. And you landed...on me. All I did was carry you to safety. Can you walk?" he says after a brief hesitation.

Nothing comes for free in this dark, cursed world, yet there is no sign of calculation or ill intent on his handsome face.

"We need to get moving. They'll catch up at any moment."

No need to ask who they are.

He slings an arm around my waist and pulls me up. We're on an empty alley leading to the white mansion glowing with old magic like a beacon in the night.

Questions and doubts about my miraculous salvation crowd my mind, but I know that we need to get going. And it seems we both agree on the direction.

The mansion looks nearly intact from the outside but groans under the centuries, its walls cracked, and ceilings sagging from the inside. It is the smell that alerts me that something is not right. Dust motes dance in the beams of moonlight that drip through the broken windows. The air is thick with the stench of rot and decay, laced with malevolent magic.

The entrance opens up to a wide hall framed with balconies. The checkered floor tiles are adorned with mosaics of unseen wildlife and plants. What's disturbing are the dark stains on them—some old, some still crimson-colored. Blood had been spilled here. The walls behind the tattered tapestries are covered with writings by a shaky hand, repeating the same sentences over and over again.

the eagle flies

the wolf's keen cry

And the words dawn and moon scribbled chaotically by fingers that seemed to have forgotten how to write.

"Look at these words! I can recognize the words wolf, eagle, moon...moon's embrace? And this looks like dawn," he remarks, studying them up close. "Written in blood, no less. Why would someone so obsessively write this on the walls?"

"It looks as if a mind consumed by madness was holding on to the single thought that still keeps it human…"

"No sign of any magical artifacts here, Talysse. Maybe we can find some stairs leading down?" Gale muses, peeking behind a pile of rotting furniture. An old chair slips and causes an avalanche of rubble, and I wince when the sound reverberates down the desolated corridors.

"I don't like this place," I say, poking with the tip of my boot a pile of something that looks like tree branches. When I take a closer look, my breath hitches. "Bones, Gale! There are human bones on the floor." He joins me and probes the pile with a chair leg. Elders above! This is a disturbing number of bones, skulls, ragged clothing and even some chainmail.

"I don't like this place too, Talysse," Gale echoes and raises the chair leg like a weapon.

"Eagle, wolf, moon's embrace." My finger follows the scribbles. "Does this make any sense to you? And who wrote this? The whole city was swarmed by Shadowfeeders and Tainted Ones centuries ago!"

"Dawn…" I tap at another word. "Dawn's first light…you are right. It doesn't make any sense."

We continue our search for clues. Distant sounds startle us a few times. Rocks crumbling or floorboards screeching—the final breaths of a dying house. Something wiggles in the back of my mind. A melancholic melody the bards at the inn play when it is close to daylight, and they want to send the last patrons home. It finds its way to my lips, and I hum it while sifting through the trash.

Gale leaps toward me, eyes wide.

"Is this the ballad of the Sun Queen, Talysse?"

I nod. One of the last Seelie Queens made her way through unimaginable dangers to the Holy City to beg the Elders for forgiveness. Nobody has ever seen her again, so legends and fairy tales waived different stories about her end. I remember a street spectacle with fireworks and confetti, where she found happiness with a mortal man and withdrew with him in some secret place, living her happily ever after.

Then it hits me.

The Ballad is old. As old as the walls of Teír Mekheret. And the lyrics haven't changed for centuries.

In moon's embrace, the wolf's keen cry,
In dawn's first light, the eagle flies.
Step on the wolf to find your way,
Eagle's mark reveals the day.

The queen had to carefully choose her steps on the traitorous mountain pass leading to the Holy City. Is it possible that the scribbles on the wall refer to the song?

The floor tiles—

Before Gale can ask, I run up the crumbling marble staircase to the balcony, overviewing the hall. I jump over the rusty chandelier chain and the piles of rotting books, their sheets scattered around like the wings of countless dead birds. Leaning on the filigree railing, I can see the whole hall beneath my feet.

"What got into you?" Gale looks up at me, brow raised in confusion.

And there, beneath the heavy bronze chandelier, darkened by time, lies the answer to the riddle. Black and white tiles, each one depicting an animal or a plant, stretch down into the corridors.

Two wolves—one on a black tile and one on a stained white one.

"In moon's embrace, the wolf's keen cry, Gale! This should be the wolf on the black tile. Black as the night, do you see?" He follows my hand, frantically pointing at the tile. His full lips slowly stretch into an understanding smile.

"It's the tiles, Talysse!" He heads to the spot I'm pointing at, and for a moment, everything seems to be going to plan.

And then Seuta pulls her damned threads again.

Thunder shakes the old building. The sound of collapsing walls echoes down the passageways and probably awakens things better left undisturbed. The sound came from the entrance. Silence settles in when the last rock rolls down an unseen slope. The minutes into eternities, yet nothing happens.

"Gale," I call hoarsely, and he whips his curly head up to me, "step onto the black plate with the wolf!"

He whips his head left and right, peering into the dark corridors, then heads to the tile. We have to recover this artifact, and this place is as dangerous as any in this city.

He steps on the black tile depicting a fearsome wolf with bristled fur, and some unseen mechanisms in the depths of the house are set in motion.

"Pressure plates! Step on the eagle tile—there!" He points with the leg chair to the far corner of the room. "It'll open something!"

Yet the doubt remains—is it wise to open a door that has been closed for centuries? Did all the dead treasure hunters who left their bones here try to do the same?

No time to think about it and succumb to fear. I swiftly make my way down to the tile Gale is pointing at and leap on it. Heavy chains rattle and move in the depths of the mansion, and screeching indicates that an ancient mechanism has just been activated. A tiny move in the side of my vision draws my attention. There stands an old altar of Seuta, still covered with dried flower wreaths, while the floor before it shifts.

A large trap door appears as the tiles nearly soundlessly slide to the side. White stairs descend into the inky darkness below.

"There!" Gale exclaims. "We need a torch or a candle; help me search. We need to save our magic." We start looking around when we hear it.

Something massive is heading our way. Something big enough to push its way through piles of furniture and rubble in the passageway opposite the entrance.

The stench gets unbearable, and then it arrives.

The first thing I see is a pale human hand crawling out of the gloom, followed by—

My breath hitches.

"Talysse," Gale calls me softly, "run."

Then he turns to face the abomination, armed with his chair leg.

The creature towers twice as tall as a man, a grotesque mass of intertwined corpses. Human limbs jut out at unnatural angles, and the stench of death clings to it. Its torso is a horrifying tapestry of melting faces, each one frozen in a mask of agony. With eyes wide and unseeing, mouths open in silent screams, the skin on these faces sags and drips like molten wax, merging into a monstrous collage of flesh. The abomination's legs are a tangle of bones and sinew, each step it takes causing the floor to tremble under its weight. Its movements are both lumbering and unnerving. The creature's head is an ever-shifting mass of features. A gaping maw, filled with jagged, broken teeth, dominates it. A set of bloodshot eyes burn with madness and hunger, a feral intelligence shining through.

I am not sure if it is the skull shape or the thick golden amulet hidden amongst the rotting skin folds, but it bears an uncanny resemblance to a man I've seen before. His eyes still follow us from countless decaying portraits and murals. Is this the lord of this mansion? I have heard that human mages of old were able to prolong their lives with spells and dark enchantments, making them nearly immortal as Fae. This one here seems to have done the same by absorbing the intruders in his unholy sanctuary.

"Run, Talysse! Get into the tunnel—" Gale points with the chair leg at the gaping trap door, too narrow for the monster to pass. But I cannot just leave him here. Not when the terror is already upon him.

"Hey, you! Ugly one! Yes, you!" I taunt. The mountain of reeking flesh changes direction and lumbers toward me. I dash left and right without a plan.

Great job. *Resourceful*, Myrtle used to call me. I wish I had a brilliant idea now to save us.

"Keep him busy for just a moment, Talysse!" Gale shouts. Risking a glance over my shoulder, I see him struggling to flip a massive bronze table. A loud rumble signals his success. What is he up to?

No time to think as the abomination, surprisingly swift for its size, is so close that its hot, reeking breath brushes my skin. Claws reach for my doublet. Sweat trickles into my eyes. I run in frantic circles around the hall, praying to all Elders that Gale's plan works.

How long can I keep this up?

"Hey, you! I know who you are! Mage Ornatus!" So Gale has also noticed the fleeting resemblance with the portraits around here? The heavy steps and dragging flesh behind me suddenly cease. Gale was right. This abomination is indeed the legendary mage Ornatus.

"I'm here to take your most precious one, Ornatus! Look, I've found where you hide it!" Did Gale go mad? I skid to a stop and turn around, breathing heavily. The nightmarish tangle of legs and arms glides over the stained tiles toward Gale.

And this crazy, amazing man stands between the overturned bronze table and the monster and looks at it with a snicker.

Elders, I've never seen someone grinning like this in the face of certain death. Gale is one remarkable man.

"Talysse, quickly," he hisses to me. "Bring that chandelier down!"

One look and I see through his desperate but brilliant plan.

I slip behind the abomination as quietly as possible and make my way up. There it is—the rusty chain I'd spotted earlier, connecting the chandelier to a wall crank. Probably an old mechanism to lower the chandelier when needed. I yank the chain with all my strength. Nothing. It doesn't even shake.

Heroy, help me! I wrap the chain around my forearm and pull, but it doesn't budge.

"Talysse, hurry!" Gale's strangled voice urges me. Elders above, the monstrosity is at him.

There! A heavy cabinet stands next to the crank. I slip my hand between its back and the wall and push, muscles bulging, joints burning, sinews straining. Every last drop of strength in my body I pour into this, praying it's not too late. Finally, the cabinet shakes and topples. It lands on the chain and raises clouds of dust. Sharp pain pierces me as I land on my knees, but the sense of triumph soothes it. The chandelier sears up, hits the ceiling, sending bricks and stones to the floor, then the chain holding it breaks.

It crashes down with a deafening rattle, followed by an agonizing shriek. I leap to the railing, pressing my ears.

The monstrosity lets out a final, blood-curdling howl. Its carcass is crushed under the chandelier, pierced by the table legs; its grotesque limbs twitch one last time and go limp. Next to it, covered in white dust, lies Gale.

I fly down the stairs, taking three steps at a time, and kneel next to him.

"Gale!" I shake him. "Gale, say something!" He blinks and rubs his reddened eyes.

Praised be Heroy, he's alive.

"Did we—" He looks at the pools of blood staining the mosaic black. "We did it, Talysse!" He slings his arm around my shoulders. For a moment, we sit on the dirty floor, laughing like lunatics.

"That was quite the plan, Gale. Now—"

"Oh, give me a break, Talysse. I just had a brush with death, and you want us to go into that tunnel?"

"Aren't you curious what's there?"

Slow clapping startles us.

By Atos, will I ever know a moment of peace in my life?

The mercenary steps out of the shadows, his chainmail and golden rings shimmering in the moonlight. Was the bastard hiding there the whole time, waiting for us to finish the dirty job?

Gale squeezes my shoulders reassuringly, still holding that ridiculous chair leg.

"Excellent job, kids! I must say I am impressed. I'd have probably done the same, but this quick thinking and teamwork was just—" He touches his lips in recognition. Me and Gale look at each other in confusion.

Then he slowly lifts a rusty ax he has retrieved from Elders know where his expression impassive.

"Unfortunately, there can be only one winner of these cursed Trials. Nothing personal, but I need only one of you to guide me to the relic. And I choose the pretty girl."

Without warning, he swings at Gale, who surprises me yet again. He grabs a handful of dust and throws it in the eyes of the mercenary, then swiftly rolls away from harm's way.

Without saying a word, Gale grabs me by the back of my doublet, lifts me with a superhuman strength, and throws me into the darkness beyond the trapdoor.

Agony pierces my joints, and I hear the mercenary curses in the background when I hit the bottom of the stairs. Then some slashing sounds that sound so odd, and something tumbles down the stairs, landing next to me.

I cup my mouth with shaky fingers to muffle my scream. The lifeless eyes of the mercenary stare at me in the scarce light filtering from above. His head, cut off clean, landed at my feet.

Then the trapdoor above me closes, and I am alone in the darkness.

TALYSSE

THE GOLDEN CAGE

"Gale?"

My voice echoes down some unseen corridors. The darkness around me is so thick that it's nearly palpable. A distant dripping of water is the only sound around.

The Shadowfeeders prefer spawning in the Wastelands, but they won't shy away from a meal trapped in stonework, too. My bruised legs protest when I stand up and summon a tiny shimmering hallo.

Elders, what is this place?

The steep stairs open to a surprisingly wide passageway. The ceiling is concealed in shadows. The green mosaic floor looks like grass dotted with colorful flowers. Paintings hang on the walls, showing a beautiful woman with long black hair and wide brown eyes. She is dressed like a queen and smiling, but there's sadness in the curl of her lips. Seems like the pounds of golden jewelry and the diamonds couldn't make it up for something.

Could that be the concubine of Ornatus? The bards are still singing about her legendary beauty and her black hair, draping to the floor. Ornatus was once a powerful mage and a holy man who took a vow of celibacy before Seuta. But he couldn't resist the great beauty of Soraya the Songstress and took her as his own, the legend says. To keep up appearances, he hid his lover away from the world, and she was never seen again.

The colors on the paintings are still vivid: there is Soraya, holding hands with a man with a shaved head and tall brow. Ornatus was not very handsome, and now the resemblance to the dead monstrosity above is very obvious.

So, he had found some dark, twisted way to keep guarding his home and his concubine centuries after the city fell to the shadows.

If that was him, then this—

These are the secret chambers where he kept her.

Or her tomb.

The thought makes me shudder. Elders know what dwells here, and all I have is a pocket full of rocks.

Looking around for a weapon, I march down the corridor, followed by my timid light spell. Doors gape on the walls, leading to chambers, untouched by time, save for the layers of dust and the delicate veils of spiderwebs. A peek into the first one nearly gives me a heart attack. A bloodied face with wide, feverish eyes and messy hair stares at me. I immediately throw a rock, and it dissipates into a shimmering net.

It was a stupid mirror.

Well, at least my aim is on the spot.

The room looks like some kind of music salon, with dust-covered instruments lying around. The violin's strings are broken, and the keys of the clavichord are ripped off as if in great anger. The rage of whoever did this still simmers in the depths of the room. Grabbing a violin and holding it like a club, I sneak to the next one.

It is a lavish bedroom drowned in feminine colors and suffocating luxury. The silk sheets still bear the outline of a lithe body, as if the woman who lived here just left. A mother-of-pearl-incrusted hairbrush is tossed at the nightstand, long, dark hairs still stuck into it. The scent of perfume still lingers, and—is this a hallucination, or is that female voice humming a beautiful melody? I whip my head left and right. Silence. Probably, my tired mind is playing tricks.

Could it be that…Ornatus's concubine is still here? He was still here! What if he had cast a similar spell on her?

Yet, there is nothing but darkness and memories around. And that faint whiff of perfume and dry roses. Moving deeper into the corridor, another sensation prickles my skin—old magic, rippling the air and buzzing with power. The artifact is close.

I search room after room—nothing. There are also no weapons or even heavy objects like candle holders. It looks as if someone has taken precautions and removed all dangerous objects. Only melancholy lingering in the corners, and extravagant objects witnessing a lonely, isolated life.

The light flickers, a reminder that my arcane powers will be soon depleted. Then I will be all alone in the dark, alone with that eerie melody. It is growing stronger now, louder than my thoughts.

The corridor ends abruptly in a pile of rocks and gravel.

Atos's hairy armpits! How do I get past it without moving tons of stone?

Hope is fading just like the light above my head.

Maybe Gale is searching for me. The man is resourceful; he overpowered an armed warrior. He'll probably find some clever way to open that trapdoor and get me out.

Still, there is one last door left. I raise the dusty violin and push the door open.

My feet sink in a crunchy carpet of dry leaves. The room is wider than the rest, and I crane my neck up to see the tall, arched vault. Tiny shimmering crystals are embedded into it, artfully arranged to mimic the stars in the night sky. They bathe the hall stretching before me in cool blueish light. Thank the Elders for the scarce light! Right on time because my meager spell dissipates with a pop. That was it. If something attacks me in this gilded dungeon, the best I can do is smack them with the violin.

Dead trees and dried flowers stretch into the hall; cages with songbirds—now only piles of dusty feathers and bones, hang among the branches.

This must've been Soraya's secret garden. The humming gets louder, and I rub my temples. I can barely tell if it's still in my head or if it resonates under the vaults.

And there, on a gilded lounger, covered with a blanket of dust, is Soraya. Ornatus's beloved.

Death has shrunk her, but her long black hair sweeps the floor and still glistens like gossamer in the cool light of the false stars. A wreath of wilted flowers still hugs her brow and some distant light shimmers in the empty eye sockets.

My heart sinks at the tragic revelation. Trapped in her gilded cage while the Shadowfeeders devoured the rest of the city, while her lover clashed his magic with theirs and became a mindless abomination, still obsessed with the idea of keeping her locked, holding her in his possession. The scribbles on the walls above—how many centuries did he spend reminding himself of the only reason he was still alive, until the words that could lead him to her became a mindless ramble, and he became a monster?

Her dry, bony fingers press something to her heart, something that pulls all my senses in like an enchanted maelstrom. It shines through her palm with black iridescence—light that consumes all colors around.

The artifact.

I step closer and reach out. Scrunching my nose, I force the mummified fingers apart, the gray teeth and hollow eyes of Soraya's skull just inches away from my face. Seconds later, the Flint lies on my palm—smooth and black, like polished onyx.

Something has changed. The humming is nearly deafening now. A smell of old dust and mold hits my nose, but there is also a trace of sweet, feminine perfume.

Quickly slipping the Flint into my pocket and closing the button, I take a step back.

A sound rolls down the corridor behind. It starts with pebbles rolling, then larger stones dragging over the floor.

Sweet Cymmetra, why does it have to be always so difficult?

Raising my violin, I prepare to turn around and face the intruder, their heavy steps already approaching, when—

I'm really born with the luck of a lamb among a horde of Tainted Ones.

The mummified remains of Soraya the Songstress slowly come back to life. Cool shimmer veils her, and her skeletal body rises, her magnificent hair dangling around her bony limbs, blown by an unnatural breeze. She's floating two feet above the floor.

Elders! What blasphemous, tainted nightmare I've been dragged into? The humming melody is a roar now, echoing under the vaults. She faces me, her jaw hanging loose, and shrieks.

"Wraiths are dangerous when disturbed. They are bound to this world by some object they value highly. Their shrieks paralyze their victims, and they relish draining them of their life force. Often, their victims become wraiths too," Friar Ben's academic, matter-of-fact tone surfaces in my mind, shaking me out of my stupor.

Keep a cool head, Talysse.

Without a doubt, Soraya is a wraith bound to the Flint. Time to get out of here. I back up toward the corridor, where the other horror is probably waiting for me. No idea what has made its way here through the heap of rocks, but even a Shadowfeeder is a better option than becoming a specter and haunting this Elders-forsaken place.

The wraith follows, floating, her jaw hanging, her hair and ragged dress sweeping the floor.

"Give it baaaack—" she screeches.

I take a few more steps before crashing into something solid.

And pleasantly warm.

My reaction is impeccably fast. The violin lands on something, followed by a satisfying grunt of pain. The makeshift weapon instantly disintegrates into dust and splinters. I take a better look at what I hit and nearly run back to the wraith. Because right now, she's the safer option.

What's before me is far more deadly than a screeching pile of old bones.

Prince Aeidas rubs his bleeding forehead, his eyes flashing in the twilight with the disturbing fluorescence only night creatures possess. His silvery hair and face are powdered with dust.

"Is this a wraith?" he asks incredulously.

"No, it's an old friend. Of course, it is a wraith!" I spit, trying to push past him. Without any success, it feels like trying to break through a wall of solid muscle.

"Then we should—" he starts, his gaze fixed on the spirit behind me.

"—burn her, I know," I say, surrendering to the thrumming call of my magic. One flick of my wrist staggers the wraith.

While I desperately search for the next spell, the prince demonstrates the terrifying dark powers the Elders have bestowed upon Fae. He stretches his hand, his long fingers spread, and a fireball forms upon his palm. The air crackles with energy, and the fireball shoots forth, a blazing sphere of fury. The battle spells of old seem to still live in the royal Unseelie bloodline.

His aim is lethal. The wraith ignites instantly; the old bones and rags dry as tinder. She shrieks, her form melting away, the smoke of her burning hair choking us. With a sigh, she crumbles into a steaming pile of ashes on the floor.

I pat my pocket, making sure the relic is still there, and look around. "All right, I'll be going now."

His fingers close around my arm, his grip tight as steel.

"Where do you think you're going, little thief?" he asks darkly.

THE PRINCE

THE WELL

I loom menacingly over her. Intimidating people is something I excel at.

"My name is Talysse." She tilts her chin up and looks me straight in the eye. Her confidence is striking, and I can't help but smirk.

"Talysse of—"

"Talysse of No Name. Daughter of traitors. The name I'm not allowed to use is Nightglimmer."

Recognition tugs at a distant memory—a ledger of names and verdicts signed without a second thought. The human's eyes, aflame with anger, search the dark garden, and she tries to shake my grip off. What is she seeking? A weapon? A way out?

"Does that name stir anything in you, Governor?" The old title drips with disdain. "My parents bore it before you sent them to the gallows. Recall them now?"

Oh.

Pure hatred blazes in her eyes now, and I immediately release her, stepping back, letting the weight of her accusation hang between us.

"Names blur when signatures number in the hundreds," I reply coolly, shrugging off the implied guilt. A future king should not apologize for his actions. "Should it mean something to me?"

How to explain to a peasant what one must do to remain in power? I did what I did. Hundreds of fates sealed. My family's hands are drenched in blood, as are the hands of anyone in power. Yet I cannot help but try to remember. Tenebris. A family sent to the gallows. I rake my fingers through my hair and shake my head. I have no memory of these people, or their crime.

Her unblinking gaze pierces me as if blinking will unleash the tears she's desperately holding back. "They meant everything to me."

The thought that I've changed the course of her life with a single stroke of the pen and don't even remember it tenses something inside me, strains it like the string of a bow.

"Am I a monster to you, Talysse Nightglimmer?" I step closer, my voice dropping to a dangerous whisper. Everyone who came to me seeking a monster was not disappointed. Her eyes—strange, mesmerizing—reflect defiance mingled with sorrow. It's the sadness and that flash of vulnerability among her fierceness that makes me want to trail a finger along her face, to wipe away the single tear she couldn't hold back.

"You wear the skin of one," she says, voice steady.

A dark chuckle escapes me. "Then perhaps you should fear me more."

Silence stretches between us, and her hand slides to the pocket, where the Flint spills its iridescent magic.

"I am a monster, bred and raised by monsters, and I would do anything, absolutely anything, to get what I want, Talysse."

She retreats, the shadows of the dead trees right behind her. "I won't let you have it."

"And how do you intend to stop me?" I challenge, taking a predatory step forward.

Without warning, she spins on her heel, darting deeper into the garden's withered embrace. For a moment, I watch her run, grinning. Bold little thief. Then I tie my hair up, wipe the blood from my brow, and give chase.

I could never resist a good hunt; it's in my blood. This game is so invigorating. She's fast, but shadows are my realm, and it's so easy to track her when she's carrying a magical relic that shines like a miniature black sun. Avoiding branches and golden cages with dead birds inside, we get to the depths of this sad place. One leap, and both of us crash into a bed of brittle leaves. She's pinned under my weight. For a moment, I stiffen, thinking that she hit her head too hard. Then she starts struggling beneath me, fiery and unyielding. The thick layer of leaves has softened the blow.

"Go on," she hisses, breaths ragged. "Kill me like you did them."

I study her strange eyes, noting every speck and nuance. She thrashes her head, trying to avoid my proximity.

"I have done a lot of despicable things, yes," my voice is low, menacing, a reminder of who's she dealing with, "and I've sent many people to their deaths, but I have done it all for a reason." For some cursed reason I need her to understand, to hear me, so I restrain her, pinning her wrists over her head with my right hand. "It pains me that it happened to your parents, Talysse," my voice drops to a whisper, "it pains me even more that I don't remember what their crime was, but the law is a law, and a governor is nothing but a servant to his people."

She's watching me now, heavy-lidded, her mouth half-open. Her heartbeat races, palpable against my chest. For a fleeting moment, vulnerability flickers in her eyes before she masks it with renewed defiance. And just when I think I've made her understand, she skillfully aims a kick at my crotch.

A deep, amused chuckle rumbles from my chest. Vicious little thief. Touching an Unseelie royalty without their permission is punishable by death. Harming one of us is punishable by a prolonged, extremely painful death, and Elders know my kind could be very creative when it comes to that. And this little human, struggling to breathe under my weight, smacked me with a violin and tried to kick me in my most sensitive parts. Oh, how I wish my knights and sparring partners had half of her courage.

"Go on, Prince, Governor, or whatever title you're hiding behind to justify your murders. Kill me and take it, as I'm not giving the Flint to you willingly." Arms pinned up, crushed by my weight, and she still tries another kick.

I lean closer, our faces mere inches apart. "Death is too final. Where's the fun in that?"

"Monsters like you don't understand fun," she spits.

I smirk. "Care to enlighten me?"

Well, that came out wrong, considering the situation. Probably Talysse feels the same way because her eyes, confused, drop to my mouth and linger there. Then, to my surprise, she blushes and whips her head to the side, dead leaves sticking to her hair.

"I am not going to kill you, Talysse. Where's the glory in that? Robbing a human girl in a dungeon with no one to see?" I suddenly release her and push myself up, my gaze lingering on her. She gasps when I grab her hand, pulling her to her feet. My touch is rough and commanding, but I wince at the thought that I could've pulled too hard and dislocated her shoulder. "Power is about flaunting it, demonstrating it. You can't do that without an audience. Come, let's find another way out."

Talysse rakes her fingers through her hair, which has escaped the braid, and brushes away leaves and dirt. Her scent—of hyacinth and sun-drenched gardens—teases me, and my nostrils flare, inhaling deeply the promise of happiness that was never meant for someone like me. That intoxicating fragrance is a cruel reminder that, in her eyes, I'm the monster who sent her parents to the gallows.

"Where did you come from?" she asks coolly, straightening her doublet. I cock a brow. Just moments ago, her life was in my hands, her body crushed beneath mine—heat stirs inside me at the thought, and I force myself to focus. Now she stands before me, her chin up, composed like a queen. This woman can take life's punches so gracefully and transform them into possibilities. So resourceful. Were she a part of my court, she'd make it far.

"I fell through the floor. Or through the ceiling, depending on the perspective. That Elders-cursed mercenary dropped a wall on me. No way we can climb back from there," I reply, my voice low and edged with another memory—that of the male scent that clung to her. The thought of some mysterious man touching her nearly makes me summon my Shadowblade. "And you?"

"That mercenary should not be a problem anymore. But the way I came in is closed too," she answers simply, scanning the quiet garden around us. I keep my expression neutral, though my curiosity burns. "Did he follow you here?"

"A...part of him did. Look, there must be a ventilation system bringing in fresh air or water pipes—"

"Let's look around." To my relief, she nods.

We walk in silence, the crunching leaves and our breaths the only sounds in this garden of sadness.

"What kind of magic made all this possible?" I marvel, my fingers brushing the marble pools of the fountains, still full of dark water and dead leaves. "This water must come from somewhere."

Indeed, just a hundred feet further, we find it. An ornate well ring stands before us. The cool air from its depths plays with the loose curls of her hair. We rush to inspect the rusty chains descending from an old mechanism.

Talysse drops a stone into the inky darkness, and we both hold our breath until the distant splash echoes back.

"It's deep," she states, her voice trembling slightly.

"There's still water down there," I say thoughtfully, sniffing the draft rising from the depths. "Fresh, running water. Do you know what that means, Talysse?"

She nods, but her face has gone pale.

"It means we have a way out," I say, but she takes a step back, her fear palpable. "What? Don't tell me you can't swim, Talysse."

Of course, she can't. A girl who grew up on the streets wouldn't have had the luxury of learning such a skill. "Listen to me, Talysse." Her name rolls off my tongue with unexpected ease. But she's fixated on the well behind me, her body tense with terror, twisting a strand of her hair around her finger. The sight of her so vulnerable, so afraid, tugs at something deep within me.

"Listen to me, Talysse," I repeat, my tone softer, my hands resting on her shoulders. Even the touch of a monster doesn't seem to shake her out of it. "I need you to trust me."

She barks a humorless laugh, her defiance still burning brightly despite the fear.

"I need you to trust me," I insist, lifting her chin with a single fingertip, forcing her to meet my gaze. Her eyes, wide and stormy, hold mine, and I feel the pull of something between us. Elder Seuta weaving her threads, entwining our destinies. "This is our only way out. I will go first. If the water is too shallow and we get hurt, it's fine—I know some basic healing spells. If it's too deep, then I will catch you."

A single bead of sweat rolls down her brow. The woman whose parents I've condemned to death is considering trusting me. By Heroy's cursed spear, I wouldn't trade places with her right now.

"It's the only way out," I continue, my voice almost coaxing. "If you prefer, you can stay here and starve, take over the job of the wraith we just burned—"

"How can I be sure you're not just going to drown me and take the Flint?" she interrupts, trying to conceal the tremble in her words.

"If I wanted the Flint, I'd take it right now, Talysse," I reply coldly, towering over her, the darkness of my threat obvious. "But I'm giving you a choice. You know what? I'll let you figure it out. I'll wait for you below," I point to the well, "but not too long."

Without another word, I summon a pair of light wisps that swirl around me, their soft glow illuminating the hard planes of my face. Then, with a final look at Talysse, I grab the rusty chain and begin my descent into the darkness.

TALYSSE

THE DARK WORLD

Biting my lip, I watch Aeidas swing his long legs over the stone well ring. His body sways over the opening, the bluish light of his wisps reflecting off his silver hair. His corded forearms strain, and just like that, he's gone, swallowed by the dark depths.

That bastard really left me alone.

With a scoff, I throw myself on the dirty floor.

Tiredness is seeping through my muscles down to the marrow. If it were a normal night, dawn would be breaking by now.

The chain still swings, clinking softly against the stone. He hasn't reached the bottom yet. The thought of what might be lurking in this pitch-black chasm makes me shudder.

Seems there is only one solution. One way out and it involves a descent into these dreaded depths, a possibility of drowning, and a murderous Unseelie. But staying here means certain death. Even if Gale has survived whatever has decapitated the mercenary, it would be difficult to open the trap door alone.

Think, Talysse.

Two options: a slow, certain death here or a slim chance at life if I follow the Unseelie. I'd take slim chances over certain death any day.

Maybe, with some luck, the water below is not too deep. My bitter laugh shakes the golden cages with the dead birds in the trees around. Me and luck, those two things never go together!

The chain rattles again. Soraya's gilded lounger shimmers coldly between the black trunks. Should I just give up, stay here, and wait for the next adventurer to find my bones? What would I say to Tayna in the halls of Atos after? That I sat and waited to die?

No. Giving up is no option.

My decision is made; I flick my hair back and approach the stone ring. Far below, the faint glow of Aeidas's wisps flickers like a distant star. The air from the well is cool, carrying the scent of wet stone—no foul stench, thank the Elders, just damp earth.

Small steps, Talysse. Focus.

Grasping the chain, I begin my descent. Darkness immediately wraps around me, thick like a black blindfold. My eyes are fixed on the faint light above, and my hands move slowly and deliberately.

It's harder than anticipated. My muscles burn, and my palms sweat, causing me to slip a couple of times, ripping nails in the frantic search for purchase. The lack of light and sound paints terrifying images in my mind—ancient, monstrous creatures lurking in bottomless underground lakes.

Then the chain rattles again, louder this time. A screech echoes from above. My heart leaps into my throat as I realize what's happening—the old mechanism is breaking, unable to hold the weight of two. When I open my mouth to shout a warning to Aeidas, it's already too late.

I'm falling.

There's no time to think, no time to panic. The icy water hits me like a wall, its coldness immediate and brutal. It fills my nose and mouth, piercing me with a thousand needles, pressing against my chest like a vise. I fight the instinct to gasp for air—a death sentence. My limbs flail desperately, searching for something, anything, to grab onto.

But there's nothing. Only the relentless, biting cold.

I open my eyes, but the darkness is profound, impenetrable, as if I've been swallowed by the ether before the Elders created the stars. The weight of the water is crushing me, pulling me down into the abyss. Hope fades, and my self-control shatters. My mouth opens in a terrified scream, my last breath escaping in a torrent of bubbles, swallowed by the dark mass of water around me.

Kicking and thrashing, I fight the inevitable. The cold is a merciless enemy, sapping my strength. Just as the last bubble and last remnant of hope leave my lips, something grabs me. A powerful force—an arm or a tentacle—wraps around my chest, yanking me upward with superhuman strength. Or is it pulling me down? Everything spins in a maelstrom of terror, and then something solid slams against my legs. I'm dragged over a rocky shore. The sharp edges of the stones cut through my pants, biting into my flesh, but it doesn't matter.

Breathe!

"Breathe, Talysse, breathe!"

Hard ground. I roll onto all fours, coughing and spitting out water, gasping for air. The air burns my lungs, but it's life. Slowly, I sit back on my heels, my breathing erratic but steadying. Only then do I look up to see what—or who—saved me from drowning.

Before me, in the haunting light of the two wisps, stands Aeidas. Strands of wet silver hair stick to his face, and his chest rises rapidly under the shirt; the wet fabric clings to his muscled torso.

Of course, that cursed Unseelie catches me staring.

"You like what you see?" he asks, panting.

"You've lost your jerkin." I shrug and take my boot off to drain the water. Anything to keep my mind—and eyes—off this chiseled torso. "Why did you save me? Did I infect you with some disease unnatural for your kind, like conscience?"

"Don't make me change my mind, human." His words are dark, but his lips stretch into a smile in the cold light of the wisps. My trembling hand pats the pocket with the Flint. Elders, it's still there.

"I will not rob you. This is your area of expertise." Aeidas crouches next to me, studying my face from too close. Too damn close to this rugged plane of rippling muscles. "How do you feel?" he murmurs, his eyes softening.

How do I feel after nearly drowning? After walking, climbing, running, and fearing for my life for a small eternity? The air in the cavern is warm, so there's at least that, but my body desperately needs rest.

But he's not getting the satisfaction of mocking my human fragility.

Instead, I just scoff, give him a thumbs up, and slip my wet boots back on. It's terribly uncomfortable, but being dead is even worse. His eyes, capturing and reflecting the scarce light, linger on me.

"Thank you. For...you know." The soft words slip unexpectedly. He remains silent for a long moment, then looks away and pushes himself to his feet.

"Very well," Aeidas declares, resuming his cold and commanding demeanor. "Let's go then. The water drains this way. I am sure there must be a way out somewhere here."

My feet are burning, and my head hurts as I follow him, stumbling on the rocks in the vast cavern holding the lake. The fatigue burns in my eyes and slurs my speech. I desperately need some sleep. But how to fall asleep with the world's deadliest predator at my side?

Aeidas walks with confidence, his dark clothes blending with the shadows around him. His broad back tapers into a lean waist. Even in plain clothes, there's an effortless grace to him. Despite his simple appearance, there's a power about him that doesn't need anything extra to be felt.

Following the underground creek, we've lost track of time. My boots are still wet, making funny squelching sounds with each step, but my hair is almost dry, draping down my back as a warm shawl.

A soft glow coming from somewhere ahead reflects on the moist stone walls. We rush forward, hoping for a way out—

And we step into another world.

Glowing mushrooms in tender pastel colors hang from the walls of the cave chamber while veins of crystal sparkle in the rocks, capturing and multiplying the light. The damp earthy scent lingers, and drips of water mingle with the babbling of the creek.

"What is this place?" I ask, unable to move. Elders, there are really wonders in the Wastelands!

"This, little human thief, is a miracle of Cymmetra!" His entire posture changes. Gone is the hinted menace in his gait and the determined line of his shoulders, replaced by a child-like wonder. I lean closer to get a better look at the blue-shimmering mushroom he's admiring. It has a long, translucent cap and a graceful stalk shrouded by a veil-like ring. It's beautiful and glowing, definitely the first of its kind I've ever seen, but to call it a miracle…

"This is Cymmetra's Veil, Talysse! Do you know the story?" He throws me a playful look, and I'm caught between suspicion and fascination. Is it another insidious Fae trick? "Legend has it that the Elder of nature, Cymmetra, was seducing her husband Atos, wearing only a veil, and running away from him to fuel his desire, a trick that always works, by the way—"

Why is my face burning? Thank the Elders, the prince is engrossed in studying the mushroom, oblivious to my embarrassment. "Atos tore her veil piece by piece, and everywhere the magical fabric landed, these sprouted! This is a mature specimen, Talysse, extremely rare," he murmurs. My reaction to his description of the Elders' foreplays is deeply disturbing. Disturbing as my imagination picks it up and—

"So, if I tap it carefully like this," he gently touches the cap with his knuckles and screeches like an excited schoolboy, "it releases its spores!"

Indeed, a shimmering haze rises from the mushroom, and he deftly collects it with his fingers. "I will just put these spores here with the others…" he rambles, oblivious to my presence. "Elders, I hope I haven't lost the other seeds when I fell—"

He fusses around, patting his pockets, and meets my stunned gaze. "What?" he asks, arching a dark brow.

"Atos's hairy armpits." It's not the spores that shock me, but his obsession with something so…tiny. Doesn't fit the image of a murderous Fae. The Unseelie Prince, in my mind, was a cold, despotic, self-centered monster, and this version of him right now is a contradiction. Well, one can be a power-hungry maniac who killed his own brother and sentenced hundreds to death and still has hobbies. I walk around, inspecting the mushrooms and trying to process this information. Maybe use it to my advantage somehow.

"Didn't take you for the gardening type," I say, letting the disbelief drip from my words.

He snaps his head toward me. "Should I be offended or flattered?" He pulls a mock-offended face that looks utterly out of place on his usually stoic features. "I love plants," he declares. "I even have a little garden—" He stops, realizing he's said too much. It's not the kind of thing you share with a rival.

"A little garden?" I ask, unable to mask my dismay. "Don't you have something better to do with your royal time, like signing death sentences or murdering?"

"One must always find time for their passions, and death sentences and murders just don't happen to be my thing." He shrugs, pulling a tiny wax paper sachet out of his pocket. "By Cymmetra, those are completely ruined!"

"Wait a minute, sending people to the gallows and murdering is not your thing?" I take a step closer, peeking into the sachet he holds. It's full of seeds, blossoms, and random plants.

What kind of trickery is this?

"We all have jobs, Talysse, just like yours was robbing naive strangers and getting them beaten up to a pulp. Mine was to keep the peace and the law in the provinces…do you think those are still good?"

"Hey, Ann's boys are usually gentle! And that was not my main job—"

"Oh?" he asks, tilting his head and presenting an ear, ending with a gently pointed tip. "Please do tell me more. Those will get moldy by the time we get to Nighthaven—"

We. He said *we—*

"I was just trying to make some money on the side for me and Tayna…those seeds will definitely get moldy, Aeidas."

"Your younger sister, right?" Shadows cloud his brow.

"Yes," I say softly, not liking this turn of the conversation. Sharing private details with the enemy is the worst idea ever.

160

"I'll just empty the sachet to put in the spores then." Aeidas breaks the silence that stretches between us. "It's just a gift for an old friend," he declares, stuffing the wax paper package into his pocket, trying for nonchalance. "Someone who's into plants, too."

"I'm sure they'll appreciate your...enthusiasm."

An old friend interested in botany? That's even more intriguing! Is it a lady friend? Some pretty Fae noblewoman with a small, coquettish garden? Surely, someone like him gets a lot of female attention, I note, frowning.

"And what friend might that be?" I palm my face as I realize I said it out loud. The last thing I want is for this royal prick to think I'm interested in his private life.

"Viridis has practically raised me," Aeidas answers, his voice distant. No mocking, no snappy comments. "He taught me to love and respect all living things," he adds, crouching. "Oh, look, this is Satyr's Wart!" He points at another modest, non-glowing mushroom. "You can eat this, it has excellent flavor!" He throws the mushroom in his mouth and closes his eyes, obviously enjoying the taste.

"No, thank you. The name itself has ruined my appetite," I declare, crossing my arms at my chest, but my stomach rumbles loudly. The participants in the Trials were not allowed to take provisions, so our last meal was at that feast. Hunger is nothing new to me, but I need to remain strong if I want to survive this, so I pick up the mushroom with the not-so-appetizing name and study it.

"I wouldn't have eaten it myself if I wanted to poison you," Aeidas says, chewing.

"Why Satyr's Wart, though?" I ask, cautiously taking a bite. Elders, he was right. The flavor is excellent.

"Sure you want that story while you're eating?"

I shake my head and pick up a handful of the delicious mushrooms. Aeidas's fingers close around my wrist, and my pulse quickens when his touch lingers an instant longer than it should.

"You don't want to get sick, Talysse," he says, and I am painfully aware of the grip of his warm fingers around my wrist. "Three are more than enough."

This prince seems to know his plants.

Uncomfortable silence settles between us, full of questions two people know they should not ask. I can't help but wonder what will happen if we find a way out. Will he kill me on the spot? Or will we just part ways, each fighting their way through the rest of the night? My heart suddenly feels heavy. Stupid, stupid heart. Some similar thoughts seem to be bothering him, too, because his head hangs somewhat…hopelessly.

"It's time to go, Talysse," his whisper is softer than the stream's murmur. "This way." He points to a dark opening. "There's fresh air coming in."

I reluctantly push myself up, not bothering to hide my exhausted sigh. The prince hesitates, and for a moment, it's as if he wants to say something—anything—but the silence between us is louder than words. And then, without another word, he turns, leading me into the darkness.

TALYSSE

THE FOREST HUT

Aeidas's superior Fae senses are right. Just a hundred feet down, the tunnel narrows, and we have to crawl into the Elders-be-blessed-not-too-deep creek to squeeze through the tight opening.

Skidding on my ass down the rounded stones of a tiny waterfall, I splash into a shallow pool.

It's still dark.

Shivering, I creep out of the cold water, looking like a water hag. Only the stars prick the velvety darkness of the sky. The moon has set, and the air is so cold that my breath comes in foggy gusts.

When nights are that long, it gets really cold. In the stables, the water buckets for the horses often freeze solid, and the Bountiful Bosom windows are getting stained with pretty ice laces.

Aeidas stands on the rocky shore and watches the silent forest around us. The dead trees are crowding us like an army.

The coldness and the lack of sleep are draining the last remains of my strength. I rub my arms and blow into my palms, eyes never leaving the tall, dark silhouette of the prince.

What is this silver-haired bastard up to?

My bloodied, shaking fingers close around a rock. It's a ridiculous weapon, but it might grant me the advantage of surprise.

"Talysse!" The stones crunch under his boots when he approaches me, and I hang on to the rock in my fist as if my life depended on it. Or maybe it does.

"You're freezing," he notes.

"N-n-no, I'm fine." It's not the stutter but the loud chatter of teeth that gives me away.

"There's shelter just a mile away." One step, and he looms over me, studying my face.

He's right. Wet clothes cling to my skin, and my lips are probably a lovely shade of blue.

The fatigue makes my brain slow like a duck treading mud. Obviously, the prince is not going with the murder plan. What a relief! My magic depends on my physical fitness, and so do my reflexes. Fighting a Fae nearly twice my size could only end in one way. And it's not a good one.

"You are shaking, Talysse."

"I am aware of this, Aeidas."

"Let's go and find this shelter, and we can make a fire." He slings his arm around me. His touch is warm and calming, grounding against all common sense. It's not the touch of a murderer but a promise of safety and warmth. He smells of night herbs and freshly mowed grass, of enchanted castles and midnight secrets and it washes over my dumbfounded sense as we drag ourselves beneath the black canopy of trees long dead. What is this sudden care about my well-being? Is this another form of Fae cruelty—making me trust him before killing me? Yet right now, the idea of shelter is not that bad, even if I have to share it with this traitorous monster.

Focus, Talysse, one foot before the other. Survive the cold first; then you'll see what fate will throw your way.

The last drops of daily warmth are gone, and the memory of the sun morphed into an icy fog that swirls around our ankles.

The Dead Hour, they call it, it's the time when the darkness has lingered so long that even the nocturnal creatures are tired. It's silent as in a tomb, only the occasional cracking of dry bunches under our feet and our panting breaking the silence. And my chattering teeth, of course.

My clothes are soaked from the final plunge in the creek, and a thin layer of ice starts forming on my doublet.

How long can I walk before collapsing from exhaustion and drifting into catatonic sleep? And giving this murderer the perfect opportunity to strangle me?

A murderer who has saved my life and loves gardening.

But I'm freezing, exhausted, and will soon collapse. Then I'll be at the mercy of the elements and the Shadowfeeders, so I'd rather take the risk and see what shelter he has spotted.

The black trunks around are receding, and we step into a wide clearing.

An old, rotting woodcutters' hut stands there, spared by some strange whim of the Elders.

Aeidas kicks the piles of dead leaves littering the threshold and forces the door open.

With a flick of his wrist, his twin wisps appear again, bathing his tall frame in cool blueish light. Something dark and shimmering solidifies in his hand. Magic buzzes around it, hinting at its deadly power.

Atos's hairy armpits!

"Is this a Shadowblade, Aeidas?"

"Shhh, Talysse," he hushes and steps into the darkness of the hut, his magical weapon raised.

Shadowblades are the stuff of fairytales, at least around Tenebris. Nobody has seen one in centuries. Legends tell of these deadly blades, forged by Atos himself for his favorite Unseelie: they can change shapes in the blink of an eye and appear in the hands of their wielder out of thin air.

And I was planning on fighting this with a rock! I bark a bitter laugh.

"Can't you stay quiet for a minute, Talysse? You want to attract all Shadowfeeders of this forest?" Aeidas scolds me from the hut.

"Don't tell me you're afraid of Shadowfeeders, Aeidas! You have a Shadowblade!"

Shadowblades can inflict serious damage on the demons, but only Sunblades can kill them, the magical weapons forged by Cymmetra for the Seelie Kings and Queens. All of them are dead, of course. Slaughtered by the Unseelie during the war.

The sound of falling objects and a soft curse spill into the night. What is happening inside?

"Are you okay, Aeidas?" A stupid thing to ask someone wielding an indestructible weapon. The air inside is cool, laced with a scent of mold. The rotten floor planks screech under my steps. The hut seems to be abandoned for centuries, left to the mercy of the tiny critters and insects but spared by the elements. Cobwebs drape from the massive beams supporting the roof, shimmering like threaded silver in the light of Aeidas's wisps; the maul of a dark fireplace gapes on the wall. The space is crowded with overturned shelves and broken clay plates. No human bones, no foul stench, no weird words scribbled on the walls this time. It appears the inhabitants left in a hurry.

A single bed, covered in rags, stands right next to the fireplace.

"Not a bad place to spend the rest of the night, Talysse!" He collects the shelves, breaks them over his knee, and piles them into the stone fireplace.

"Indeed. I've seen much worse."

He throws me a long, thoughtful look.

His blade is gone. Dismissed.

Thank Cymmetra. Something about this weapon, about the lethal power harnessed into it, unsettles me. For a moment, I imagine how he must look in battle when all the charm of a prince is stripped off, and the raw, murderous essence of Fae royalty is unleashed. It must be quite a terrifying sight. Oblivious to my presence, he snaps his fingers and sparks fly into the kindling. The flames lick the dry wood, and soon, the hut is bathed in soft golden light.

I stretch my hands, basking in the blissful warmth.

"You better take those wet clothes off," he says over his shoulder.

"I know you cannot resist me, but in Tenebris, gentlemen should buy me dinner before asking for this," I spit, trying to calm the wild beating of my heart.

"Is that before or after your friends from the back alley smack them with a club?"

I shrug. "Depends on the job."

"Oh, there are other jobs? Now I'm curious. What else is on the menu? Pickpocketing men while you kiss them?" He chuckles, throwing more wood into the flames.

Elders above, his guess is so close. "Pickpocketing is not my trade. My looks are very…memorable." I point at my white hair strand without hiding an amused grin. The silence stretches, and the prince rises and takes a step toward me. The warmth of his body, combined with this cursed scent of his, tempts me with promises of dark, forbidden pleasures.

"Indeed," he murmurs. "Your eyes are so unusual for a Satreyan."

His gaze drops to my wrist, where Mother's bracelet pulsates with soft magic.

"Look, I'll just sit by the fire and get dry—"

"Talysse," Aeidas clicks his tongue, "I'm surprised you're such a prude. The fire will die in an hour. You'd better take advantage of the heat now and dry those clothes. And no worries, I've seen ladies without garments before." His voice is low and raspy now.

Oh, I bet he did. Plenty of them. Even if he wasn't the heir to that cursed throne, his looks are enough to lure flocks of Unseelie ladies into his bed chamber.

Disgusting.

"Or you can stand there and catch your death." He shrugs.

His glowing sage eyes pin me, and the right corner of his lips curls up, displaying a sharp fang. He looks like a predator ready to pounce, and for one maddening moment, my exhausted brain thinks that he'd *make me* take these clothes off. A thought that sends a wave of heat through my core. He starts unbuttoning his midnight-colored shirt, his gaze relentlessly fixed on me.

"I've seen…gentlemen without their garments, too." I lift my chin and glare back at him defiantly.

A deep, devilish chuckle rumbles from his chest. "Did you now?"

"Yep, the last one was the blacksmith's apprentice, a handsome young man with hair like straw, very proud of his physique—" Rambling nonsense is often my last resort when in trouble. But I'd say anything just to keep myself distracted from this shameless display of magnificence before me. And of danger too—his Ancestral Mark: red like blood and carved into his flesh. The Sacred Mountain, split in two, and the moon crescent over it; letters of some long-lost language swirl around it. Royal Seelie and Unseelie are born with this mark, a reminder of their guilt.

My gaze crawls back up to his face. He's watching me, his eyes bright green now, like the fields in spring.

"And how was he?" the prince asks, hanging his shirt on a hook on the mantelpiece. Elders help me. The light of the fire gilds every dip and every swell of pure, lean muscle, painting a contrast between the two dips on the sides of his stomach, which narrow down to a—

"Quite disappointing. Myrtle told me about some interesting trick he can pull off." Aeidas listens with a smirk, and to take my mind off the fine dusting of dark hair disappearing into his low-rise leather pants, I start boldly unbuttoning my shirt.

"Hmmm, which trick might that be?" He purrs but quickly looks away when my fingers fiddle with the second button.

"He probably had a bad day. I'm afraid I'll never find out." A lie. Myrtle told me about the way he can use his tongue, which made her scream with pleasure. Something I've never experienced with a man and something that makes me very, very curious.

Aeidas kneels before the fireplace, throwing more wood in. His eyes are fixed on the flames when I hang my clothes on the hook. Standing behind him only in linen panties and the lacy band holding my breasts together, I rake my fingers through my hair, grateful that it's so long and provides some cover. His scent of midnight dew, woodsmoke, and secret gardens makes my head spin, and I quickly step away.

The air deeper in the hut is still cold, and the rags on the bed are teeming with life. Tiny shapes dart to the cobwebbed corners when the old covers are gone. I pile them all on the floor, together with the mice nests, raising clouds of dust and moths, and look around for something to cover myself with.

While the prince is breaking planks and branches over his knee and feeding them into the fire, I manage to pull out some moldy but well-preserved blankets from a trunk.

"As a lady, I'm claiming the bed!" I strew some dry leaves from the floor on the bed planks, throw the covers over them, and smile at my job. That would do.

"Oh, that's not how it works, Talysse," his deep voice rumbles so close to me that my skin sprouts goosebumps. "It's too cold to sleep alone." Atos, take me! Warmth pools from my core and settles lower, when the meaning of his words reaches me. His eyes are nearly black when I turn to face him, and there is tension in the line of his strong shoulders.

He's right. The fire is not enough to keep us warm, and standing here, my breath is visible again.

"Let me keep you warm," he breathes, leaning in closer. Slickness spreads between my thighs.

What is wrong with me? He is Fae royalty—a natural-born predator, shaped by nature and by the Elders in a way to be irresistible.

"We don't know how long the night will last, Talysse. And we have firewood for less than an hour. Let me warm you." His long, thick lashes cast shadows over his eyes, but there's still that predatory glimmer in them.

"I will not touch you in any...inappropriate way; you have my word."

With fatigue comes madness because I nod. And because some hungry curiosity gnaws on my insides.

He's right, it's too cold under the thin cover, eaten by the moths, and I'm shivering when I stiffly lay down, facing the wall.

"You humans get cold so easily," the prince whispers when he slips underneath the cover.

"How many humans have you bedded?" I snap, letting out a soft moan when the rugged plane of his chest molds onto the bare skin of my back. Another maddening low chuckle.

"See? It's already working. You're much warmer now," he murmurs into my ear and slings his heavy arm over my waist. I'm hyperaware of the places our bodies meet.

Elder Seuta, what twisted games are you playing?

He makes a tiny feral sound when I struggle to pull away. A hard, callused palm presses against my abdomen and pulls me back into him.

"May your night be short, Talysse," he rasps in my ear, his hot breath stiffening my nipples under the breast band.

Well, how to sleep in a situation like this? The hot, hard plane of his chest glued to my bare back; every slow, deep beat of his heart tangible; his fingers resting just inches away from my soaked folds.

Praise the Elders; he's still wearing pants, yet there's still the hard outline of something massive pressed against my nearly bare ass.

I'm panting, my nipples painfully straining against the breast band. Body and mind are fighting over melting into him, surrendering to his warmth, or packing the blanket and moving to the floor. Murderous thoughts also cross my tired brain, already walking the thin line to madness.

He is my enemy.

A ruthless, power-hungry Unseelie who sent my family to death.

But how to convince my body that this is wrong? That his arms around me, his even breathing, that wretched feeling of safety I've never experienced before—that this is all a sin?

Those are troubles for the daylight.

"You're safe with me, Talysse," he murmurs as if talking in his sleep.

And he's right. Sleeping in the arms of a Shadowblade wielder must be the safest place in this damned world unless he's trying to kill you, which might be the case here...

Then he does something mesmerizing and terrifying at the same time.

His callused fingers start drawing tiny circles on my lower stomach, gently, like butterflies, and he whispers into my ear, "Sleep, Talysse."

THE PRINCE

DEATH AT DAWN

Time has stopped here, in the golden warmth of this forgotten hut.

Talysse's supple body is melting in my arms, her skin so soft. Her long hair cascades down the stained, tattered covers like black silk. It's impossible to resist such a temptation, and I inhale deeply, savoring the smell of hyacinth and sunshine. Of something pure and beautiful, like a sweet dream you cannot remember in the morning but desperately try to fall back asleep just to return there.

Something not meant for a black heart like mine.

The hands that hold her are drenched with blood. How many innocents have I sent to their deaths? How many lives have I destroyed?

Guilt gnaws on me, just like every other night, and the shadows around us thicken.

I might be a damned sinner without any hope for redemption, but I've promised Talysse that she's safe here with me. So I prop myself on an elbow and watch over her sleep.

Even villains like me have the right to dream.

The plunge in the cavern lake has washed away the grime from her face, and the freckles on her skin draw unknown constellations. She's fast asleep, yet I still draw soothing circles on her stomach, in awe at the way she trusted me. Having someone in my arms, at my mercy, trusting me so blindly is a new experience.

She'll be dead soon; that's the way the Nightfall Trials go, either by my hand or—if the Elders are merciful to me—by the hand of someone else. The thought of hurting her disturbs me deeply; it's like a briar rising from the gloomy depths of my soul, its thorns ripping at my heart, drawing thick, red blood. I choose to ignore this darkness and focus on the warmth of her body molded into mine, her even breathing, and that tender, maddening scent.

My damned body, so unused to closeness, reacts.

I curse softly when my cock strains painfully against my pants, afraid she might feel it.

The fairest court ladies have clawed their faces over my attention, using all the tricks of the Unseelie seduction, yet I have never felt such fire inside me.

And it is so wrong.

She hates me for what I did to her family.

And I have a trial to win.

Any Unseelie would flip her on her back, pin her down, and have his way with her. Fae bodies are different from humans: stronger and more resilient, and people might get hurt in the passionate games with us. In the eyes of my kind, she's just another human, after all, the pest we've been controlling and exploiting for centuries.

The temptation to pull her in even closer, feel more of her soft skin, makes me restless.

Elders, I need to get away from her.

Carefully peeling myself from her, I pull the cover over her shoulders, throw the last piece of wood in the fire, and open the door.

Frigid air hits my face at the doorframe. The cold wind howls between the trunks of the dead trees. The moon has set, and the bottomless night sky shimmers above me; the stars flicker like distant reflections from another world on the surface of an endless inky well. Before heading into the freezing gloom, I turn around one last time. Talysse lies there, drenched in the golden light of the dying fire, her lips parted, her dark hair framing her freckled face, her impossibly long lashes casting shadows over the apples of her cheeks. Something stirs inside me, something better left undisturbed, whose power frightens me.

The door closes without making a sound, and the night swallows me. I rub my face with the heels of my hands and take deep, controlled breaths. The chilly air floods my lungs and restores some of my lost self-control.

It's past the Dead Hour, and the night creatures are tired of their songs and struggles. Like all living beings, they withdraw for some rest and pick up their music later, as if Cymmetra herself has planted tiny mechanical clocks in their heads.

But this silence is unnatural.

I venture deeper into the woods, the clearing with the hut behind me. The distant chirping of crickets mutes with an odd pace, as if a large animal is moving, scaring the tiny critters.

Heroy, stand by me; this might be a Shadowfeeder.

The Shadowblade soundlessly slips into my hand.

Then its scent hits me.

A concealed stench of death and decay, of cruelty and bloodlust, masquerading as innocence. An ancient evil is making its way toward the hut.

And I know very well what it's after.

A tiny silhouette—something one could easily mistake for a small animal and underestimate the immense danger—glides between the trunks.

"Lord Deirhaîm, you can walk freely," I shout into the night. "If it is me you seek, you've found me."

The boy smiles timidly, his crimson eyes capturing the starlight in an unsettling way. He would have grown into a fine male.

Too bad his kind doesn't grow.

"No need to stick to the shadows, Lord Deirhaîm," I repeat, leaning on my Shadowblade. The coolness of my sword, made of condensed magic and shadows, is a comfort in my palm.

"A fine night to stroll and spill some blood, Prince Aeidas. Some...human blood." His voice is anything but childlike; it's a voice you'd expect from something that just crept out of a crypt. The boy approaches me, sniffing the air like an animal, then licks his ruby lips. "Mmmm. I can smell her from here. Delicious, isn't she?"

I casually lean the blade on my bare shoulders and plant my feet firmly in the scorched soil.

Lord Deirhaîm barely reaches my waist but grins at my defiant stand. "Let's share her. Let's hunt her together, Prince Aeidas. You can have your ways with her, and then—then I'll have mine. I've noticed how you look at her." His words slither from his mouth like a viper unfurling. The thought of Talysse with her throat torn out by this monster, drowning in her blood, unsettles me. Wouldn't that be the perfect solution, though? Letting someone else do the dirty work instead of delaying the inevitable?

The clarity of the answer strikes me like a lightning bolt.

No.

She hates me, and she has every right. But I'll be damned if I let her die.

"No."

The air shifts around him, the distance between us crackles with tension.

"Do you think I need your permission to get her, Princeling?" He sounds more like a beast now, a reminder of his true nature. Without giving in to his taunting, I raise my blade.

"Will you—" he licks his lips in anticipation, and his canines—ivory daggers—flash in the scarce light, "fight me for her?" A flicker of savage excitement ripples through his face.

Instincts kick in. My feet assume a fighting position, and the Shadowblade drops to the boy's face.

"You should know better than to stand between someone like me and their prey," the child growls, a feral and inhuman sound.

Indeed, I know.

The creature before me is more deadly and unpredictable than a Shadowfeeder.

Vampires are cursed by the Elders. Legend says they tricked the gods into letting them taste their blood and stealing some of their powers. For that, they were punished, and everything they have is a twisted parody of the Elders' gifts. Even their immortality is not given but bound to their consumption of blood. They are forced to walk the night and crave the lives of all. This is not a boy before me but a millennia-old demon who sees us all, both humans and Fae, as livestock. A rich and powerful demon, though, with an army very useful to the crown.

What leaps on me is no longer human—it's a monstrous abomination towering at eight feet, a beast with claws like scythes meant to tear flesh from bone and fangs that could crush a skull. Patches of brown fur cling to its gray, leathery skin, and its eyes blaze like gateways to hell. Its guttural growl reverberates through the woods, a sound so primal and terrifying it could freeze even a Shadowfeeder in its tracks.

I barely manage to roll to the side as it barrels toward me, my blade poised to strike. But the creature is unnervingly quick for its size, skidding to a halt and whipping around with a feral snarl.

It lunges, and before I can react, it's on my back.

Elders!

Pain explodes across my shoulders as its razor-sharp teeth sink into my flesh, tearing through muscle and sinew. The smell of my own blood mixes with its rancid breath.

"Atos take you," I growl, feeling its acid spit eating through my flesh. The pain explodes, throbbing and blinding, but my instinct doesn't let me succumb to panic.

Gritting my teeth, I will my blade morph into a dagger, feeling the comforting shift of magic in my hand.

The beast's chokehold tightens, its foul breath hot against my neck as it hisses in my ear, "Royal blood is a rare delicacy. I'll bleed you dry, then take my time with her—"

The thought of her—mangled, screaming—drives a cold spike of fear through me. My grip on the Shadowblade tightens, the hilt slick with my blood, as I slowly force him to loosen his grasp.

I can't lose her.

Not now.

With a savage roar, I plunge the dagger deep into its thigh. The blade cuts through the dense muscle, and the creature howls, a sound so piercing it rattles my bones. Acidic spit dribbles from its fangs, burning through the skin of my shoulder, the agony nearly blinding me. I twist the dagger and rip it upward toward its hips, the blade tearing through flesh with a sickening squelch.

The creature's howls turn into shrieks of pain, and its grip weakens, the chokehold loosening just enough for me to shake it off. The Shadowblade morphs into a lance, the weapon lengthening in my grasp as I spin it in a lethal arc. The beast is fast, its hulking form dodging my first strike, but not fast enough to escape the two vicious slashes that carve through its abdomen.

Black blood spills from the gashes, steaming as it hits the ground. Now, this is a sight for sore eyes.

"Maybe you'll bleed first, beast," I snarl, a savage smile curling my lips as I launch myself into a somersault, the world spinning around me in a blur of motion. I land behind its back, and just when the Shadowblade descends to the abomination's shoulder blade, the beast spins around faster than anticipated, its massive claws lashing out.

What a fatal miscalculation.

Pain erupts in my side as its claws rake through my flesh, and I'm thrown backward, crashing into a tree trunk. My vision blurs, my head dizzy as I struggle to rise, but the demon is on me in an instant, its colossal weight pinning me down. I can barely breathe under the crushing pressure, and my limbs scream in protest as I try to free myself.

And just when I think it cannot get any worse, it does.

"Aeidas?" Talysse calls from the clearing. "Aeidas, are you there?"

My blood curdles in terror.

"Do you hear that, Prince? Dinner is served," the vampire hisses and releases me.

Cold air fills my lungs as the beast suddenly lets me go and leaps toward her, frenzied. Not wasting a second, I push myself up and give chase.

Talysse stands in the middle of the clearing, her form shimmering as if reflecting the starlight.

Deirhaîm leaps on her in one swift move, his claws raised like daggers. Elders, she'll be dead before I can reach her. My blade morphs into a spear, and I send it flying. The abomination reaches Talysse just when the Shadowblade finds its mark, piercing it with lethal precision.

It's too late.

My heart pounds as I race toward the monster, each breath a searing reminder that I've failed.

With a scream, I yank the blade out with a wet smack, morph it back into a long sword, and swing. The vampire's head rolls into the soot on the forest floor.

I step back to avoid the massive collapsing body crushing me and lunge forward, bracing to see a mortally wounded Talysse.

Skidding in the soot, I come to a stop, looking around confused, then rubbing my eyes with a bloody fist.

She's gone.

Vanished.

"Aeidas? Are you hurt? Say something!" her voice, laced with worry, calls to me.

A good fifty feet away from here.

My mind stutters. How can she be there? How is this possible?

I glance at the empty space where she was just a moment ago, the spot now nothing but a patch of disturbed soot. And then I see her—alive, whole—standing in the doorframe, golden light spilling around her like a halo.

I chuckle.

Relief and disbelief crash over me, but the revelation that she's more than she seems stirs something deeper. This human...she's full of surprises.

Weaving illusions is a rare gift, and to do it so skillfully, without any guidance, is far more advanced than any human magic. To the hell pits of Atos, it is more advanced than most Fae magic around!

This oddity requires a more thorough investigation. Yet another reason to keep her alive for a while.

182

I dismiss my blade and stride back to the hut, my wounds throbbing, the poison working its way through my body.

Above us, a purple shimmer veils the sky, and the stars flicker, paling.

The sun is rising.

TALYSSE

NIGHTHAVEN

We're sitting at the doorstep of the hut when a group of Unseelie riders arrive with the first rays of the sun.

The body of the demon is quickly decomposing in the sun rays in the clearing, attracting swarms of flies.

"Prince Aeidas, Talysse the Nameless." The lead Fae soldier dismounts and bows low before his lord, acknowledging me with a polite nod.

"Her name is Nightglimmer. Make sure you address her properly next time," Aeidas says, a dark threat lacing his tone as he holds the improvised bandage I've pressed onto his wound.

"As you wish, Your Majesty," the soldier quickly responds, his eyes darting to the other riders as if seeking reassurance, but they avoid his gaze. He surveys the scene: the large, decapitated body in a puddle of drying blood and me sitting beside the prince, alive and unharmed.

"It's dawning. All survivors of the first Trial are invited to rest and recuperate in the palace of Nighthaven until the next long night."

Atos's hairy armpits! The thought of setting foot in the Unseelie capital sends a shiver down my spine. Father always spoke of it as an ancient, treacherous place where the common laws of nature don't apply.

"Very well. We ride immediately," Aeidas declares with the same cold, imperious tone he used in the Governor's Palace.

Did he just say ride? That's too bad. Seems I have an excuse not to go after all.

"Sorry to decline this invitation, but it seems like I'm staying here. I cannot ride." Eyes, wide with disbelief, land on me.

"That's out of the question, Talysse Nightglimmer," the messenger interrupts. "Orders are for all contestants to gather at the palace."

"You cannot ride?" Aeidas asks, a hint of amusement in his voice. "I thought you lived in the stables!"

What an ass.

"Cleaning horse manure is different than riding. Or are servants in Nighthaven treated differently?" I spit out through clenched teeth. "But that's okay, I'm staying here."

"She will ride with me," the prince declares, and before I can protest, he swings onto the saddle of a massive black horse the Unseelie have brought forth.

"I'd rather take my chances alone, thank—" The air is forced from my lungs as his arm wraps around me, pulling me up onto the saddle as if I weigh nothing. The shock leaves me breathless.

The words die on my lips as the horse surges forward, racing through the woods. Does this cursed beast have wings? Clinging to the front of the saddle is a welcome distraction, as I'm painfully aware of the prince's muscular form pressed against my back. His arm remains around my waist while his other hand expertly guides the reins.

Elders. He's not wearing a shirt.

And there it is, that dreaded warmth in my core, that cursed need to feel more of him, the murderer of my parents. I feel every contraction of his chest, and—Elders help me—something hard and thick pressed against my ass.

Do not be naive, Talysse.

He's Fae royalty. Bred to seduce, deceive, dominate, and rule over weak minds. To him, I'm just a pawn in some twisted game.

"I still find it hard to believe you cannot ride." His hot breath brushes my ear, sending all the wrong signals to my body. I growl in frustration. The acceleration pushes me closer to him, and every jolt in the road brings us dangerously nearer as if the damned beast has an agenda.

"My father had many horses. He was about to teach me riding when someone spotted the Seelie hiding in our barn—"

I cut myself off, realizing that it sounds like I'm seeking pity from him. That was not my intention. The reminder was for me: that beneath this bronzed skin and breathtaking physique lies a heart as dead and black as the desolate woods stretching on both sides of the road. His arm tenses around my waist, and I steal a glance at his face.

His black brows knit together, cold eyes fixed on the horizon.

"Power is not for the weak of heart, Talysse," he says, his voice deep and firm, a rumble from a calloused place in his soul. "I won't deny that my family and I have spilled rivers of blood. You won't understand, but it was for the greater good. If it brings you any satisfaction—" He seeks my gaze, and for a moment, I catch a flicker of vulnerability—Elders above, remorse?

I must be imagining things.

"—they all seek me out in the night. The lives I've destroyed, the villages overrun by Shadowfeeders, the growing devastation in these lands. And now, seeing how I've destroyed your life will make my nights even worse, Talysse. Your eyes will join the screeching of gallows, the thuds of heads rolling down the scaffold, the pleas of wives, and the screams of orphaned children." His voice drops to a whisper, lost in the wind. "One thing keeps me going, Talysse, and this I promise you: it all happened for a reason."

A lump forms in my throat. Somehow, the vulnerable, remorseful Aeidas frightens me more than the cold, despotic one. I can deal with a cruel monster, but not with someone who regrets what he did. Hate is easy; it comes naturally to humans and Fae. But walking the gray zone of your enemy's motives is…dangerous. Dangerous because you might understand the reason behind their dark deeds and lose everything that has driven you forward. Everything that has defined you.

This fear steals the snappy comment from my lips, and we ride in silence. My mind tormented, my body responding in maddening ways to his touch.

Elders, how did I deserve such a perverse, refined torment?

The sun climbs higher, its soft rays soothing my troubles. The charred soil and black trunks of the dead forest give way to a dull, rocky plain encircled by barren hills. Ahead, a fortress of dark stone glints like a polished onyx spear tip. Silk banners unfurl in the wind like thick snakes preparing to strike. Even from this distance, I recognize the crest they bear—identical to the Ancestral Mark of the Prince, pressed against my back. We are nearing a bastion of the Unseelie.

Aeidas's jaw is set, his eyes narrowed, silver hair whipping in the wind. His cheeks are flushed, more color than usual. He spurs the horse into a gallop, drawing me closer as if concerned I might fall. Breathless, I search desperately for anything—anything—to keep my mind off his firm embrace and the ripple of muscle behind me.

"That creature you slew—was it a vampire?" I ask, grasping at the obvious, but Seuta is my witness; I can't think straight with his jaw resting on my head and his silver strands tickling my face.

"It was." His whisper brushes my ear, and I look away, hoping to hide the goosebumps on my neck.

"And he is...dead now?"

"He's been dead for centuries. Now he cannot harm anyone anymore," Aeidas breathes.

The horse's hooves clatter over cobblestones, and the polished black walls rise before us. Soldiers and civilians spill out of the tall gate, rushing to meet us.

"What is this place?" I do my best to conceal the note of uncertainty in my voice. Riding with the Heir to the Unseelie Throne doesn't make his kind any less threatening.

"It's the doorstep to Nighthaven. You're safe here, Talysse." Somehow, the royal bastard reads my mind. He removes his arm from my waist and waves at the crowd. The thunderous wave of cheering nearly makes me slip from the saddle.

Aeidas! They chant. *Wildling!*

He deftly pulls the reins, and for a few terrifying moments, the black beast rises onto its hind legs. The city wall seems ready to crack from the force of the applause.

Seems like this show-off is pretty popular around here.

The town behind the walls looks surprisingly dull—simple square buildings devoid of decoration or hints of luxury. But its Beacon is new and tall, and crystals of the halo grid are placed on every street corner. If only Tenebris had defenses like this against the horrors of the night!

Barracks and gray one-story houses line the steep cobbled road. Crowds roar all the way to the city square. A tall granite monolith rises at its center, and the magic vibrating around it fills my mouth with a metallic taste. Lines of Unseelie soldiers in polished cuirasses, bearing the Ancestral Mark's heraldry, secure the perimeter.

Aeidas pulls the reins, and I squint against the bright sun, studying the artifact. The three massive rocks resemble a doorframe, and strange glowing runes are carved into the weather-worn stone.

"Have you ever traveled by portal, Talysse?" the prince asks, and I scoff. He knows very well that Fae portals aren't accessible to humans. They're locked away and heavily guarded in their black bastions. The only way a human can reach Nighthaven is by winning the Nightfall Trials or being sold as a slave.

The warmth behind me vanishes suddenly, and I nearly slide off the saddle. That would've been quite the entertainment for the Unseelie crowd.

Aeidas is off the horse, and I squeak pathetically when his large hands wrap around my waist and pull me down. Flailing, I grab his shoulders for support—sweet mother Cymmetra—how can a body be that hard? I slide down the rugged plane of his torso, heat spreading between my thighs. We stay like this for a brief moment, eyes locked, my breast pressed against his bare chest. He releases me quickly, looking away, but not before I catch the heat in his sage green eyes. Crossing his arms, he points at the obelisk.

"Well, Talysse," he says, his voice once again cold and imperious, "it's time to show you my home."

*

I stumble out of the portal, my senses numb by the roar of raw magic. The blinding lights dancing before my eyes dissipate, and the knot in my stomach loosens a bit. Elders, that was something I'd be happy to repeat. The world is still spinning, but firm hands seize me before I can fall. The touch is familiar, unwelcome, and it sends a jolt through my body—like a spark waiting to ignite. There's no need to look to see who it is; my body already recognizes this particular touch, and it reacts in frustratingly unpredictable ways. I slap Aeidas's hands away and shake my head to clear my thoughts.

The portal has brought us to a circular square, similar to the one back at the outpost bastion, but far more crowded.

The royal guard, clad in armor bearing the royal coat of arms, is easy to spot. They are everywhere, holding back colorful crowds of Fae. It seems like the whole capital has gathered to see the contestants who survived the first of the Nightfall Trials. Merchants and street performers take advantage of the gathering, and music mixes with excited chatter and the shouts of the townsfolk. The aroma of roasted meat tingles my nose, and my belly responds with an angry growl. Just like before, the crowd roars when they spot their prince, and Aeidas lifts both hands in greeting.

The noise nearly makes the roof tiles of the buildings around fall off by the sheer force of their chant.

"Aeidas! Wildling! Aeidas!" They chant, applaud, and stomp their feet. I suddenly feel small and terribly vulnerable. Here I am, surrounded by the kind who killed my parents, at the mercy of a ruthless prince with an unclear agenda.

And why, in the name of Atos, do they call him the Wildling?

My fingers close around the magical Flint in my pocket, the smooth surface cooling my emotions. He didn't take it away from me, though he had many opportunities. He could have left me in the dark garden of Sorayah the Songstress, or let me drown, or let that child monster have me and claimed my victory as his, but for some unknown reason, he didn't.

Fae are traitorous and self-serving, and this one here has more refined ways. He will try to deceive me soon; I know it in my bones. Maybe he's making me trust him in order to get some sick pleasure from breaking me later.

We climb a wide street with smooth pavement surrounded by ornate granite buildings. Artfully carved onyx statues of the Elders and some unknown Unseelie Kings line the street, their glossy black eyes following our procession.

The street ends at the feet of a monumental black staircase leading to the most magnificent building I've ever seen. It is a symphony of towers, steep roofs, breakneck stairways, arched bridges defying gravity, and wide, ornate windows. It is breathtaking. Noticing that I have fallen behind, the prince turns around and—to my embarrassment—chuckles when he sees the awe written all over my face.

Just great. The human girl from the stables sees big houses for the first time. I look pointedly away, straighten my doublet, and follow him on the steps leading to the palace, where a group of courtiers is already awaiting us.

Stepping through the grand doors of the Fae palace, I am immediately enveloped by an aura of ancient, crumbling decadence. The entrance hall looms vast and imposing, its polished dark jade floor gleaming under flickering light, like the surface of a murky lake that might hide unseen depths. The crystals of the chandeliers catch the light, casting a kaleidoscope of colors onto the vaulted ceilings high above.

Walls of onyx, etched with intricate, timeworn patterns, guide the procession through a labyrinth of endless, spiraling staircases. Each step on the polished black stairs echoes with whispers of centuries past, their handrails adorned with delicate carvings of mythical creatures and ancient runes that seem to pulse with a life of some old, forgotten magic.

Magnificent tapestries hang from the walls, masterpieces woven with threads of gold and silver, depicting the Fae's history—battles of old, coronations of long-forgotten kings, and the serene beauty of enchanted forests before the Hex. The draft moves them, bringing the scenes almost to life as we pass.

The palace halls stretch endlessly, their high vaults arching gracefully overhead, supported by slender columns of jade. Sunlight filters through tall, arched windows draped with heavy velvet curtains, illuminating the dust motes that dance in the air and casting long, eerie shadows that play tricks on the eye.

Every corner of the palace whispers secrets. The scent of old books and the sharp tang of magic lingers in the grand halls. Mirrors, darkened by time, with frames encrusted in jewels, are lined up along the walls, and I catch a glimpse of my reflection. Elders, I look tired. I take a deep breath, struggling to keep up with the prince, carried away in a conversation with one knight in black armor. The air is thick with the scent of old stone and the faint aroma of incense and wilting flowers.

Seems like our march through the melancholic beauty of the palace is nearly over when we enter a wide corridor with ornate doors on both sides. Looks like some kind of quarters and my suspicion is confirmed when the guards halt before a door.

"Your chambers, Talysse Nightglimmer," the knight in unmarked armor declares and pushes the heavy door open.

Relieved that I'll be finally left alone with my thoughts and that I'll get a chance to rest, I rush in.

Without hesitation or a word of goodbye, I slam the door behind my back. Yet two glowing sage eyes still pierce me, and his touch still lingers on my skin.

Beyond the heavy oak door lies an intimate and shadowy haven. The opulent darkness of the room is disturbed by the warm glow of the flames of a black marble fireplace. The walls, draped in deep velvet tapestries of midnight blue and onyx, seem to absorb the light. The air, perfumed with the scent of burning wood and faint incense, is pleasantly warm.

In the center of the room stands a magnificent four-poster bed, its dark mahogany frame intricately carved with twisting vines and mythical creatures. The canopy above is lined with heavy velvet curtains in a rich, deep purple, edged with delicate silver embroidery. I pat the soft mattress and brush my fingers over the layers of sumptuous fabrics—silk sheets in deep garnet, a plush ebony comforter, and an array of pillows of various shapes and sizes.

To the side of the fireplace, a high-back chair upholstered in dark green brocade invites you to sit and ponder, its wood polished to a deep, glossy sheen. A small table beside it holds a crystal decanter filled with an amber liquid and two matching goblets.

The floor, covered in polished onyx tiles, reflects the room's splendor, like the surface of a dark lake.

I've never seen such opulence before, as if every piece is created by the hands of Elder Raynisse herself.

Still busy taking in the details of the room, I hear the door open too late.

A human girl, no older than fourteen, slips into the room with the quiet grace of someone used to moving unnoticed—her presence a sudden intrusion into the shadowy space. She's wearing a plain but new cotton dress, and her light brown hair is braided on both sides of her face. She looks like any other normal young girl, and there's something in her bearing that reminds me of Tayna if it wasn't for the terrible scar covering half of her face. It looks like her skin melted or was ripped off, and a thick pink band covers it, hinting that she's lost her eye, too.

"M'lady." The girl curtsies with a pleasant smile, and I scold myself for staring. "I will be your maid during your stay in the palace. I am so excited to be of service to you, m'lady," she chirps, puffing the pillows on the enormous bed with the black, silky sheets, "they say you won the first trial and got the Flint!" She looks at me, her single brown eye wide open, glowing. I'm already preparing an excuse to send her away, but her excitement stops me. How often does this poor slave girl have the chance to talk to someone, especially another human?

"Drop the m'lady, I am Talysse. And you are?" I ask while unbuttoning my doublet.

"I am Ayrene," she squeaks with excitement, and I realize that her smile is infectious.

"Well, Ayrene, you remind me a lot of my sister," I remark, shedding the doublet and fussing with the buttons of my worn-out lacy shirt, which sports a couple of holes after the Trial. This bed there is calling my name, and I can't wait to feel the coolness of those sheets.

"Do I?" She gleams. "What can I do for you m—Talysse, m'lady? Should I stitch up these holes? Or draw you a bath?"

"A bath would be perfect," I agree, realizing that I'm looking for an excuse to keep her around, despite the fact that my knees are giving in from the fatigue.

"On it, Talysse!" The girl folds the silk screen at the far corner of the room and reveals a crystal tub and some copper pipes connected to a strange hearth. She throws some firewood into the opening and opens the valves. "It heats the water." She points at it proudly. While the water steams and fills the beautiful tub, she fusses with the jars on the shelf above, sniffs, and throws some petals in it.

I watch her, my clothes piled on the floor. "Aren't you a little young to do all this?" I ask, crossing my arms. The air is filled with the soothing aroma of iris and chamomile.

She dips a finger to test the water and looks back at me, glowing. "I'm fifteen, Talysse. My brother is thirteen, and he's helping at the stables," she adds proudly.

"And where are your parents?"

Oh, snap. Should've known better than to blurt out a question like this. I immediately recognize that look, that telling silence.

"It's all right, Ayrene, you're not the only one who lost her family to the Unseelie." I walk to her and place a palm on her shoulder.

"To the Unseelie?" Her single dark eye flashes incredulously, and she puffs her lips. "It was a horde of Tainted Ones, m'lady Talysse. They attacked us, Ma put us on a horse, but I slipped. The horse dragged me for a while, m'lady...Talysse. That's why I have this face. Aeidas saved us. He came down on them with his Shadowblade and took the whole horde all alone. But he arrived too late for Ma and Pa." I blink, dumbfounded. "Do you know why they call him the Wildling, m...Talysse?" I shake my head. This conversation is becoming far more interesting than anticipated.

"Why?" I ask, dipping my toe in the water. It's fragrant and hot, a luxury I haven't had since my time in my parents' mansion.

"You need help getting in? No? Okay." She watches me tensely when I ease myself into the water, petals floating on the surface. Elders bless this girl. This is heaven. "They call him like this because he prefers spending more time exploring the Wastelands and working in the palace gardens than in his court." The memory of the glow in his eyes when he was collecting the glowing spores flashed before me. This...makes some sense in a very odd way.

"I was very young, but Raynar, my brother, was even younger. We set off to the Free Cities with Ma and Pa, but our caravan had just one mage, inexperienced they said. It was over in seconds." I squeeze her tiny hand, but she pulls it out and starts massaging fragrant oils into my scalp. She continues on telling the story with an even voice, "Prince Aeidas came from nowhere and saved us. Then he brought us here. The court healer worked for nine nights on my face, but she couldn't save my eye—" I swallow drily, my eyes welling up. Poor young ones, the torture they must have been through. "But I am good, as you see. Raynar, on the other hand," her voice breaks, "he will never be the same again. He hasn't spoken a word since that night, Talysse, m'lady, and he is a little bit slow. But he's a good boy, and he helps. He works at the stables, did I tell you that? He loves sweets. Bring him some if you have the chance. I feel like he's...forever stuck in that night, Talysse, and this pains me." Fragrant foam is dripping into my eyes and I am grateful for this, as it hides my tears. This could've been me and Tayna.

"I am sure that he knows that you're safe, Ayrene. Are you happy here?"

"We are, m'lady. We are happy to serve the prince. And he taught me reading." I whip my head to look at her. She's not joking. Children cannot lie in the way adults do. And this girl is telling the truth.

"And you're...free to go if you wish?"

"Yes. But where should we go? We're paid handsomely for our work, and the prince is treating us fair. We're safe here. Working for him, we're off-limits for the rest of them. I cannot bring myself to attempt another trip to the Free Cities."

I lean into her skilled touch as she continues babbling. "Aeidas, Master Viridis, and Desmond are my friends. They say that soon things will change for good, Talysse. They want to make trees grow back out there; they want to make the nights shorter. But we should not speak of this. See, I'm small and can sneak around unnoticed, so I hear things." She winks at me. Well, now she sounds delusional—probably, this girl's ordeal has messed with her head, too. "You have beautiful hair, even prettier than the Fae ladies; no wonder the prince looks at you like this—"

She's washing the fragrant foam off my hair, yet I still open my mouth and nearly choke.

"Looks at me like what, Ayrene?" I mumble, my eyes still closed.

"Well, rumor has it that you caught his eye, m'lady Talysse, and that they found you after the Trial with no clothes on—" I grab the edge of the bathtub, struggling to get out, not sure if I want to protest, or just be alone. Who is spreading these outrageous rumors? I need to find them and make them shut up. I was completely dressed, and Aeidas—well, he was still bleeding from that nasty bite.

"I personally don't believe this, m'lady Talysse, as our prince, handsome as he is, has never been in the company of a lady longer than—"

Well, this is more than enough. Wiping the foam off my eyes, I urge her to rinse my hair off and dismiss her.

"I will be back at Nightfall to help you with your gown and hair, m'lady Talysse; rest now!" She curtsies and hurries to the door.

"Help me with what?" I ask incredulously.

"Help you look even better for the ball tonight, m'lady Talysse." She glows and closes the door behind her back.

Atos's hairy ass.

A ball in this viper's nest, where everyone will stare at me—the prince's latest conquest.

I step out of the crystal tub, wetting the polished floor, and change into an airy nightgown Ayrene has prepared for me. Then I slip between the crisp sheets, smelling of lavender soap. Exhaustion pulls me under as soon as my head touches the feather-filled pillows.

Still, even as sleep claims me, the distant echoes of music and laughter haunt my dreams.

Another trial, a far more traitorous one, is just around the corner.

TALYSSE

THE UNSEELIE COURT

The nightmares are back.

Instead of my parents' lifeless bodies, there is a horde of monsters hunting me. I am clutching Tayna in my hands and we're riding a horse, and it is so terrifyingly big and fast. The animal is scared, galloping without a care of the two tiny humans on its back, and I slip down. Still tangled in the reins, the horse doesn't stop, and I scream until my throat is dry, aware that I've lost Tayna somewhere along the way. Then Aeidas comes out of nowhere, waving his Shadowblade, but instead of helping he swings it at me—

"M'lady Talysse?" Ayrene is at my bedside, lighting the candles in the silver candelabra. "It's almost Nightfall; time to get ready for the ball. It'll be a short night, a time to celebrate. Here, I've brought you snacks."

"Snacks" is a magic word for me, and it is incredibly smart of Ayrene to keep me distracted with the honey-walnut cookies and quince compote spread over thin slices of fresh bread while she combs and braids my hair and squeals over the dresses we found in the mahogany wardrobe.

When she walks me to the mirror opposite the bed, I subconsciously scan the room for magic. This vision in a white silk dress threaded with silver cannot be me. The dress has a generous cleavage plunging deep and displaying more than I'd feel comfortable with, but this is the extravagant Unseelie court, so I'd better blend in. Long transparent sleeves, split from the elbow down, sweep the floor with each move. The hem of the flowing white skirts is encrusted with sparkling crystals, its pattern reminding me of the paintings the frost draws on the windows in the winter mornings. The delicate fabric shows the lithe line of my legs and pools around my sequined slippers like fog.

Ayrene has added some color to my lips and cheeks and painted my eyelashes black, which makes my eyes pop out. Maybe it was the whole day of rest, but there's a sparkle in my gaze that wasn't there before.

"Do you like it, m'lady Talysse?" Insecure, the girl is touching up my curls which cascade down my shoulders, rows of pearls and diamonds snaking between them.

"If I like it?" My brows shoot up in dismay, then pack the girl and swing her around. "I love it, Ayrene! Are you sure you don't have magic? I came in here looking like a Tainted One, and see what you've done!" She palms her forehead. "Oh, I nearly forgot! A last but very important detail! The prince asked me to give you this," I glare at her, "tell her to put the Flint in there, he said, and never to part from it!" She hands me a tiny brocade pouch with a long cord intended to be worn around one's neck. "And I agree with him, m'lady Talysse; put the relic in there and never take it off! Contestants are not allowed to attack each other before the beginning of the next trial, but I am sure there are enough wicked minds here plotting to steal it. Keep it safe, and don't wander the castle alone," she finishes, hanging the shimmering thread around my neck, and I wince at the touch of her cool, small fingers, so much like Tayna's.

"Promised," I declare solemnly, wondering what game Aeidas is playing. There must be some tricky, sinister plot behind all this. "Now show me to this ballroom." I brush my skirts, straighten my back, and brace to leave the safety of my chambers.

Two silent Fae guards in unmarked black armor escort me to the ballroom.

"Shadowblades," Ayrene whispers in my ear, "the prince's most loyal men." Everyone has heard of these fearsome warriors, Aeidas's private army of knights, assassins, and spies.

Ancient magic and secrets much older than the royal family lingers linger in the corners of the Unseelie palace. Some corridors and halls seem to be used daily, while others are covered with layers of undisturbed dust and cobwebs. It is a maze, or my guards have chosen a route to confuse my senses, but we're skirting around some sections of the palace, descending and then climbing back up just to avoid certain halls or areas.

"I cannot go any further, m'lady." The girl pulls my hand and turns back to leave. "Don't walk the hallways alone; don't follow the whispers, Talysse! I will see you later!" And she's gone.

The Shadowblades urge me to keep up with their wide strides, and we reach an area more lavishly decorated than the rest. A group of extravagantly dressed Unseelie courtiers stands around and glares at us. The way they look at me is giving me the chills. It's not the ridicule in their beautiful, cruel eyes; it's the way they stare and lick their lips as if I am on the menu tonight.

Well, nothing new to me. I close my fingers around the pouch at my neck, turn around, and grin, adding an exaggerated curtsy. This stuns them; some look away, and others respond with fake smiles, baring blood-chilling sharp fangs. But at least the whispers behind my back die out.

The scent of hot food alerts me that we're close. My guards stand before a tall mahogany door with golden ornaments. They look at me as if awaiting confirmation, and I nod, surprised by their thoughtfulness. They push the heavy door open.

Chin held high, I enter the ballroom.

Every inch of the banquet hall is covered with black marble, capturing and reflecting the light of the crystal chandeliers like the night sky. The walls are adorned with intricate gold filigree.

At the center of the hall stands a long, grand table, its surface a gleaming expanse of onyx inlaid with veins of gold. It's loaded with an extravagant array of delicacies: roasted game birds, their crispy skins glistening with honey and spices, platters of exotic fruits, and decadent pastries in various shapes and colors. Goblets of Fae wine, shimmering with an otherworldly glow, stand before each guest.

The guests, clad in deep velvets, silks, and brocades, are carried away in conversations; the air around them is heavy with fine perfumes and incense. The women wear gowns adorned with gemstones that sparkle like stars, their hair styled in elaborate twists and braids. It's such a relief not to feel overdressed anymore. Ayrene knew what she was doing—seeing the cut of the gowns and the hairdos of the court ladies, I easily blend in. Music fills the air, a haunting melody played by unseen musicians. The delicate sound of a harp, intertwined with the deep tones of a cello, creates a symphony that resonates with the very soul of the palace.

The closest groups of chatting courtiers grow quiet as soon as I'm near them. A human attendant in an impeccable silk uniform shows me to my seat. At the far head of the table sits the royal couple—they look ancient and otherworldly and tired, their eyes haunted. No piles of sparkling jewelry, layers of luxurious fabrics and clever garment cuts can compensate for the lack of color in their faces and their detachment from the surroundings. They've lost their eldest son, but there's more to their resignation than that. It seems like they're done with everything. As if Death is sitting next to them, and they don't mind.

When the attendant pulls my chair back, Gale peeks from behind a stuffed peacock and winks. Praised be the Elders! I can't hold back my grin. So, he escaped the cursed mansion of Ornatus too. Next to him sits the Dark Dryad, silent and mysterious, and the shifter, busy with a bloody chunk of meat.

The Warrior Pony Princess is here, too, in a gold-threaded dress that adds sparkle to her eyes. She's talking softly to the blond man, both holding goblets of Fae wine. Her eyes darken when she sees me. I pat the pouch on my chest and wink at her. WPP's gaze spells murder, and she leans into her friend, starting a heated discussion.

Two Fae are out: the creepy vampire child and the Huntress, and just one human, the mercenary. Nobody will miss them. Leaning back, I raise a gold-rimmed crystal goblet of Fae wine to my lips, scanning the hall. One contestant is missing tonight, probably planning a grand entry.

"You'd better be careful with that wine, human," the dark-haired Fae male on my right says with mocking concern. "It's not for your kind; it may come on a bit hard." Great, some Fae-splaining. He has handsome but cold features and predatorily sparkling ruby eyes.

"Thanks for your concern, dear sir, but you might be surprised by my abilities," I respond, sipping the wine casually, its intense flavor nearly choking me. Compared to the poison sold at Bountiful Bosom for copper a jar, this is a divine elixir. One of Godey Goldtooth's cats drowned in a barrel once, and they found the poor thing after we drank the last drops. "It just added more flavor." Godey shrugged and started charging a copper more for the next barrel of burning poison.

"My cousin is right, Talysse of Tenebris." the Fae male on my left leans in, too close. There's a family resemblance, but his hair is red, cut above his shoulders. "Fae wine goes to human heads and makes them do foolish things."

"Not that we would mind," the first one adds, amused. "They say you didn't find the magic trinket yourself but fucked our prince and received it as payment." His cousin cackles, and I casually reach for a pastry tray, knocking a large crystal decanter of deep purple wine right into his lap.

"Oh, apologies." I meet his enraged gaze without flinching. "Seems like you're right. This wine is really getting to my head." The arrogant prick curses, pushing his chair back and leaving the table.

"You'd better get that cleaned up; it looks like it will leave a stain!" I shout over my shoulder, then return to my meal.

"That was...amusing," the red-haired male says, helping himself to a load of marinated wings of some unknown creature. "There's a fire in you. I can see the appeal. But tread with care, fiery human. You've just made an enemy."

I shrug without bothering to answer, enjoying a spoonful of divine pickled vegetables instead. Suddenly, all conversations muffle. Steps echo behind my back and everyone's staring at something. I throw a look over my shoulder, and nearly choke on a pickle.

Regal and magnificent, clad in a midnight silk shirt, unbuttoned to display his Ancestral Mark, Aeidas strides toward the table. The inky velvet pants hug his powerful thighs, accentuating the way he moves—with the casual elegance of an assassin. He doesn't need any crown to show his royal status. There's something in the straight line of his broad shoulders, in the way he holds his head and his eyes— cold and distant now. Some people are born to rule, destined for it by the Elders. And even if he were born in a barn, he'd have found a way to get his crown.

What makes me quickly down the rest of the wine goblet, is the Unseelie walking next to him. She's gliding on the floor, her long silver hair dragging behind her like a train. Her pale rose dress encrusted with pearls brings out her perfect complexion, and her violet eyes seem to be speaking to each one of us: flattering, seducing, promising.

"This is Sorcia, his late brother's promised. Rumor has it she's set to marry him," the red-haired male explains as if he had noticed the tightness in my chest. "She's the greatest beauty in the kingdom, a daughter of a powerful house, and don't be deceived by these delicate hands. She has a mind of steel and teeth. She'd torture you, mangle you, cook a delicious soup out of you, and feed it to the prince you're ogling so unashamedly." His cruel cackle slices me like an icy blade, and the way the prince serves her wine helps her in the chair, plunges it deeper into my chest. Aeidas settles between the ethereal female and his mother, every inch the cold, ruthless Prince of the Unseelie. His eyes wander around, and when they clash with mine, something flashes in their emerald depths. Quickly looking away, I push my chair back and go around the table, followed by many curious gazes.

"Gale." I place a hand on his shoulder, and he looks up at me; the warmth of his smile immediately makes me feel better. "Shall we dance?"

"Talysse, I was just about to ask you myself." He rises, takes my hand, and guides us to the open space where some couples are already swirling to the haunting melody. There's a sway in my step—the annoying Fae was right. This wine really got me.

Gale's hand rests on my hip, the other holding my hand. We're so close I can see every amber sparkle in his almond eyes. His golden earrings capture the warm light, and he whips his head to flick the unruly curls from his forehead.

"I am so happy you made it out of these Elders-forgotten tunnels, Talysse," he murmurs, and there's sincerity in his voice. So refreshing and heart-warming in this court of lies.

"I can only say the same, Gale. How did you manage to kill the mercenary?" His gaze drifts to the distance, his dark brows furrowing. And he takes too long to answer.

"Oh, Ornatus did half of the job. The old bastard was not entirely dead. All I had to do is get the ax and take advantage of the chaos." He chuckles nervously and my gut is telling me he's keeping something to himself. Full of secrets, just like the Fae. Disappointment and some inexplicable sadness weigh on me. The joy of seeing him again melts like ice in the morning sun. "And you? Are the rumors true? You retrieved the relic, striking a very unusual alliance? Be careful with him, Talysse—"

"I believe I treated her fairly despite my reputation," a deep voice, nearly a snarl, resonates behind him. Gale's face freezes in a mask of pure hatred for a second, but he quickly replaces it with a fake smile.

"May I have this dance?" Aeidas asks coldly, and it is clear to all of us that this is not a question but an order. The beautiful Sorcia, her palm resting against the bare skin of his chest, her thin, graceful fingers lightly caressing his Ancestral mark, looks at me, her fine white brow raised.

"Oh, it's the daughter of those traitors of Tenebris who hid the last Seelie of the province!" Her long white lashes flutter. "You don't look like your sister at all, dear!"

"Her name is Nightglimmer," the prince growls. Sorcia shudders. It's barely detectable, but it's there. She fears him.

"How do you know how my sister looks?" I hiss, taking a step toward her.

"My job is to know things, Talysse," she hisses, an unspoken warning concealed in her words.

Aeidas removes her palm from his chest. "Go get some refreshments, Sorcia," he orders her in the same cold, imperious tone he has just used to ask me to dance. The female's face twists for a second, her beauty contorted by something monstrous. She hesitates but shrugs and turns her back, the angry clicking of her heels raising many brows.

When I look back up, Aeidas is towering over me, his silver tresses brushing his shoulders.

"May I?" he asks, his eyes suddenly darker. I nod and cast an apologetic gaze on Gale, who stands there, his hands balled into fists, knuckles white. His lips are drawn into a polite smile, but there is tension in his posture as if he's restraining himself not to do something foolish. Completely oblivious or uncaring about the distress he has just caused, Aeidas hand lands on the small of my back and pulls me in closely, a gesture so rough and claiming that it draws murmurs from the spectators. Butterflies flutter in my stomach; no, those are no butterflies—those are moths with thick black wings, threatening to tear my guts apart.

It is the wine.

It is the wine, not him.

"I've seen the little scene you made," he says softly, tucking some loose strands behind my ear. "Are some of my

210

courtiers giving you trouble?" There it is again, that snarl in his voice, making the hairs on my nape rise.

"Nothing I cannot handle," I answer carelessly, grateful for the conversation that provides some distraction to the reactions of my insidious body to his proximity. My palm rests on his pecs, close to where Sorcia's fingers lingered just a minute ago.

"I see you're not shy to display our Ancestral mark, Your Majesty," I say bitterly, suddenly irritated by the memory of the arrogant female.

"It's a reminder of what is lost, Talysse. A reminder of what needs to be done," he answers cryptically.

"You speak as if you regret the Hex," our hips are so close that heavy, sleek warmth is crawling down my spine, "yet the Unseelie are the ones who profit the most from it. You are the undisputed rulers of this world, and everyone depends on your mages to protect them." He slides his thigh between mine and guides my body to a graceful arch. The feeling of his hard leg muscles, clad in soft velvet against my already slick center, nearly draws a moan.

"I will not deny it." He takes my fingers and swirls me, then pulls me in, my backside firmly pressed against him. "The Hex gives us control, yet there might be some among us who seek change."

"And yet you're participating in these Trials, hunting down humans with magic? Humans who could protect cities and trading caravans?" His hands are on my waist, and he lifts me, swirling me around, then lets me slowly glide down the rugged plane of his body.

"The reasons to participate in the Trials are my own, Talysse, and I'd watch my tongue if I were you," he rumbles.

"Sure, I should not forget whom I'm speaking to." Another swirl, and he's leaning me over his thigh again, and it's so damn hard to resist the urge to shamelessly rub myself against him in front of his whole Atos damned court. The crowd of courtiers, watching our dance with curiosity, will be delighted.

"You better not do that," he breathes in my neck, and suddenly, I think he can read minds.

"Do what?" I ask, drawing some intrigued gazes from the nobles standing around.

"Forget whom you're speaking to." The unspoken warning is subtle but stings like a whip. The crowd around us grows, and they're all listening, eyes shimmering, fangs flashing. Suddenly, it all gets too much. Is it the sweet venom of his presence, the incense smoke burning my eyes, or all the malevolence of this court, but the room starts spinning.

I'm tired and confused. Exhausted of hearing lies and being followed by malevolent eyes all the time.

Elders, I need to get out.

"Aeidas," the poisonous voice of Sorcia echoes behind me when I stumble away, "care for a dance?"

How convenient that this viper appears now.

Applause erupts when I curtsy and flee the dance floor. There—a door and the shimmer of the Blessed light beyond it. It leads to a wide balcony. The night sky is veiled by the golden glow of protective magic, casting an otherworldly hue over the city at my feet. Below, the Fae capital sprawls across the hillside in a series of terraces, each layer a symphony of gothic spires and domes of black granite, intricately carved and adorned with gold filigree.

The quiet streets meandering between the buildings are glimmering in the soft glow of enchanted lanterns. Winding staircases and arched bridges connect countless terraces, their paths lined with lush flora, the night breeze washing its tender perfume over the city. The gentle hum of arcane energy permeates the air, mingling with the distant sounds of nocturnal life.

Far below, the inhabitants of the city move like shadows, their elegant forms barely discernible in the dim light. I hate to admit it, but the entire town is a mesmerizing blend of shadow and light, of untamed magic and ancient power, an addictive mystery, just like its prince.

The fresh air does its soothing magic, and the light dizziness of the Fae wine is gone. Time to go back or—

Heavy steps echo over the checkered floor, startling me. Looking back, I expect to see Gale or even Aeidas. Instead, steely fingers close around my neck, lifting me clean off my feet.

"You owe me an apology, human," the courtier I spilled wine on growls. I dig my nails into his fingers, my feet kicking in the air. The lights of the crystal chandeliers of the ballroom—so near and yet too far, spin before my eyes.

Stay calm, Talysse.
Panic has never saved a life.

He's too far for a kick in the crotch, so Myrtle's golden move, which has saved me countless times before, is out of the question. The only other option at my hands is my magic.

Get him away from me, I demand from the silvery lake inside me. And it instantly obliges. My fingers shoot out a sweep of arcane force. The Fae prick releases me, landing heavily on his back and sliding on the smooth tiles. Dazzled, he's shaking his head while I straighten my dress and prepare to go back inside.

"Hopefully, I haven't caused much of an inconvenience, but I'm afraid you might wish to change again," I snap when skirting him, but the bastard is fast. He reaches out and grabs my ankle, pulling me down. My skull hits the floor hard, and lights flash before my eyes. In an instant, he's straddling me, his hands closing around my throat.

Well, now he's in the perfect position for a kick in the crotch. The noble is so full of himself that he thinks that he got me this time, or he's used to abuse helpless palace damsels.

"Surprise, fucker," I murmur, angling my knee for the perfect kick in his most cherished possessions. And it's delivered with cruel precision. The air leaves his lungs with a terrifying sound, and he rolls to the side, whining.

Pure music to my ears.

I scramble up, touching my neck where probably bruises are already blossoming, and once again head to the door when a move catches the side of my eye. He's coming at me again, his resilience stunning. And the sheer ferocity in his eyes. But most disturbing is the flash of steel in his hand. Just two feet away from the safety of the ballroom, he grabs my hair and pulls me back with such force, spilling the jewels Ayrene has braided in my locks.

"Now you die, human whore," he whispers and swings the blade right when I'm frantically scrambling the last flickers of magic inside me.

Elders! I frantically seek my magic, but it's depleted, and squeeze my eyes, expecting the blade to sink between my ribs.

So this is how I die.

A second passes, then another.

Nothing happens.

"Cousin, this is unwise. Release her at once." I crack an eye open to see the red-haired noble. Both are locked in struggle, presenting me with the perfect opportunity to escape. I slip into the banquet hall unnoticed. It's much louder now; everyone seems to be dancing and laughing.

"Take me to my chambers," I request from the silent, black-armored guard, and he leads me down the corridor, the noise of the party dying out behind our backs.

We navigate the usual maze of arches, abandoned halls, spiraling stairwells, and decadence. As we reach the doors of my room, a tall shadow peels from the wall.

"Leave us," Aeidas orders, and the silent Fae salutes with a fist to his heart, then disappears.

"You left so soon, Talysse." His voice is low as his eyes seek to capture mine.

"I'm surprised you noticed that; you seemed to be in good company—" I nearly bite my tongue, but too late, the snarky remark has already slipped.

He crosses his arms and responds with a low, indifferent tone, "I have my royal duties, even to those who have not much left to live."

"Do you mean me?"

"Does it matter who I mean?" His voice is still cold, but his eyes have a soft glow when he's studying me.

His riddles are tiring me, and I try to push past him, but a hard grip around my arm makes me stop in my tracks. He spins me around, so now I have no choice but to look up, irritated, and meet his gaze. And nearly stumble, taken aback by the rage burning in it.

"Talysse—" his knuckles travel along my jaw and he gently turns my face up, "who did this to you?" he rasps.

"Nobody important," I chirp with exaggerated carelessness, "he's taken care of."

A deep, bestial growl escapes his heaving chest.

"I will ask again, Talysse—who hurt you?"

Is it the fierce protectiveness in his voice or the way his callused fingers tenderly brush the skin of my neck, but my knees are about to buckle? There is that tone—that promise that heads will roll, and he'd watch it with a smile.

"Does it matter, Aeidas? I don't have much left, as you said," I repeat with irony and try to escape his careful yet steely hold.

"Was it Galeoth?" His fingers are at my chin now, forcing me to look at him. And by the demons of Atos's Underworld, he's a sight to behold when he's furious. His eyes are deep verdant now, his pupils wide, his massive arms vibrating with barely leashed power. His jaw is set, and the right corner of his lip curled up in a snarl, displaying the sharp edge of a fang. "Did Galeoth hurt you, Talysse?"

"Gale wouldn't hurt me," I snap back. Not now.

Realization straightens the furrow between his perfectly shaped dark brows.

"It was that drunkard Haeddyn and his cousin, right? I saw you spilling wine on him—" His finger travels up, pausing for a moment on my lower lip, and he cocks his head. "You taught the arrogant bastard a good lesson," he murmurs. His gaze softens and lingers on my lips. "Goodnight, Talysse. I have…business to take care of." Darkness drips from his last words as he melts into the shadows of the passageway.

I stand there for a moment, panting, my fingertips resting on my lips, then open the door to my chambers.

TALYSSE

THE ROOM OF REFLECTIONS

My thoughts flutter around like a swarm of moths on a moonless night.

The brush of Aeidas's knuckles still lingers on my skin, and I shake my head, reminding myself that this male is the Crown Prince of the Unseelie, the one who holds the life of my little sister in his hands and that I should not fall for his deceptions and his lethal beauty. That's what Fae do best: ensnarl us with their sweet talk and feral sexuality, turning us into mindless thralls doing their bidding. I let the delicate dress drop and carefully remove all the jewelry Ayrene has given me.

The night is warm, and the Halo over the city reflects on the golden ornaments of the ceiling. I pull the heavy curtains so that the soft light of the silver candelabra and the fire are the only light in the room, then throw on a transparent nightgown, probably intended for some royal concubine. My cheeks are flushed, and the peeks of my breasts are tight, straining against the airy fabric. And there is a sweet, hot heaviness between my thighs. The poison of this beautiful monster is already working in my body.

I snuggle between the crisp sheets, the softness a stark contrast to the turmoil inside me. Squeezing my eyes shut, I bury my face in the pillow, but sleep eludes me. Tossing and turning in the bed for something that feels like hours, I finally surrender to a maelstrom of dark thoughts that eventually drag me into a sweaty, fitful sleep.

*

Something wakes me up. There's no need for magic to realize that something is very, very wrong. My teeth chatter uncontrollably, and I pull the covers tighter around me, noticing the foggy huffs of my breath. The candles have long since burnt down, and the only light should come from the gap between the curtains. But this is not the soft light of the Halo. This eerie, silvery glow—is something different.

Sitting up, I rub my eyes, trying to make sense of the glowing mist pooling at the ornate feet of the tall bed. It carries with it strange, disembodied whispers and climbs up, forcing me to press my back against the filigree headboard.

What kind of twisted nightmare is this?

The cold, flickering tendrils reach my feet, and the murmurs become more distinct, bidding me to rise and follow. It's a command that snaps my willpower like a dry twig. As my toes touch the cold floor tiles, I flinch, but my body moves like possessed. Unable to stop myself, I open the door and peer into the gloomy corridor. The mist muffles all sounds, and the guards that usually patrol this palace wing are nowhere to be seen.

Elders, let this be some bad dream, not some wicked Unseelie sorcery.

The haze guides me through a labyrinth of neglected passageways, crowded with dusty old furniture. "Open the door," the voice in my head orders, and I push a low copper-plated door open. The only light in the wide hall comes from the mist and from a tall, square object in its center.

"Come closer, Talysse," the voice beckons, and my body obeys like a puppet on strings. "Look into the mirror."

A haunting vision of myself glares back from the cold surface. My lips are blue, and my hair is tangled. One strap of the transparent nightgown has slid off my shoulder, revealing the dark peak of a breast. My reflection blurs and elongates, and suddenly the prince stares back at me, his eyes cruel and glowing with a malevolent glimmer. Questions make their way to my lips, but my jaw remains stiff. Aeidas steps out of the mirror, its surface rippling like the waters of a dark lake.

"Who are you, really, Talysse?" There's a metallic echo to his voice.

Something wicked is at work here.

His hands rest on my shoulders, devoid of their usual warmth. Images of my past swirl around us. "Show me!" he commands, and tears run down my face as I see my mother humming in the garden, my father in his study, showing me maps of all the lands he longed to see. The burn of the hot milk spilling over me as I try, unattended, to take it off the stove, and my scream ripples through the empty hall.

"So, this is how you got this scar." The mirror prince chuckles, his cold fingers trailing down the pink, uneven skin at my side as if he relishes in my pain. Panting, I see my mother consoling me, taking off her bracelet to place it on my childish wrist.

"This will make the wound heal faster and the scar less visible," she whispers, drying my tears.

"Interesting," the Fae whispers. The visions turn visceral. The feet of my hanged parents dangle before us, and a knife is pressed against my sister's tender neck. "Show me who you really are, Talysse," the prince hisses, and the knife his doppelgänger holds against Tayna's skin slices deep, severing cartilage and bone. My parents' lifeless corpses stalk us, their eyes open, black and empty like an abyss full of suffering, their whispers holding poisonous accusations.

Death.

Everyone is dead, the whole world is dead, and it is all my fault.

Shadowfeeders crowd the room, followed by a horde of Tainted.

"Tell me who you are, and I will make it stop." This isn't Aeidas's voice anymore; it is a feminine, shrill, commanding voice that sounds oddly familiar. "What is the prince up to?" it inquires, and the Tainted Ones surround me, sniffing me, licking my skin. Saliva drips from black teeth and rotten lips, and claws scratch me—first timidly, then slicing deeper.

"There is more that you keep to yourself. Tell me WHO YOU ARE!" The prince is gone now; there is only me and the Tainted Ones. Their stench and bites drown my screams.

My lungs hurt, and darkness consumes me.

*

"Talysse." First, I recognize the voice, then the touch. His hands are warm now, not like—

My eyes snap open and focus on the last person I expected to see here.

"Gale?"

How, in the name of the Elders, did he get here?

The world slowly gains contours. The mirror room, roughly hewn into the bedrock, is the same, minus the creepy mist. The mirror still stands, dark and ominous, in its center.

Was this all just a nightmare? Quite a vivid one, as my scar still bears the mark of Aeidas's icy fingers.

"What in the hell pits of Atos are you doing here? Were you sleepwalking? Or someone took you here? Was it the wretched prince?"

"Sleepwalking…yes." A plausible explanation. "And you? What are you doing here?" I ask, rubbing my temples.

"I wanted to see more of the infamous Unseelie palace." He brushes off my question and helps me up. There's more to this than just curiosity, but I'm too dazzled to ask. Gale wraps an arm around my shoulders, and I'm grateful for the warmth.

"What happened, Talysse?" he insists softly. "Who showed you the Room of Reflections?"

"How do you know what it is called?"

He ignores my question, and his steps are rushed as he leads me out of this cursed place. "Let's take you back to your room, Talysse; it is not safe for you here."

"But it is safe for you?" I arch a brow while letting myself be dragged along the dusty passageways.

"It takes more than an old Unseelie trinket to harm me." He shrugs, and suddenly, there's something to him: a fleeting shadow greater than his mortal frame, a murmur of forbidden spells.

We've reached the familiar corridor of my chamber, and a couple of guards walk by, throwing us a look.

"Can I come in, Talysse?" He leans on the doorframe and looks down at me intensely. The guards in unmarked black armor, Shadowblades, I remind myself, stand there, watching us. "We need to speak," he insists. With a tired nod, I relent. Well, sleep is out of the question anyway.

He whistles when looking around my chamber in awe. "I can see that someone is clearly favored here! My room looks like a barn compared to this!"

"Why do you want to talk about, Gale?" I fill two glasses with some of the amber liquid from the decanter next to the fireplace.

He settles in the soft chair, ankle over his knee. He's wearing only a loose linen shirt and pants, his unruly curls tucked behind his shoulder, his enchanted golden earrings shimmering in the twilight. There's an odd glow to his eyes that makes me wonder once again why he was wandering the Unseelie halls alone.

Throwing myself on the bed, I cross my arms over my chest. Still wearing the scandalous nightgown, I am feeling a bit uncomfortable.

"Listen, Talysse, just want to tell you that you can rely on me in the next trials," he says softly, sips on the fiery drink, and grimaces. "Elders, this is some strong shit."

"You have quite a low opinion of someone who had to wrangle street rats the size of a pig for a piece of bread, Gale." His cryptic talking and the whole aura of mystery around him started frightening me. I take a generous sip and nearly spit it on the floor. He was right; this is stronger than anticipated. "You know how these trials work. Alliances are temporary. There could be only one winner. Soon or later, we'll have to slaughter each other."

It's a ridiculous concept while we sip our drinks in the light of the dying fire. But we both know it's true.

"Or not," he says, pushing himself up from the chair and placing his palms on both sides of my thighs, leaning on the bed. The warmth of his closeness washes over me. "Trust me, Talysse." His voice is soft now, and his amber eyes locked with mine. "Things…are about to happen. You better be ready. I want you to pick the right side. Remain loyal to your nature," he whispers in my ear, and I'm suddenly afraid. Alone with another contestant, who's acting mad. Maybe he'll try to take the flint away from me?

"What in the name of Atos are you talking about, Gale?" I ask, cautiously pulling away.

"There are things I cannot talk about among these walls, Talysse." Noticing my uneasiness, he backs up and starts pacing the room.

"Look, if this is your way of warning me that the Trials are botched and that—"

His laughter spills in the night, disturbing as a pot dropped in the silent kitchen.

"No, Talysse, no. The Trials are not botched. The stronger one will prevail," he adds darkly. "Just...just stay alert and choose wisely." He drags a palm over his face and halts, hesitating as if debating whether he should reveal more. Then he turns on his heel and heads to the door. "The most dangerous thing in these Trials is that prince of yours," he hisses, his hand on the doorknob, and I don't like the sound of yours. "Stay away from him, and you'll be safe."

Elders.

When I look up, he's gone.

*

The final hours of the night stretch into pondering over his words, creepier than my experience in the Room of Reflections.

Ayrene slips in with the first sun rays, balancing a tray loaded with fresh bread, cheese, fruits, and berry jam in her thin hands.

"Good morning, m'lady Talysse," she chirps. "Slept badly, didn't you? All of us had a restless night."

My hand, holding a warm slice of bread generously spread with jam, freezes.

"What do you mean?" Was everyone affected by the magical mist?

"The prince lost his mind last night and executed two of the lords," she declares solemnly, pulling the drapes and letting the sun in. I drop the bread and cover my mouth with my hands. "He said that they've attacked a guest under his roof, ignored his orders, and interfered with the Elders' will. Their heads are on spikes in the Southern courtyard," she adds morbidly. "People said they died slowly, and I was listening to their screams in the servants' wing."

"Who were they?" The food turns to sand in my mouth. Those two idiots didn't deserve such a harsh fate. Or did they? Do self-centered monsters who raise their hand at a woman deserve mercy? Would I be kinder to Tayna's new suitor if he harms her?

"Lord Haeddyn and his cousin, m'lady Talysse. Did you meet them last night?"

I bark out a cough.

"So, it is true then! They hurt you, and the prince killed them! This is so romantic—" She bats her eyelashes. Living in this cruel court has clearly messed up the poor girl's idea of romance. And right and wrong, too.

"There's nothing romantic about people dying, Ayrene." My appetite is suddenly gone. Dealing swift and cruel justice is something one could expect from an Unseelie, but to do it with such ferocity is another thing.

"How did they wrong you?" the girl asks, her tone slightly defensive.

I open my mouth, but the door flying open stops me. Aeidas stands in the doorframe, shadows pooling at his feet, the sting of his angry magic biting my skin. Ayrene curtsies and hurriedly leaves.

Elders, he looks so smug. His silver hair is tied up on his nape, his jade gaze merrily sparkling. He's still wearing the silk attire from last night, but his sleeves are rolled up, and I cannot miss the telling crimson sprinkles on his forearms and his collar.

"You killed them—" I breathe.

"I made sure they will never disrespect or harm anyone," Aeidas explains calmly. "I want you to feel...safe while you're here. Safe when I'm close, Talysse."

"You cannot kill them just because they tried to...whatever they tried to do. I had the situation perfectly under control. And I've had far worse experiences in Tenebris back alleys."

He pulls the chair near the fireplace with a growl.

"Tell me more of these...experiences. All these vermin deserve to be gutted. Do you remember their faces?"

I bark out a laugh, but my jaw drops, realizing that he's been dead serious.

"Aeidas, we're in the Trials." The notion of the bitter truth sobers him up. He cannot avenge me because I'd be dead soon. Or he would be if I'm lucky enough.

"You had a visitor last night?" he snarls, pointing at the two glasses, still half full with that terribly strong brandy.

"It was Gale. He...came to tell me that I can rely on him." I keep my night visit to that horrible Room of Reflections to myself. Don't want to send the prince on a murder spree, searching for the culprit behind my spellbound walk last night, the one pressing me with those questions.

A vein appears on his regal forehead. "Are you afraid of me, Talysse?" he suddenly asks, his fingers digging into the armrests of the chair.

How to explain to the Unseelie Prince without sounding preposterous that I am not afraid of anything that could harm me physically? I died that day when the sling broke my parents' necks, and some bitter, relentless version of me still continues breathing, fighting, and shielding Tayna from the cruel world. Protecting the few I love is what's driving me, not the usual self-preservation instinct, so—

"I am not, Aeidas." It sounds sincere.

"Very well." The tense line of his shoulders smoothens. "Because I want to show you something," he adds and looks away, "something that's…important to me. Will you be ready in an hour?"

"Yes," I breathe, stunned by the way he rakes his fingers through his hair and heads to the door in wide strides. The Unseelie Prince has just invited me to spend time with him, and…looks nervous about it?

Suddenly, it's hard to remember why I hate him. I have to open my black book of painful memories to remind myself that this is the Fae who ruined my life. This is the Fae who'd end it if given the chance.

And just like Gale said, he might be the most dangerous thing of these Trials.

THE PRINCE

AEIDAS'S HAPPY PLACE

"Are you wearing Raynar's clothes?" I ask when we descend the tunnels leading us deep into the heart of the palace. The white cotton shirt and soft, neutral leggings look borrowed from Ayrene's little brother. How odd. All the dresses worthy of a queen in her wardrobe, and the little human thief has chosen the clothes of a servant.

"Did you change your clothes and washed because there was blood on them?" Talysse responds with a question.

Shrugging, I urge her to follow me.

"And do you kill everyone who disrespects your...guests with your own hands?" she presses on.

"Not all of them, but I kind of enjoyed this one," I answer with a smug grin. Should've taken more time with the drunk fool, but the bruises on Talysse's neck drove me into a frenzy. The message is clear now: raise a hand at her, die painfully.

And yet, there can be only one winner of these cursed Trials. Only one of us will walk out of this alive.

"Weakness will be your undoing. Attachment is a weakness. Loyalty only belongs to the dynasty. Those are the laws I've lived by all my life, Talysse. Cruel but necessary."

She halts in her tracks. "Attachment is weakness," she drawls. "Hmm, I wonder how Lady Sorcia sees that."

"Jealous much?" My chuckle purges the darkness of the bloody, sleepless night. It's so invigorating.

"Me? Jealous of a noble lady ogling your crown and rubbing your Ancestral Mark as if it is some magic lamp that makes wishes come true?" Talysse snorts. "I'm just puzzled by the double standard here."

"Lady Sorcia is aware of that." The tunnel descends steeper. The sconces on the ancient masonry recede, but I stride confidently through the gloom. "But she seems to have forgotten these rules when she bought an assassin to kill me." Talysse's throat bobs.

"So her head will join soon poor Lord Haeddyn in the courtyard?" Her fear is palpable, and for a moment, I feel like the monster she believes me to be.

"Not yet. Her little plot requires a more thorough investigation. She's too vain and superficial to come up with this alone," I murmur, keeping the rest of my thoughts to myself. There are more involved in this, and something tells me she'll lead me to my brother's murderer. "So, she's in the dungeon now, pondering over her mistakes. And you have me all just for yourself today."

Talysse snorts, but her footsteps are lighter, more hesitant. When she hears the sounds of the crickets and the damp scent of soil mingling with the fragrance of flowers wafts from the depths, she halts.

"Where are you taking me, Aeidas? Are those—" she rushes forward, "—fireflies? What sorcery is this?"

"It's my happy place—"

"And a great place to dispose of a body!"

"Disposing of a body is such a waste. Heads on spikes make an excellent decoration. And a statement."

"You are really a monster, Aeidas." She punches my forearm.

The anticipation adds a spring to my step, and I do not waste any time wondering why it is so important to me to show her my secret. "Come, there's someone I want you to meet."

We stroll through a wisteria tunnel, the purple blossoms brushing against our heads, and I lead her further into the depths of the royal greenhouse.

White pebbles crunch beneath our feet as we follow the path winding around thickets of vibrant flowers and bushes with thick waxy leaves, deeper into the centennial emerald forest ahead. The damp crystal roof lets in beams of sunshine, but the thick branches swallow most of the light, casting dappled shadows. Low among the grass, moss, and blossoms, tiny creatures live their secret, hurried lives in the glow of fireflies and light wisps.

"What is this place, Aeidas?" Talysse murmurs, looking around with wide, bewildered eyes.

"It is a sanctuary. Since the Hex struck, the royal house created this, and I've taken it upon myself to save as much of the living world as possible." Digging into my pocket, I pull out the sachet with seeds and spores from Teír Mekheret.

"It's so unexpected that your kind values…places like this."

I bend over to gently remove a centipede from the path. "What did you think that my kind values?" I inquire.

"Power? Murder? World domination?" she muses, brushing her fingers over the low-hanging blossoms.

"Well, even villains need a hobby, Talysse. Like you, for example. What do you do when you're not robbing people?"

"I…tend tables," she confesses reluctantly, and we stroll deeper into the gardens. For a moment, I try to picture her carrying trays with food. Is she happy? Is she flirting with the patrons? And what, in the name of Atos, is with my damned curiosity?

"That's surprisingly mundane. Come, Talysse, let's meet a friend."

We walk by clusters of roses, their petals dots of deep colors among the eternal green around, and delicate orchids, their lean forms glowing softly in the twilight. Lilies of every color line the path, their fragrance mingling with the earthy scent of ferns and moss. Foxgloves taller than me stand like sentinels, their bell-shaped flowers nodding gently as we pass.

We arrive at a clearing where an ancient magnolia tree spreads its gnarled branches, its pale pink blossoms luminous in the dim light. Here, the air is thick with the scent of honeysuckle, and the soft rustle of leaves is louder than all my worries. Straight beds of bluebells and snowdrops frame the clearing, and I smile, feeling the buzz of soft, ancient magic at work. Talysse does, too; she whips her head left and right until she spots him.

Amused, I watch her eyes widen as she takes in the bark-like skin flecked with patches of moss of the ancient Dryad. Viridis is busy poking holes in the ground, a pile of bulbs at his root-like feet, ready to be planted. He's wearing a straw hat with a wide brim and a bunch of lavender blossoms tucked behind his ear. He senses us and rises, stretching his long, sinewy limbs, and his ancient fern-green gaze rests on her.

"Talysse, meet a dear old friend and a tutor who has taught me a great deal about this world, about the place all living beings have in it." Talysse's brows skeptically climb up at this statement, but I ignore it. Soon, she will see. "Kings and nobles rule the world outside this paradise, but here is only one true king: Viridis the Dryad, tending to these gardens since times no Fae can remember."

The Dryad studies Talysse with curiosity, golden bees swirling around the thick green vines of his hair. His fingers are working on something I cannot see.

"A pleasure to meet you, Viridis. I believe that Aeidas has something for you." She nods with a pleasant, genuine smile that makes the clearing a bit brighter. When I hand him the sachet with seeds, the Dryad places an elaborate wreath of bluebells on her head.

"A crown for the princess," my friend says and dips his chin respectfully.

"Viridis likes talking with riddles. He gets confused sometimes," I whisper to Talysse, as she still seems to be stuck on the word princess.

"A real prince," the old Fae praises me, peeking into the sachet and making me blush like a youngling, "loyal, dutiful, and tending to his lands." Murmuring some unintelligible words, he goes about his work. Talysse takes a deep breath and lets her gaze wander around the Dryad's garden.

"This is your friend who likes plants, hm?"

"Isn't it obvious? Technically, he is a plant." My clumsy joke gets me a reward—her smile is infectious.

"So this is your happy place, Aeidas?" Talysse cups the bluebells and waves away a couple of fluffy, curious bees.

"It's more than this. It's the place that made me who I am. I've spent more time tending to these gardens than training for my royal duties." Viridis fusses about with his seeds, humming a strange melody, completely oblivious to our presence. "Come, there's more to see." I point behind my back to the hidden path, the one only a few know about.

She follows me with unease through the prophet's laurel bushes, the gentle murmur of a stream and the rustling of the leaves the only sounds around. Butterflies the size of my palm flutter over the blossoms, and it's suddenly all more colorful when it reflects in her eyes. The plants around grow wilder, untamed by the blessed hands of Viridis, and it gets darker.

The two oak trees stand before us like sentinels, making us slow down our pace. Their heavy branches drape to the soft grass, and light wisps dance among them. The place is unusually quiet, as if even the cicadas and crickets don't dare to disturb the sacred silence beneath the leaves.

"My parents planted these trees when me and my brother were born." Talysse pauses, swallowing the question everyone's too eager to ask.

Good for her.

"Do humans—" I ask while making my way through the foliage beyond the oaks, following a barely traceable path, "—dream, Talysse?"

"Of course we do," she answers simply, confused by the question. My smile stretches as I take her deeper into the gardens. It's time to show her just how big Unseelie can dream.

Her steps falter when the path opens into a hidden clearing at the heart of the garden. There, nestled amidst a riot of flowerbeds brimming with roses, lilies, and foxgloves, stands my quaint wooden cottage with a straw roof. Its timbers blend with the surroundings, and golden light filters through the trees, casting a warm glow over it.

Ivy is creeping up its sides and colorful blossoms spill from window boxes. A small, stone-paved path leads to the front door, flanked by lush beds of lavender and marigolds.

I turn around to see why she's not following, and my heart sinks. Talysse stands there, indecisive, her fingers closed around the pouch with the flint.

"What is this place?" she asks.

"It's a place of secrets. If you want to know the truth about my kind, you must enter." I take a step toward her, and she flinches.

"Does anyone know of this hut?" She takes a slight step back. I shake my head, and she pales, clutching the flint.

"I wouldn't spoil my floorboards with your blood, Talysse. If I wanted to kill you, I'd have done it already out there." Elders, that came out wrong.

"You said you trust me, Talysse." One more step, and I loom over her, irritated by that look in her eyes, brandishing me as a monster.

Fear is something I understand well. She's alone with the brutal prince who massacred her family, tortured and slaughtered a courtier just last night, and probably—if she believes the rumors—murdered his brother. Her enemy. And here, she's at my mercy.

The way she slightly backs off when my fingers close around her forearm pulls some strings in my black heart. The overwhelming need to reassure her that she's safe with me, that I'd never hurt her, flushes over me. But I can't promise her that.

"Talysse." My hands at my sides, I realize how menacing I look, not only because of my size and my ability to summon a deadly weapon out of thin air. And just like that, she turns on her heel and darts into the thicket.

That's a bad idea.

No Unseelie can resist a good chase.

The dormant predator in me, a remnant of times when my kind stalked the night and fought beasts over food and shelter, awakens. This might get dangerous and she's fragile human, a tiny voice inside me warns, but it's quickly muffled by the roar of my blood. This human is *not* that fragile.

Drawing the tip of my tongue over the sharp edges of my canines, I give chase, relishing in the thrill of the hunt.

TALYSSE

THE COTTAGE

Branches whip me and pull my hair as if that beautiful and cursed place is doing Aedias's bidding.

Where was the way out of this unreal place? My flower wreath is lost somewhere, and his steps are getting closer.

I am sure that sometime during his life at the tyrannical Fae court, the prince has lost his mind. After gruesomely murdering two of his own people and putting their heads on spikes, he brings me to this secluded place, away from witnesses. He'd probably pin my disappearance on the old Dryad, who's not clear in the head anymore.

I swiftly change directions like a mouse trying to outsmart the cat, but alas. In a blink, the prince is on me, straddling me, pinning me to the cold, damp grass. We're both panting, our hot breaths mingling.

"Talysse," he rasps, his eyes completely black now, a predator ready to carve out my heart, "why are you running?"

I try to free myself from his iron grasp, wiggling like a ferret. The weight of his hard, muscled body over mine stirs other very wrong sensations.

"You know very well why I'm running, you murdering monster—"

"I brought you here to make you see, Talysse."

"Oh, and you couldn't do that somewhere else? Was that Dryad digging my grave?" He closes his fingers around my wrists and pins them over my head while I still try to wiggle myself free, but every friction makes me crave more, and I whip my head to the side, so confused about this contradiction between body and mind.

"Don't be silly, Talysse. Give me a chance to show you that I'm more than…a murdering monster." He tightens his grip around my wrists and vulnerability flashes in his eyes. I cease my thrashing, searching for more of it. Searching for something that would prove him right.

There's no denying the pull between us: it's the dark, lethal curiosity that lures the traveler to get closer to the chasm and peek into it; the morbid fascination of the explorer making him venture deeper into the cavern maze, though he already knows that there's no way back. My heart and my body betray me when he's near, and when he's so close that I feel his mad heartbeat, I cannot lie to myself.

"Are you really?"

"Elders damn you, woman." His lips brush against my ear, sending a jolt of undeniable, guilt-loaded pleasure down my spine; a pleasure I try to fight by angling a knee and aiming at his—

"Why are you fighting? Just listen to me, Atos, take you!" he curses and, to my utter embarrassment, sees through my plan to kick him in the royal jewels and forces my legs open, settling at my center and robbing me of the possibility of hurting him. For a moment, we stay like that, staring at each other, searching our eyes.

"Will you listen?" His voice drops to a low, hoarse whisper.

"Mmmmhm—" is all that escapes my lips as I suddenly become hyper-aware of the thick hardness rubbing against my already painfully throbbing labia. He's hard. The realization hits me like a visceral lightning bolt of need, and I arch my back into him.

"You are safe here with me, Talysse," he murmurs, and his hot breath, combined with his scent, makes the hairs on my nape stand up.

"We're enemies, Aeidas. Only one is to walk out of this alive." His eyes linger on my lips when I say that. Closer. Maybe reminding us of the obvious will bring us both to our senses.

"We are. But I gave you my word that nothing would harm you under my roof. And I've brought you here to make you understand—" He looks away, eyes closed, and muscle trembles in his jaw as if he's battling something. Something dark and primal.

His body tenses, and I'm trembling beneath him, reining all my willpower into not rubbing myself against his hard length. Elders, even Myrtle, would blush at this whole situation.

"Make me understand what?" I mumble, grateful I managed to form a question.

"Why I'm doing all this," he says simply, and for a brief moment, he sounds nearly human. Lonely, tired, and misunderstood. He releases my wrists, dragging his knuckles down my forearm. His eyes have a soft, radiant glow I see for the first time.

"I will not hurt you, Talysse. Not now, not here. I swear it on my Mark." He pushes himself up to his knees and looks at me, head tilted to the side, a faint smile on his face. Stupid must be my middle name because I believe him.

"Let's go now before you destroy all my flowers."

"You've planted these?!" Leaning on my elbows, I look around. The flowerbed we've landed in is stunning, even if we broke a few forget-me-nots.

"I'm spending a lot of time here, remember? Come on, Desmond must be wondering what's going on."

"Who is Desmond?" Instead of answering, Aeidas stretches his hand to help me up and guides me to the cottage. Someone drops a metal plate inside, and the sound of the dish rolling around is followed by soft curses.

"You'll see soon enough."

*

"Desmond, I've told you not to smuggle food here; we'll get cockroaches," Aeidas scolds his invisible friend when we enter. Carefully, I step over pieces of cheese strewn on the thick moss-green carpet, the silver plate lying on the floorboards.

"How's that a bad thing? Cockroaches are delicious!" a tiny, disembodied voice announces, startling me.

The wide space is a definition of creative chaos. There are tables piled with books, maps and paintings on the walls, trapped light wisps hanging in garlands from the wooden beams, and dozens of flowers and plants in pots, but no sign of Desmond.

The scent of blooming trees and books hangs in the warm air. Fireflies dance in the thick cascades of leaves draping from the ceiling.

I approach the paintings hanging on the dark plank walls—lush green forests and crystal lakes shimmering in the sunlight, creatures big and small flying, swimming, running.

Aeidas slumps into a soft chair; his lips curled up in amusement.

"Where is your friend?"

"He's probably watching you, making sure you're not a threat—"

"Are you sure she won't hurt me?" the tiny voice squeaks again, this time from a working table near me.

Elders, how bad did I hit my head?

A pink, hairless rat climbs a tall tower of books. He's dressed in a dramatic red velvet vest and bows politely, his tail twitching nervously.

I rub my eyes, then open and shut my mouth.

The prince's laughter spills into the room, a sound much merrier than I'd imagined.

"M'lady." The rat faces me, studying me with sparkling beady eyes.

I slap my cheek not so gently and glare, unable to say a word.

"Is she mute? Or is it true that humans have no manners?" Desmond's voice dripped with mock concern as he shuffles closer to the table and glares at me with his black eyes, nearly spilling an inkwell over the apparently priceless maps strewn around. "My name's Desmond," he tries again, drawling the words as if I'm slow.

"Apologies. It was unexpected—" I shuffle my weight from one foot to the other, making a conscious effort not to stare.

"That I speak? Oh, long-term exposure to magic when the prince was experimenting in his youth, but tell me about you! You're the first lady he brings around—" The rat makes himself comfortable on top of the table, obviously enjoying the attention.

"Shut up, Desmond," Aeidas cuts him off, obviously not keen on letting him rat out on his solitude. "Talysse, this is a dear friend of mine and a former pet—"

"Pet is a very diminishing way to call me, you know," the rat squeaks, the fir on his tiny head bristling,

"The experiments with shadow magic gave him—" Aeidas starts. My eyes dart between them. Is this some kind of a trick?

"The ability to give wise advice and guidance to hollow heads like you," Desmond adds, grooming his tail with fake indifference.

"The ability to think and talk—" Aeidas shuffles in his chair, his patience obviously tested.

"I was able to think perfectly before your experiments, too, thank you very much." The rat lifts his snot haughtily.

"So a dear friend and a..." He opens his hands in a surrendering gesture.

"An advisor. And you are?" Tiny beady eyes lock with mine.

"I am Talysse." This is probably a delirious and incredibly vivid dream. Hopefully, I made it to the safety of my room before passing out.

The rat glares at the prince, and the latter just shrugs.

"Do tell me, dear Talysse, is it true that the cats in the human towns are as big as lynxes?" Desmond asks politely. His posture and demeanor remind me of a miniature courtier, and I nearly burst into laughter.

"Lynxes? I have never heard of such a creature before." I thoughtfully tap my lips with a finger.

"Lynxes. Majestic creatures, though Desmond might disagree. Gone, like many others." His voice drops. "Which reminds me of why we're here. Talysse. There is something I need to show you."

"Look, this is a lynx, Talysse!" The squeaky voice calls me to another table he's swiftly climbing. The rat points with his tiny, distressingly human-like paw to a book filled with colored pictures.

My eyes widen. A graceful creature with beautiful eyes stares at me from the colorful page. So many lives were wasted, and the whole world turned into a wasteland due to the Fae desire for more power.

"I brought you here to show you how it was, Talysse." Aeidas is close behind me, the warmth of his body seeping through my shirt. "Take your time and look around; see all that's been lost." He gestures to the books and the paintings.

"All of this is lost because of the Fae, Aeidas," I state the obvious.

"I do not deny my kind's fault, nor do I reject the responsibility," he states, his fingers brushing his Ancestral Mark, "yet some of us are missing...all this."

Well, that's news.

"Isn't Unseelie profiting from the curse? Keeping us all on a leash, dependent on the magic you control?" A deep furrow appears between his dark brows, and, to my surprise, he nods in agreement.

"Some might call me a traitor to my kind, Talysse, but I would do anything in my power to bring it back. I will go down in history as the king who would break the Hex."

Wait. What?

The silence stretches, thick and charged, between us. Even the birdsongs and the chirping of cicadas and crickets have ceased.

Now I understand why he brought me here to share this. He would lose his crown and his life if his family and this whole wretched court learned about his ambitious plan. All Unseelie and their allies are interested in keeping the status quo, controlling and milking the resources of all provinces while offering them meager protection against the dark.

This is far more dangerous than those cursed Trials.

"Why confide in me, Aeidas? Because I'll be dead soon, and you need justification if it happens to be by your hand? Will you sleep better after if I join your cause now?"

"I cannot...stand when you look at me like I'm a power-starved maniac." The prince drags a palm over his face. "I need the crown to bring all this—" he gestures around, "back."

Desmond's beady eyes study me, and he raises a furry brow. The rodent also seems conflicted with Aeidas's choice to trust me.

"That's why you brought me here? To convince me that it all is for a noble cause? That I should gladly sacrifice myself?" I bark a bitter laugh. "Fae or human, you men are all the same. Always chasing some noble cause without caring for the lives lost in the process. Good luck with getting your crown, Prince, but I'm also planning to win this. And I'm not doing it to chase some shadows on the wall, but for something very real: saving my little sister from marrying a monster and giving us both a dignified life."

His eyes glitter like gems reflecting starlight. A smirk stretches his lips, and for some reason, it annoys me. His rat climbs up his shirt and settles on his shoulder.

"I've never expected you to surrender, Talysse. You might be an outlaw, but you'd never settle to be a pawn in someone's grand plan."

"Mock me as much as you want for having dreams that are...down to earth, but your plan has a fault."

He crosses his arms and smiles with that royal confidence that I find maddening. "Oh. And what might it be?"

"As a crowned king, you might have all the resources to search for ways to reverse the Hex, but it is impossible. Many have tried."

He brushes the rat off his shoulder and walks to one of the thick books lying on the table. It's larger than the rest, its yellowish pages brittle. Overwhelmed by my cursed curiosity, I follow and take a peek.

"The Gospel of Seuta—" I gasp. He nods.

"A very damaged one, one of the few which still exist." His long fingers brush the pages with fainted pictures and unreadable text.

"Seuta—the Elder of fate and relationships—" Desmond clears his throat and Aeidas rolls his eyes, preparing for a lecture, "—was so outraged by the fratricidal war between the Fae, that she convinced the other four Elders to unleash the Hex and doom this world."

"And I will feed you to the kitchen cat if you interrupt us again. I found this in Seuta's oldest temple, and it nearly cost me my life to retrieve it. The sanctum of this holy place is now overrun with shadows and foul things," Aeidas whispers, gently flipping a brittle yellow page. "It's written by Seuta devotees, probably in the first years of the Hex. Look at this, Talysse. The prophecy was much longer, but this is all I managed to recover before the page crumbled:

When shadow dances with the light,
The curse of old shall lose its might.
   ++++++
As moon and sun in silence blend,
Their union marks the curse's end.
In darkest depths and highest skies,
The hidden path shall arise.

My finger follows the pale letters. Fascinating. "Does your family know about this, Aeidas?"

He shakes his head and starts pacing around, tension locked in his shoulders.

"Imagine how many clues like this are out there, Talysse. Imagine what a king with an army devoted to this could achieve!"

"It was believed that there's a spell hidden in our Ancestral Marks," he says, back turned to me. "Yet all it contains is a fragment of a sentence that just doesn't make sense. So there must be another way, another answer out there."

I lean onto my knuckles over the book, re-reading that cryptic phrase again. By Seuta, how I hate riddles.

"There is more." He stands before another thick book, his dark lashes casting shadows over his cheeks when he looks down. "The nights are getting longer, Talysse."

My heart skips a beat.

So our fears are confirmed.

I peek behind him, looking down at the pages. It is some kind of journal, with dates and moon phases skillfully drawn on every page.

"We've been keeping records for ages. Soon, the sun will set forever." His voice, usually so confident, now wavers with a rare vulnerability.

There's no deception, no trickery in his eyes. I suck in a ragged breath.

Soon, the sun will set forever.

I break out in a cold sweat.

"Out there is more than Shadowfeeders and Taint, Talysse. You should see it! Life is out there, dormant and beautiful, waiting for the right time to wake up—"

He's not a monster anymore. A different kind of monster, perhaps, but not the blood-thirsty, power-starved one I believed him to be.

"How much time do we have?" My voice trembles.

"Nobody knows for sure, but if we trust this simulation, no longer than three full moons."

Elders!

Three full moons until eternal night settles over Phyllesia and the rest of the world.

And then there'll be no escape. Even if Tayna and I make it to Free Cities, how long until the darkness and hordes of Tainted Ones breach the walls? How long until we starve?

"Do you see why I'm doing this now, Talysse?"

The lump in my throat doesn't allow me to speak.

"Will walk you to your room," the prince says simply, and we leave the safe coziness of the cottage, a stark contrast with the dark visions of the future.

Maybe he's wrong? Maybe there's a way. If I survive the Trials, I'll find a way.

We walk the cold marble corridors of the palace and it feels like the door of my tomb is sealing shut, leaving all my hopes and dreams in shambles.

TALYSSE

A MIDNIGHT SNACK

As soon as Ayrene leaves my room with the empty dinner plates, I climb into the bed. The cold sheets immediately remind me of the dreadful mist that took me to the Room of Reflections.

"It's the last night before the Second Trial," Ayrene reminded me while brushing my hair. "I pray to Atos you sleep well, m'lady Talysse."

But there are other things far more terrifying than the magical mist which dragged me to the Room of Reflections.

We're all living on borrowed time.

But how accurate was Aeidas's estimation?

The predictions of that frail white-haired court mage have been correct so far. Probably, she has access to some similar documents, and she's managed to establish some kind of a pattern. The sky spheres appear to move randomly, but for the wise and skilled ones who have centuries-old records, there must be a way to foresee any changes coming.

Soon, the sun will set forever.

Pulling the covers up to my chin, I notice that my fingers are shaking. To prove that things can always get worse, tendrils of silvery ghostly mist filter beneath the door.

Elders. Not again.

Just when the swirls of malevolent magic reach the bedposts, the door of my room flies open.

"Talysse." Aeidas stands in the doorframe, shirtless and chiseled like a marble statue of Elder Heroy, his long hair messy and draping his bare shoulders. "Are you all right?" The cold chills running down my body are swept away by a sudden heat wave.

"Are you seeing this, too?" I ask, my voice trembling. He nods, a furrow forming between his brows. His gaze follows the mist, which quickly withdraws down the scarcely-lit corridor.

"And I have a suspicion where it comes from," he says darkly. He shuts the door and looms near the bed, looking down at me. "Are you unharmed?" he asks, his voice a soft whisper. "Did it...speak to you? Or show you something?"

I hesitate but decide to tell him about the previous night. The furrow between his eyes deepens.

"She took you to the Room of Reflections," he rumbles, the knuckles on his fists turning white.

"Who is she?"

"Someone who'll pay dearly for all her crimes after I have no further use for her," he spits through his teeth. Standing in the light of the dying fire, he looks again like the cold and brutal Fae Lord I've seen in the Governor's Palace.

The silence stretches between us, dark thoughts buzzing around like angry wasps.

It's obvious that sleep is out of the question.

Suddenly, Aeidas claps his hands, startling me, and says in a far more cheerful tone, "You know what? I have an idea." His jade eyes light up with a mischievous glint.

"What?" A lump gets stuck in my throat. Oh, I might have an idea or two, too. One that Myrtle would very much approve of.

"The kitchens are empty at this time of the night, and we both need a snack—"

Atos's stinking hell pits, who would expect such a suggestion from a murderous Fae prince? The absurdity of it makes me blink. But the word "snack" does its miracle. I crawl to the edge of the bed and throw a light blanket over my shoulders to cover my too-revealing nightgown.

The door creaks open and we tiptoe the corridors of the sleeping castle, the Aeidas guiding us around night guard patrols and creaky floorboards. He speeds up his pace when crossing some darker halls. "The palace is old, full of echoes from the past," he whispers. "Legend has it that Atos himself built it. Some rooms are sealed off—too dangerous. Others are avoided, like the Room of Reflections."

The Elder of the Underworld, the ruler of the Kingdom of the Dead and Lord of the Winter has built this place! My head spins. Ancient magic lingers here and mine responds to it somehow, giving me goosebumps or raising the hairs on the back of my neck.

We finally reach the kitchen, a grand space with old stone walls. The scent of roasted meat, herbs and pine coals still lingers in the air. It's dark; the fire in the enormous hearth has nearly died out, and the prince lights a few candles.

We both startle when we see a tiny silhouette with beady black eyes sitting on his hind paws behind a plate, generously loaded with food.

"Seems you got caught red-handed, Desmond!" Aeidas chuckles while the guilty-looking rat wipes his paws in the tiny brocade jerkin he's wearing.

"My metabolism works differently than yours!" The rodent defends himself. "I need snacks all the time."

"Did you trap poor Lord Nyxie again?"

No need to ask who Lord Nyxie is—an upside-down bucket that moves across the tiled floor and an angry meowing from underneath it explains it all.

Desmond looks smug. "That stupid cat always falls for the treat and the broomstick trick." He shrugs, returning to his meal.

"Take a seat, Talysse." The prince pulls a chair at the long wooden table near the hearth. I settle, unable to take my eyes off his shirtless frame, his torso gilded by the light of the dying fire. He throws some wood in, hangs a tea cattle on a hook over the flames, and starts rummaging through the cupboards.

"Let's see what Desmond left for us," he says over his shoulder, and soon, there is a pile of cheese, cold meat, tomatoes, and fresh bread before me. All served neatly in a gold-rimmed plate. Even the clean linen napkin on the side is there.

"You seem quite experienced with this," I note, enthralled by his confident moves before the hearth. He places a grid over the flames, puts a pan over it, and—my eyes widen—prepares to fry some eggs. The fire bronzes his bare torso, and I swallow drily, watching the cords in his forearms strain as he breaks the eggshell at the rim of the pan.

Desmond clears his tiny throat next to me, and I look away from that mesmerizing sight of the prince stirring eggs, a white towel over his shoulder, his eyes narrowed with concentration.

The rat is glaring at me, brow raised.

"Looks like you're already drooling, Talysse. Well, I will take my leave then. Aeidas, m'lady," he bows dramatically, "make smart choices. The second Trial starts tomorrow," he declares ominously, then jumps down from the table and scatters away.

The prince slams a plate with steamy scrambles eggs on the table and sits opposite of me, pouring us some hot tea in translucent porcelain cups.

"You seem awfully experienced at this," I repeat, piling cheese on my bread slice.

"Sneaking off to the kitchen with beautiful ladies? Not really."

Elders, please don't make me blush. "But I was doing this a lot with Desmond and Viridis, as the solemn meals in the dining hall never appealed to me. Viridis is an excellent cook. Me and my brother were crazy for his food."

"So you can cook too?" I burn my tongue on the hot eggs and curse my gluttony.

"Better than expected from a prince." He shrugs, his eyes flickering with amusement. "And you? What are your secret talents?"

"Well, I am quite good at relieving people of their possessions." We both chuckle, and I try to pierce a cherry tomato with the fork. "Before my parents died, they did their best to give me a fancy high-born lady education, and I developed a love for reading. Tenebris has a nice library in the Temple of the Elders, a remnant of the time when the city was big and important."

"A well-read human then." He smiles, wiping his fingers on the kitchen towel draped over his shoulder. His silver strands touch his shoulders, and I feel the need to reach out and tuck them behind his pointy ears. "Who were your parents?" he asks with genuine interest and nearly makes me forget that his name was on the document that sent them to the gallows.

"My mother was kind and graceful. She has never raised her voice." The tea tastes divine. "She was from the Free Cities and always talked fondly of this place. Especially of the sea. She had that large seashell, and she swore she could hear the waves when she pressed it to her ear." The dam of memories has burst. The room has become quiet after he released Lord Nyxie, only the crackling of the fire breaking the silence. The prince has stopped eating, watching me attentively. There's something in his eyes that I've never seen before, like the flash of a gold coin at the bottom of a clear well. "It remained in my parents' mansion, and you will not believe how many times I have considered sneaking in and stealing it. I hope it's still there."

"And your father?" Aeidas asks, putting the fork on the plate and leaning forward on the table as if trying to catch my every word.

"My father was a merchant. He traveled a lot and brought us amazing gifts and even more exciting stories. He protected us fiercely. When they came for them—" My voice breaks, and I pinch the bridge of my nose.

"I am sorry for this, Talysse," he says softly and takes my hand. The warmth of his touch corners the shadows of the past.

A sad smile stretches my lips, and he responds with the same, both of us realizing the hopelessness of the situation we're in. And I believe in him. I know deep in my guts that he will try to change things. Maybe even break the Hex. But his way to this goes over my dead body. And most likely, over Tayna's, too.

But now there's tea and warmth, and there is still some time to daylight, some hours before the beginning of the next trial.

"And how was growing up in a palace?" I ask, not pulling my hand away.

"Lonelier than you think. You have already met my closest friends—a gardener and a talking rat. I was bred and trained to be the right hand of the king, Commander of the Shadowblades—an elite squadron of warriors and spies. I had more freedom than him," he adds, his gaze staring into the distance. No need to ask who he means by him. "And fell in love with the Wastelands, with plants and growth, all creations of Cymmetra. And no, I didn't kill him," he adds so softly that I am not sure if I heard him right. "You are the first person I confess this to. I haven't killed my brother. I watched him gradually turn into a monster, a power-hungry maniac, and I knew the time would come when I'd challenge him for the crown, but not like this."

"Why haven't you told anyone that you haven't killed him?" Elders, how could he keep this to himself when the whole world is calling him a murderer behind his back? His hand over mine is burning.

"Because murdering an opponent is the normal way of Unseelie succession. It makes me more respectable and feared, just like—"

"Winning the Nightfall Trials," I end the sentence for him, and it all clicks into place. So that's why he is in the Trials. Not out of bloodlust or desire to hunt and torment others.

"Hey, the conversation got quite gloomy, didn't it?" He winks. Seuta guard my heart, but he winked at me! "How about you help me clean up?" He suggests and pushes to his feet, leaving my hand cold and missing his touch.

It is a good idea. Our shoulders brushing, soon we are laughing again, soap bubbles flying around, while scrubbing the steel pan together. He fits me with a foamy beard, and I create a tall, bubbly crown and solemnly place it over his silver tresses. Then we put the washed dishes away.

"Put the cups in the tall oak cupboard over there," he orders while drying a plate with the towel. I pass in front of the fireplace and freeze, feeling his burning eyes on me. My blanket is draped over the chair's backrest, and I'm in my translucent nightgown, the light of the fire making every detail of my body visible. He is at me in one leap, not touching me; his eyes are black under the heavy lids.

Elders help me; I am breathing heavily, enveloped in the warmth of his bare chest, the heat of the hearth behind me, and this otherworldly, intoxicating scent of his. His fingers, soft from the warm water and smelling of soap, graze my jawline and linger at my chin, tilting my face up so that our eyes meet. His gaze slowly takes in my features as if trying to memorize them, lingering on my mouth.

His lips part, flashing his fangs, but they are anything but threatening now in the warm glow of the hearth. I marvel how they would feel if used gently on my...heat pools from my core, reaching that place between my legs, that already aches with need. Slowly, very slowly, he leans in, and his lips brush against mine in an unspoken question. They are softer than I thought.

The kitchen around me disappears in a maelstrom of candlelight and soap bubbles, and I part my lips, granting him access. He slides his tongue in, crushing me against the hard plane of his body. His powerful arm snakes around my waist, pulling me in closer—if that is even possible—and his hand finds my nape. He deepens the kiss, his broad chest rising rapidly, and our tongues swirl together greedily, each one unable to get enough taste of the other. He tilts my head in a position, granting him maximum access, and deepens the kiss with the ferocity of a warlord, claiming his spoil of war.

This is all too much; my knees soften, and slickness spreads down the inner of my thighs. I bet he smells it, Fae senses and all. And I don't care. I want him to know how much I want this. I respond with a moan to his row kiss, and this sets him off.

With a swift move, he wraps my legs around his waist and carries me to the massive table. He gently sits me there without interrupting the onslaught of his tongue, and I moan again, realizing that I am naked beneath the transparent gown and feeling his massive length pressed against my slit.

A deep, animalistic rumble reverberates from his chest when I grind against him, rubbing my soaked, swollen labia against his pants. The fabric is so thin that I can feel the veins along his massive cock, his wide crown, and the drops of his need staining the light cotton.

I moan again, louder, as his hand cups my breast, a calloused finger twirling around my nipple, and slowly and deliberately slide my clit along his hardness.

Foreplay and lovemaking are nothing new to me. I had a few tumbles in the straw with young men, driven by pure lust and curiosity. They had all left me wanting, needing, and missing something I could not put my finger on. But nothing, nothing could compare to this. My moans are genuine, not the sounds of pleasure Myrtle fakes for her customers, and my need is burning me on the inside.

Once again, I slowly glide my nub along his throbbing length, and he responds with a well-aimed thrust. His lips suddenly leave my mouth, and I open my eyes in protest. But then the straps of my nightgown slip down, and burning soft lips trail a path to my right breast. I grind against his cock like a woman possessed when his tongue explores my nipple, licking, gently suckling, and grazing the tender flesh while his hips work with mine in some savage harmony. All thoughts and alarm bells are muted in my head. All I want is this magnificent male inside me.

"So beautiful," he murmurs, and the sound of his voice is nearly enough to send me over the edge. "Let me see you, Talysse," he whispers hoarsely, and before the meaning of his words reaches my mind, he is on his knees before me, his hot breath brushing my wet and painfully open folds. "So beautiful." And then flicks his sinful tongue along my slit, pausing at my clit.

Leaning back on my elbows, I bite back a scream. He takes his time exploring me—licking every single rim before returning to my clit. There, he starts working with a maddening rhythm, circling it, teasing it, and gently sucking it in. It takes an embarrassingly short time for me to come undone and fall flat on my back, eyes rolled up, unable to say anything but his name.

"Aeidas," I call, and it is a plea and a prayer at the same time.

When the world around me gains shape again, he rises to his feet, wipes his lips with the back of his hand, and looks down at me with a devilish smirk. Once again, he is the Crown Prince of the Unseelie, tall and commanding, prepared to do anything to get what he wants. The outline of his massive cock is so mouthwatering that I know, humiliating as it is, that I will beg him to return the favor.

But his eyes are suddenly cold again, staring at something behind me.

"It is dawn, Talysse."

I push myself up and look back to the tiny kitchen window. Pink light streams in through the iron bars.

We both know what this means.

At dawn, we become enemies again.

And for the first time in my life, I curse the daylight.

TALYSSE

DEATH IN THE MIST

There's barely time to wash the scent of the nightly encounter off, don my old clothes—freshly laundered and pressed—and head to the courtyard.

The crowds are cheering behind the steel-plated lines of Unseelie soldiers, their armor sparkling in the rays of the morning sun. Banners with the coat of arms of the crown fly in the warm breeze, and the royal couple is already walking among the contestants. Gale waves at me when our eyes lock. The Odryssian man and the blonde woman at his side watch me like hawks. Betting those two have some sinister plan. The prince is there too, standing tall before his knights in black armor, his face cold and beautiful.

Mage Aernysse Stargaze emerges, her white hair shimmering pink in the rays of the morning sun. Silence sweeps the crowds as she raises her frail arms.

"You are all wondering what the next task will be," she says with a dramatic smile, revealing rows of sharp, black teeth. "The Elders revealed it to me during my meditation at the River of Fire. You will be escorted to the Bone Coast, where you are charged with finding the Candle of Azalyah."

A murmur ripples through the courtyard. Not much is known about the Seelie Princess Azalyah, who lived on one of the islands around the Cradle long before the Hex. She loved reading so much that she often spent her nights lost in a book. Someone gifted her a magical blue-flamed candle, which, once lightened with enchanted light, can burn forever. It's been rumored that its light would probably hold Shadowfeeders at bay, but as it's been lost for centuries, nobody knew for sure except, obviously, Aernysse Stargaze.

"May the Elders be with you." Her voice, rasped by the centuries, scares the birds from the roofs nearby.

This voice—

Recognition paralyzes me. This was the voice from the Room of Reflections. So this is what Aeidas meant. The hag has some sinister agenda of her own.

Black, windowless carriages pull over into the courtyard, and we are all herded to different vehicles that will take us to random parts of the Bone Coast.

Finally, I will get to see the sea. Will it sound like the shell Mother owned?

The monotonous sound of the wheels and the hoofs pulls me into a deep, dreamless sleep.

As soon as the carriage comes to a screeching stop, the door swings open, letting in swirls of fog and some odd, putrid smell. There are hot springs close to the Bone Coast if my memories from Friar Ben's geography classes were right. The water has healing properties and there were many bathhouses and beautiful villas here before. Nobody is mad enough to wander this Elders-forsaken place anymore. The hot spring water spills over the even area of the coast now, creating treacherous swamps that swallow the poor shipwrecked who survived the deceiving waters of the bay.

The carriage disappears into the white shroud, leaving me alone. A lonely howl drags into the night.

I shudder. Welcome to the Bone Coast.

The fog is so thick it feels almost palpable, consuming all sounds. How to search for a magical artifact here when I can barely see my own feet?

After a few uncertain steps, a faint sound reaches me. It reminds me of cinnamon-flavored milk and evenings around the fireplace while Father is reading, and Mother is braiding my hair; it reminds me of a certain magical seashell that made this sound when pressed against the ear.

The sea!

The grass beneath my feet gives way to rocks, and when the moon rises somewhere above the mists, my boots are sinking in fine sand. The sea breeze picks up, clearing the fog around me, and the sound of the surf grows louder.

There it is, powerful and endless, foam framing each wave biting the shore. The moon extends a silvery path over the unruly water, daring me to enter. Shipwrecks stretch their bones out of the indigo waters, a morbid reminder of just how treacherous the bay is. Their skeletal remains stretch into the horizon, the distance between them dotted with dark, swirling holes—the legendary maelstroms of the Bone Coast. Nowadays, ships sail protected by multiple magical beacons against the long nights and captains make sure they avoid the dangerous bay. Yet, the currents are so powerful that sometimes they are sucked in and crushed against the razor-sharp rocks.

Debris are scattered all over the moonlit beach: crates, rotting boats, and even some ships broken and torn as if by some unknown sea leviathan.

Maybe the relic is somewhere here? Searching all these piles would be time-consuming. What's more disturbing is that there's no sign of magic around, no light buzzing in the air, no metallic taste in my mouth.

The moisture of the sea air soaks my clothes and hair, and the evening breeze makes me shiver. Nights around here seem to be cold. I'm poking the piles of rubble around, overturning boats, opening rotting crates, and disturbing colonies of crawling, wiggling coastal creatures, but there is nothing. There are many corpses around—skeletons picked clean by the animals, their bones still covered in tattered remains of clothing are scattered around. In the hollowed chest of one of them still sticks a rusty dagger—the last witness of some unknown tragedy. I pull it out, pleased with my find. Its blade is dull but still potentially useful. It's a small comfort in this hopeless landscape.

My feet are already aching when I near the hot springs, their putrid smell stinging my nose. The fog still lingers here, reaching to the middle of my calves. A distant howl sends chills down my spine. This isn't an ordinary wolf. The normal wolves have adapted to the long nights and learned that they should remain silent if they want to live. This beast is probably tainted, so if I don't perish by its fangs, its taint will turn me into one of the Shadowfeeders' thralls. The hair on my nape and arms lifts.

A low growl reverberates through the mist just behind my back, and cold sweat trickles down my back. From the dark veils of the fog emerges a wolf. Its eyes glow a menacing red, its fur hanging in tattered patches, its teeth bared in a snarl. There's a shamble in its step, a certain mindless ferocity that confirms what I feared. This is definitely a Tainted One.

The wolf lunges, jaws snapping shut with a sickening crunch where I stood just a heartbeat before. I roll to the side, the cold ground scraping my arms, breath choking in my throat. I've landed badly and pain explodes in my shoulder, sharp and unrelenting, threatening to drag me under. Every muscle screams as I scramble to my feet, my vision blurring with the effort. The beast is already recovering, its glowing eyes locking onto me.

Panic has never saved a life.

The monster is much stronger, but I have other advantages. All Tainted creatures are husks driven by mindless ferocity. They're easy to trick.

I call upon my magic, and the silvery waters inside me weave an illusion around me to blur my form. The wolf hesitates, confused by the sudden distortion.

My limbs trembling, I hurl an illusion of myself charging at the beast. The demonic wolf snarls and leaps at it, passing through the phantom form and landing in a heap of confusion. Taking advantage of its disorientation, I close the distance, the dagger clutched tightly in my hand.

Now or never.

Atos take it! It recovers much faster than expected, swinging its massive head toward me. That was close! I leap back, narrowly avoiding its snapping jaws. My heart races.

Cold terror courses through my veins. Exhaustion weighs my limbs, and my magic will soon be depleted.

So precious little resources in these Wastelands! Rocks! I crouch and grab a handful of round pebbles strewn between the patches of grass and toss them into the swirls of mist. The beast whips its head in that direction when they hit the ground.

Heroy, guide my blade!

This is my chance.

I dart forward, aiming the dagger at its vulnerable neck. The beast senses my movement and twists, but I manage to drive the blade into its shoulder, penetrating its patchy fur. The rusty metal bites into flesh, and the wolf howls in pain and fury.

The wound isn't fatal, but it slows the beast down. It turns on me, black blood dripping from the gash, its eyes burning with rage like glowing embers. Its jaws snap terribly close to my hand, so all I can do is yank the blade out and flee.

Atos take it.

There's no time for a calculated, planned move. The demon tenses its muscles for a leap.

Summoning the last drops of arcane power, I create an imperfect illusion of myself right in front of it, feinting an attack. As the beast lunges at my distorted image, I dive to its side, driving the dagger deep into its neck, aiming for a vital artery.

It thrashes wildly, trying to dislodge the blade, but I hold on, ramming it deeper and twisting the dagger until my palms bleed. With a final, bloodcurdling howl, the beast collapses, fountains of black ichor coloring the grass.

Breathing heavily, I pull the dagger free, wiping it on the grass before collapsing next to the monster.

This Trial makes the first one look like a walk to the Temple of the Five.

No time to linger around the cadaver, spreading its tainted ichor around. There might be more lurking in the mists around. I push myself up, massaging my sore shoulder, and scan the foggy coastline for any more threats. The rusty dagger, though battered, has proven its worth.

I head to the sea and kneel in the shallow water. Its salty coldness bites my shaky fingers. Its touch—so purifying and fresh, washes away the taint and the aches in my muscles.

The night has grown quiet, only the soothing sound of the waves disturbing the silence. No more howling, and, thank the Elders, no human voices or steps. I splash my face, braid my hair, and sit a little in the silence, trying to calm my still-racing heart. The sulfuric stench of the hot springs grows more intense, it tickles my nose, reminding me it's time to go.

It's probably past midnight as I sharpen that weird sense inside me that can pick up on magic. And aim it at the nearly impenetrable wall of fog. Nothing, just distant bubbling of water and stench that makes my eyes water. My feet feel heavier—I should've probably walked for miles. Each step gets trickier: reeking puddles of green water gape before me. It's the marshland, and one wrong step could be lethal.

The blow to the back of my head comes suddenly and sends me flying forward. The mud rushes to meet my face. Then a starry explosion blurs my vision.

What is the name of—

"Finish her!" a cold female voice commands just behind me, and rough hands grab me, turning me around like a rag doll. The white flashes of light reside, and I face the hatred-twisted Odryssian man, the Warrior Pony Princess's loyal shadow. As expected, she's right there, peeking behind his shoulder, her eyes glittering with malice.

"And here ends the story of the girl from the stables, who thought she could charm the prince," she hisses. The Odryssian raises a rusty sword, going for my breastbone, and all I can do is stretch my left leg and kick him. Hard.

Damn it, I missed the golden spot, but this throws him off for a moment. The blade slices into my left thigh, and I gasp; visceral, mind-numbing pain searing through my flesh. I press a hand against the slash and wince when I feel the hot gush of blood. Clumsily, I roll to my side and leap to my feet. An apocalyptic headache erupts in my head, and my surroundings blur—that blow to my head was really something.

"You just refuse to die, don't you, you flea-infested peasant!" WPP aims a spell at me, which hisses into the fog like an angry viper. Elders, that was close. Summoning my own magic, I seek cover in the thickening mist. It buys me the moment I need to come up with a plan.

Breathe, Talysse.

Breathe.

The last remnants of magic hum within me, ready to be spilled.

It worked with the wolf, it should work with them, too. An illusion of me charging at the Warrior Pony Princess appears; the fog veils make it even more realistic, and the woman swings at my doppelgänger, slicing empty air with her thick stick. Still standing in my original spot, I squeeze my last droplets of arcane energy, creating more copies of myself, each moving in different directions before dissipating into a shower of sparks.

"Tricks and shadows won't help you!" the Odryssian man shouts. Elders! He's somewhere on my right, hidden in the thick mist.

"You know what they would do if they don't find your body, stable girl?" the blonde woman asks. "They'll assume you abandoned the Trial and ran away, and they'll come for your family—" Her face is concealed, but I imagine the cruel smile curling her beautiful lips.

"And we'll make sure they won't find you, Talysse of Nowhere!" The Odryssian chuckles.

Tayna! My teeth grind painfully. I cannot let this happen.

Trying to put some distance between us, I navigate the fog carefully, blending in with the surroundings. A wide puddle of dark water gapes before my boots—it looks like one of the deadly ones that could swallow whole horses. Interesting.

"Fancy armor, fancy magic, and yet here I am, still standing," I taunt. "The Flint still around my neck." Just as predicted, my voice lures the blonde woman, and she charges at me, her silhouette cutting through the fog.

"Don't follow her! She's tricking you!" the Odryssian warns her with a snarl.

Very well. Those two are really easier to confuse than the Tainted wolf. All I have to do is take a step to the side and let the fury of the WPP do the rest. She splashes into the murky lake, and as if orchestrated by Seuta herself, a low, menacing growl rumbles from the mist nearby.

"Tomira! Where are you? The wolves aren't real! Find her! She has the Flint!" the Odryssian shouts, panic rippling his voice.

The thick, reeking water rapidly devours his friend. Her scream for help ends with a bloodcurdling gurgle.

"Tomira? That's not funny!"

Oh, I disagree.

From the shadows, a pack of frenzied Tainted wolves emerges, their eyes glowing with an unnatural light, teeth bared and dripping with black, venomous ichor.

And I know very well they are not an illusion.

"They are not real!" The Odryssian's voice has dropped to a whisper. "The wolves are not—"

Pressing my palms to my ears, I run, stumble, fall, then rise and run again as far as possible from the fountains of red blood slicing the fog and the sounds of crushing bones and tearing flesh and sinews.

When his desperate screams and pleas die out in the distance, I realize that dreadful as it is, his death has saved me.

My heart is in my throat, and my legs are about to give in, but my mind is strangely clear. Blood trickles down my thigh.

Away from the mist, near the sea, I drop to my knees to wash my wounds and come up with a plan. Where am I? The rotting boats and piles of wood and algae appear the same, but this part of the beach is new to me.

The cut is deep and throbs in a very bad way. The salty water makes me gasp and nearly collapse in that foamy area where the sea bites the land with primal ferocity.

Clouds gather above, and the wind howls, whipping loose strands of hair against my face and tugging at my doublet. The waves swell from the depths, hurling themselves at the beach like vengeful sea demons, all teeth and claws.

The sea can be fascinating and terrifying at once. The ghostly bones of the shipwrecks scattered in the bay are still there, but something—

Something is different now. It's faint at first, like the flicker of a dust speck in the sun.

The silvery lake inside me swells. It senses it, craves it, and reaches out to it.

My laugh is long and bitter, like that of a madwoman, and it scares the seagulls dozing on the beach. The flatter of their wings and their outraged cries are swallowed by the wind.

It's there, on a half-sunken ship deep into the bay. Its stem piercing the starry sky, mocking me. The shimmer of ancient magic is brighter now. There, deep underwater, close to the keel, is the candle of Azalyah.

Too bad I cannot swim.

THE PRINCE

THE MONSTER FROM THE DEPTHS

It stinks of sulfur like the hell pits of the Underworld, and death lingers everywhere. Bones crunch beneath my boots, and my senses catch echoes of the laments of the lost souls who found their end here.

Aernysse claims that the Elders themselves give her the tasks for the Trials, but I have my doubts. She is coming up with these twisted scenarios by herself. And she's tasked us with collecting these cursed artifacts because she needs them for something. Something not good. Some trap by the old hag probably to get rid of the throne heir? Surely, my brittle parents are easier to manipulate and would trust her venomous lies. She has tried to hurt Talysse, to wring out my secrets from her, and for that, she'll be punished. When all this is over, I'll have some questions for her myself.

When all this is over.

The thought is poisonous like a viper's bite, it nags on my heart, rotting it from the inside.

My stride hastens, and my eyes scan the desolate coast.

This place is hopeless and lethal, swarmed by tainted wolves, but slicing through them with the Shadowblade is effortless, and I'm grateful for the distraction.

The cool salty breeze coming from the watery graves of Rhessian Deep is invigorating. The waves are ferocious, biting the coast as if trying to claim the remains of the countless shipwrecks back. I let the foam wash over my boots, listening to the music of the surf. The sea will always be there, even after our cities crumble to dust and memories. There's something about this bay, its savage beauty made greater by the death lurking in its depths, all the bones and ruins scattered around contrasting the eternity of the sea. The silver ladder of moonlight over the water is mesmerizing to watch but—

Wait.

My nostrils flare, and all my senses focus on a certain spot in the black water: a faint vibration in the breezy air, a distant call of magic old and forgotten.

The Candle! Too bad it is beyond the shallows, deep into the traitorous water. Maelstroms swirl around it, open and hungry like lethal black flowers. This would be a challenge even for an excellent swimmer like me.

I rummage through the rubble around and find a halfway well-preserved boat, and quickly empty it from the bones and rags rotting inside. The oars are gone, but there is a wide plank lying inside that can work. When the boat is afloat, I jump in and push away from the shore. The dark water around me is unruly, steering the bow to the side and sometimes spinning it as if warning me about the dangers ahead. Not that it would make me change my mind. Rowing with the plank, I go deeper, and the waves are swelling, nearly as tall as houses now. My tiny boat climbs up before crashing down. Not for a second do I falter.

Just like in a battle, my mind is locked in survival mode.

Live through this and bother with strategy and consequences later.

The beach is shrinking, yet some instinct makes me look back. There's someone or something there.

Inhuman, malevolent eyes watch me.

A seven-foot-tall beast stands on his hind feet, his muscles glistening in the moonlight.

Watching. Waiting.

"Woodrick." The wind steals my words.

The Elders are smiling upon me tonight. What a treat! I will get to kill a shifter. Probably one hired to end me. One I want to kill before he finds Talysse.

Make yourself look vulnerable.

Make them strike first.

Moving to the bow of the boat, I place my weight just when it plunges into the abyss of darkness and foam. Just as predicted, it capsizes instantly. Ignoring the biting cold and struggling with the insidious current, I swim underwater in the direction of the coast. Reaching the shallows, I let the surf wash me ashore, then roll on my back and start coughing and spitting water. It's a stupid trick, but then again, Woodrick is not known for his brains.

The show must've been quite convincing, as the stupid beast buys it immediately. He knows he has to be quick and take advantage of my weakened state, as my Shadowblade is well-known and feared.

He may be quick, but it's not enough. I'm on my feet in the blink of an eye, pierce him mid-leap, and step away not to be crushed by his heavy, muscular body. The red glow in his eyes fades, and I scoff, disappointed, before dispatching my blade. I was expecting more of the kingdom's most feral shifter.

The pockets of his tattered pants are empty: no evidence that my enemies paid him. Another disappointment. Letting the sea claim his body, I sit on the soft sand, still panting. Sacrificing my boat for this kill was worth it; Talysse shall be safer now. The thought of her lying dead somewhere on this cursed beach makes me want to spill blood and burn cities, shatter mountains and grab Atos by the throat, demanding he return her to me.

The waves are roaring now, and the pungent scent of seaweed stings my nose. Gathering rotting planks and barrels, I try to tie them with a rope and build a raft. The powerful currents have brought whole underwater forests to the surface. The smell gets more intense—seaweed and salt. Something odd draws my gaze—a straight path of foam leading from the coast to the shipwreck holding the Candle.

By Heroy's beard! What's going on there?

Damned be all Dark Dryads and their powers! Just like us Shadowblade wielders, their magic comes from Atos himself and the night—the Unseelie element, before it got corrupted by the Hex.

But this particular Dark Dryad is clever and takes full advantage of her power over plants. Her inky frame is blurred by the distance but still recognizable. With her hands up, she is summoning thick, twisted vines from the bay depths. They writhe and entwine, building a narrow but relatively safe path over the tall waves.

She's building a fucking bridge of seaweed.

I wave my hand and deepen the shadows around me, my body melting into the gloom, and head her way. When the Dryad steps on the shaky bridge, extending over the tempestuous maelstroms and crashing waves, I follow.

The night becomes a demon, summoning howling winds and crashing waves. The Dryad's lithe figure shrinks in the distance as I set foot on the narrow bridge, swaying precariously over the stormy sea waters. The thick seaweed vines are slippery, and each gust threatens to plunge me into the roaring abyss below. A few controlled breaths steady my step, and the Shadowblade slips into my hand, its dark glow pulsating with power.

The wind is screaming in my ears, salty droplets blurring my vision. The coast behind me fades. The skeletal remains of the shipwreck grow with each step, the magic of the artifact inside calling me. The bridge shakes violently, and suddenly, she stands before me, her eyes glinting with malevolence. She twists her fingers, summoning more roots and vines from the very fabric of the bridge, causing it to groan under the added weight.

She looks like a dark, twisted version of Viridis, her cracked lips stretching into a smile, displaying sharp, blackened teeth. Dark Dryads are remnants of a sinister Unseelie experiment during the war, who tried to turn the peaceful forest dwellers into ruthless weapons; one of the many evils my kind has unleashed upon this tormented world.

The sea itself seems to rise up in anger.

What, in the mercy of the Elders, is that?

From the turbulent waters below, a colossal Kraken breaches, its massive tentacles slamming the surface, sending tons of water into the air. Its eyes are black as a starless night, and its roar echoes like thunder over the crashing waves. Me and the Dryad exchange a look; her eyes are wide in terror, confirming that the beast is not just another trick of hers. The monster is Tainted. It has somehow sensed us—two intruders entering its domain and has risen from the abyss to punish us.

Seems like I'll face a worthy opponent tonight after all. The Shadowblade shifts, morphing into a sleek, deadly spear. I dodge a lash of the Kraken's tentacle, thrusting the spear into its slimy, writhing flesh. The beast roars in pain, but another tentacle comes crashing down, knocking me off my feet. I push myself up before plunging into the black water, and the Dryad resorts to her cursed magic, sprouting sturdy vines that writhe around my feet.

"Not today," I growl, summoning the Shadowblade back to its sword form and slashing through the vines pulling me toward the chasm. The cursed Dryad, seeing an opportunity, directs the Kraken's attacks toward me. She maneuvers herself in front of me and rolls sideways when a tentacle comes crashing down. I manage to free myself from the seaweed and evade it in the last moment, by some mercy of the Elders. The beast is enormous but devilishly fast.

The bridge sways violently. Rolling to the side, I avoid another tentacle and swiftly parry the Dryad's strike. Her arms have morphed into two long, heavy clubs overgrown with thorns. The Kraken, enraged, sends another wave of tentacles crashing onto the bridge.

It's a miracle the thing still holds.

A battle with such odd opponents demands odd solutions. And praised be Heroy, I could be quite creative.

I let the Shadowblade morph into a whip, wrapping it around one of the Kraken's tentacles. With a powerful yank, I use the beast's own strength to pull myself back to my feet. A swift kick to the Dryad's breastbone sends her stumbling. The rewarding crunch of bones makes me grin.

The nightmare from the depths lashes out again, and this time, I'm ready. The Shadowblade changes back into a sword and slices through two tentacles in a single, fluid motion. The beast screeches, thrashing violently and causing the bridge to sway even more. Fountains of dark water, taller than the Beacon in Nighthaven, rise and fall.

Black blood showers.

I got him good.

One more slash will send this cursed demon back to the hell pit that spawned it.

A mad smile curls my lips. Nothing makes me feel more alive than a battle like this.

The Dryad recovers from my kick, dark blood dripping down her chest, and summons another surge of vines to bind my legs, pulling me down. Struggling against the tightening grip, my blade changes form once more, transforming into a swarm of sharp, ethereal daggers that fly through the air, cutting through the vines and striking her with precision.

With one final, desperate effort, she attempts to overwhelm me with a mass of writhing roots and vines, but the Kraken, in its agony, slams into the bridge with such force that it begins to collapse. Seizing the moment, I summon the Shadowblade back into a spear and hurl it with all my might at the Kraken's head. The weapon pierces the beast's eye and sinks into the soft flesh. The leviathan's deafening, final roar rumbles over the water and echoes over the desolate beach before its massive carcass sinks back into the depths.

The bridge, now barely holding together, sways dangerously. That Atos damned Dryad is still struggling to regain her balance. Her resilience is stunning. One swift movement and the Shadowblade is back in my hand. I deliver the final blow, sending her head tumbling off the bridge into the churning waters below.

My muscles and lungs burn as I run toward the shipwreck, the wind pulling me back.

Elders, let that bridge hold a little while longer!

The vines snap, and holes gape just before my feet, but I don't slow down, my gaze fixed on the shipwreck ahead.

I swing my legs over the decaying railing just before the vines disintegrate and sink back into the churning black water. My left foot falls through the dilapidated planks, but I make it to the captain's cabin, sliding on the wet planks. The door is open, and there's something odd about the gloom beyond.

The floor screeches as I enter, and the moldy air tickles my nose. Rags, bones, maps sealed in wax cylinders litter the narrow space, and crabs the size of dogs scatter into the corners.

Now I know what was so odd about this place. The magic inside me swells and quietens.

The Candle of Azalyah is gone.

There is nothing here. While I was busy fighting the Dryad and the Kraken, someone took it.

I roar in frustration and run back to the deck, peering into the dark horizon. No boats in sight. Whoever took it is already beyond my reach.

With the Dryad's bridge destroyed, swimming is the only option to reach the shore. Cursing my luck, I rip a wide plank from the deck and jump into the black waves below.

Every muscle aches, but I press on. The shore looms closer, and with a final burst of strength, I pull myself onto the wet, sandy beach, collapsing in exhaustion.

It takes a while to calm the trembling in my limbs, to regain the steadiness of my breath. Searing pain jolts up and down my thighs, but I push myself back up. Walking the desolate beach, stumbling over debris and bones, I'm obsessed with one single thought, so irrational, yet so right: to find Talysse.

A faint magical shimmer ahead pulls all my senses by an invisible thread.

Am I hallucinating?

The Candle is within my reach again.

I hasten my pace and gasp. On the beach, lifeless, her lips blue, lies Talysse. And next to her, half-buried in the sand, is the Candle of Azalyah.

TALYSSE

THE SANCTUARY

The sea is terrifying.

The waves are roaring, and the salty wind whips my face. The water is freezing. I bite my lips to muffle the chatter of my teeth as I shove the heavy boat into the churning water, every muscle in my body screaming with exhaustion. The oars rattle in their rusty loops, and I pray it can get me across. The tide picks up the boat, and I jump in at the last moment, grabbing the oars.

The salty spray stings my eyes, but the soft magic of the Candle of Azalyah is still there across thundering maelstroms and waves as big as a house. Elders help me. The boat rocks violently beneath me, each wave threatening to capsize it and plunge me into the black abyss below. I clutch the oars with white-knuckled hands, my heart pounding in my chest like a trapped bird.

I can't swim. What the hell was I thinking?

For Tayna. For Myrtle and her little son. For the faint hope of a future.

The deeper I go, the more the waves rise, cold and unforgiving. Every time the boat tips, my stomach lurches, and a scream claws at my throat.

Stay calm. Focus. Breathe. Survive, just like always.

The wind roars like a beast, and the waves crash against the boat with deafening force. Water splashes my face, cold as ice, and I gasp for breath, choking. I try to steady myself, but the boat bucks again, nearly throwing me overboard.

Panic surges. My mind races with visions of the dark, bottomless depths teeming with unseen horrors. The thought of being pulled down, of drowning in the icy blackness, sends a shiver of terror through my entire body.

I will die, and nobody will even know what happened to me. My bones will join the many at the bottom of this Elders cursed bay, picked clean by the crabs.

And then they'll come for Tayna.

And Aeidas—

Aeidas. The thought of him awakens a tiny spark inside me. Gentle warmth spreads from my core. I wish to see him again, to try his scrambled eggs, to…

Nonsense. He will slay me with that terrifying magical blade of his at sight.

I am on my own. And I need to make it to that cursed shipwreck.

My shoulders are burning as I push the oars harder. The stars above me, cold, distant, and impossibly beautiful, seem to mock my suffering.

Each stroke is a battle. The wind fights me, pushing the boat off course, and the waves seem to rise up in defiance, slamming into the hull with bone-jarring force. My muscles ache, but I push through the pain, driven by sheer desperation.

A particularly large wave crashes over the side, drenching me in freezing water. My heart skips a beat, and I scramble to bail the water out with my hands. The boat feels heavier and more sluggish, and the fear of sinking presses down on me like a weight.

Please, please let me make it. The mocking wind steals my words. Who would help me? The Elders, who doomed this world to darkness?

The minutes stretch into eternities, each one filled with the relentless fury of the sea and the ever-present threat of the depths. My breaths come in ragged gasps, my throat raw from screaming into the wind. The waves grow more ferocious as if sensing my hope and seeking to crush it. The boat tips dangerously, water sloshing over the sides.

I pour every ounce of strength into rowing, my palms raw and bleeding. The ocean fights back, a final, desperate assault. A monstrous wave rises before me, and I brace myself, eyes wide with terror.

The wave crashes down, and I know, with crystal clarity, that this is how I die.

It all happens so fast.

The world turns to freezing, dark chaos. The boat capsizes, and I choke on seawater, my mind screaming in panic. I paddle mindlessly the boiling water around me when another wave rises, a mountain of dark water. It hurls the boat in my direction, and something heavy slams against my temple. Probably the oar.

Then I start sinking.

It's all lost.

I beat the darkness with my arms and feet, unable to figure out which way is up and which way is down. My lungs scream in pain, and white stars from the blow blur my vision.

The Elders grant me a merciful vision before my end: two strong male arms closing around my chest, pulling me up with such force, that the last breath escapes my lips. And to my surprise—before darkness swallows me—I am flying. And the sound of powerful wings is stronger than the wind.

*

"Talysse?"

This cannot be. I am dead. Is Aeidas dead, too? Because I am sure he's shaking me awake, his concerned face just inches away from mine. He is warm, smells of sea and magic, his wet silver hair loose, and the moonlit beach doesn't look like Atos's Underworld.

"Talysse, speak to me!" There is a plea and pain in his voice and a hint of rage, a barely concealed promise that the world would suffer should I not wake up. I remain motionless, too weak to move, melting into his warmth, relishing in his wild heartbeat.

He is the type of man who would drain seas, split mountains, and burn cities for love. I see it in the glint of his eyes, in the relentless curve of his lips, in the fluid way his body moves.

Fate is cruel, placing me between him and his dream.

Too bad he is an obstacle to my escape to the Free Cities with my sister.

Too bad the sun will set forever soon.

Someone else has drawn this path for us, has thrown the dice, deciding our destinies, and all we can do is relish the tiny stolen moments before we have to face each other and the inevitable death of one of us.

"Aeidas?" I whisper and brush my knuckles along his stubbed jaw to make sure it is him and not some nasty trick of these cursed lands. A feverish sage flame burns in his eyes as he sees the wound on my thigh.

"Who…" he is heaving when he points at the slash on my thigh, "who did this to you?"

His growl is a promise of a violent death for the fool who harmed me.

"He's already taken care of." A proud smile curls his full lips as he leans closer.

"Was it the pampered Odryssian and his mistress?" He sneers. "I knew you could handle yourself well in…tight situations."

"Like tricking rich boys? Atos's hairy warts, you should see me and Myrtle."

We cackle and drink on each other's warmth.

The beach has gone suddenly quiet, even the wind has found some other place to torment.

We both feel the air shifting. The haze of our breaths mingles.

There. Just a hundred feet away. Behind the decayed remains of something that was once a beautiful siren's face, a magnificent ship bow, now looking like a rotten corpse, eaten away by the elements. The darkness beside it thickens, stretches, and becomes dense.

"Aeidas," I whisper, "Shadowfeeders."

Faster than lightning, he grabs something from the sand next to me and stashes it in his pocket. Then he gathers me in his arms and dashes toward the sand dunes, away from the sea, away from certain death or worse. The wound on my thigh burns, my muscles are jelly, and my head is still spinning.

"You could've just left me there, you know."

"Shut up, Talysse, I'm busy saving us," he spits through clenched teeth. "Are they catching up?" Hot springs' vapors veil the surroundings, but I can still see the beach. Two Shadowfeeders aimlessly wander the empty shore.

"They're searching the beach," I breathe, "they're not following."

He lets out a grunt; the muscles pressed to my body, straining.

The sound of the waves has died out behind us, and the landscape among the thick putrid mist has changed dramatically. The floor is solid rock. Round holes filled with clear water are steaming around, and they look really inviting. Crumbling walls appear from the mist—ghosts of buildings long gone—colorful ceramic tiles still cover the floors. Seems like we've reached the luxurious bathhouses that stood here before the Hex.

My head rests too conveniently in the curve between Aeidas's powerful shoulders and his neck. His skin is covered in a thin layer of sweat now.

"Aeidas," I call softly, and he nearly stumbles, "you can put me down now. I can walk." He obliges, cautiously letting my feet touch the floor, his arms still around me.

"We need to find a place to clean your wound and spend the rest of the night," he says, raking fingers through his salt-tousled strands. Was he also trying to reach the shipwreck?

"Spend the night? I need to get back to the beach—" I protest, ignoring the oddly hot throbbing in my thigh.

"You found the Candle, Talysse." He digs into his pocket and pulls out a simple wax candle as big as my palm. It looks so inconspicuous, yet the arcane streams pulsating around it nearly blind my magic-sensitive eyes. I open my mouth and close it.

"No idea how you made it to the ship and back when you cannot swim, but I guess there is more to you than meets the eye. Here—" He hands me the Candle. "It's yours, Talysse. You nearly died retrieving it."

The silence between us thickens, just like the vapors of the hot springs. Two of the artifacts are in my possession, and all he needs to do is reach out and grab them.

One heartbeat, then another. Nothing happens. His dreadful blade doesn't solidify in his hand. He doesn't strike me. His fingers don't close around my throat.

Will I be fast enough—my magic against his Shadowblade? Should I create the illusion of some tainted wolves and distract him, then bolt into the mist? He cocks his head and studies me, his chest still rising rapidly. Is he considering how to end me? I take a step back, and sparkles of magic fly around my wrists as I brace for an attack.

"Listen!" Aeidas brings a finger to his lips. "There's water running somewhere close. And shelter." Then he turns on his heel and dives into the mist.

The Candle weighs in my pocket. Chills run down my spine at the memory of the raging waves against my boat, the cold darkness swallowing me, and the horror when I couldn't tell where the surface and the bottom were. Then, the feeling of being pulled out and up into the sky, the majestic swings of two powerful white wings. What creature came to my rescue? And how did it know that I am after the Candle? Did it retrieve it for me? Or was this some devious Unseelie setup?

Thoughts for another time when there are no Shadowfeeders after us. I limp after Aeidas and find him standing before the low opening of a cave, his head tilted, listening to any sounds coming from the inside. Soft bluish light filters from the depths, and even my human senses can hear the distant splashing of water.

"There's clean water inside. It's safe. Come on. I want to see that slash." He crouches and disappears into the opening.

Folded in two, I squeeze through the narrow passage. The air gets warmer, and the faint sound of splashing water suggests a hidden waterfall ahead. The low corridor suddenly widens, revealing an underground chamber the size of my parents' dining hall.

Elders.

Glowing mushrooms cascade down the walls, their light casting a soft glow over the cavern. My boots sink into thick, velvety moss that carpets the floor. A gentle waterfall spills into a shallow, oval lake, its clear waters shimmering under the light of clusters of luminous crystals embedded in the cavern walls.

The water looks inviting, almost beckoning me to step in and let the soothing coolness wash over me. Delicate ferns and exotic, glowing flowers line the lake's edge, adding dots of color. I take a deep breath. The air is filled with a sweet, earthy scent, mingling with the refreshing mist from the waterfall.

Iridescent butterflies flutter around, their wings catching the light. The gentle hum of the waterfall and the occasional chirping of crickets make it appear as some serene sanctuary beyond space and time—a perfect haven to heal and escape from the world above.

"Disrobe, Talysse," the prince commands, arms crossed at his chest. "Let's wash and check that wound."

I open my mouth to object, but the throbbing in my thigh and the heat flushing my skin make me consider his words. That slash needs to be cleaned; Elders know what filth was on that blade. Drawn by the crystalline water, all of my clothes land on a pile on the mossy floor. Unable to tell if the heat inside me is fever from the infection or something entirely else, I step into the pool.

The water barely covers my breasts. The warmth soothes my aching muscles. I rub away the sweat and sand, letting my hair float free, before submerging my head to wash away the blood and salt. The throbbing in my thigh slows down. When my face breaks the surface, a splash next to me makes me rub my eyes and look straight into the solid, bronzed plane of his pecs.

"Let me see this slash, Talysse," he murmurs, his eyes reflecting the ethereal glow filling the cavern. I swallow hard and nod, realizing that my nipples tighten painfully and it is all too visible in the clear water. His hands close around my waist. He lifts me and places me on the edge of the pool—my bare arse on the soft moss, my feet still in the water. I press my knees together and bite my lip, breathing heavily, tormented by flashbacks of our moment in the palace kitchens, but his eyes are on the cut slicing my skin. He brushes his fingers along the wound, softly whispering some unintelligible words. Sparks follow his touch, and I let a ragged breath out, stunned by how replenishing the sensation is.

"Viridis has taught me a bit of healing magic. My kind is not very skilled with it. It's a Seelie art, but it worked well on you. Here, take a look." Aeidas's hands rest on my knees now, and his touch sends trembles along my skin, which is craving more. "How does it feel?"

The slash is nearly gone; transformed into a pink line along my thigh. The prickle of magic still lingers over it, but the poisonous hot pulse inside is gone.

I drape some wet hair over my shoulders to cover up. What a stupid move. I think it is obvious how it feels. My nipples are hard, my breasts heavy with need just by watching him nearly naked, so close to me. Every detail of his powerful body is visible in the clear pond: every line of his stomach, every scar, and every stroke of his royal mark. His broad chest narrows down to a lithe waist, and there, something hard and massive is straining his loincloth. Slickness spills between my thighs onto the thick moss, and I look away, embarrassed. Surely, he can smell me. The prince is even closer now, looking at me hungrily, his fang digging into his lush lower lip.

He is my enemy, I remind myself. It would be best if I get dressed and head into the night outside.

Yet nobody would know if I stayed just a little longer. It's only me and him here.

Then I do something shameless and crazy, something Myrtle would applaud. Mad as it is, it feels right, and it's the only way to quench that thirst inside me since that night in the kitchen. I part my knees, granting him a full view of my glistening, wet, bare sex.

"Talysse—" That's my name, yes, but it's followed by a sound that simply cannot be human. Or Fae. It is a deep, bestial growl, a promise for sweet, sinful, violent things.

Visceral things I crave and fear at the same time, no matter that my mind sounds alarm bells, screams how devious and selfish Unseelie are, how this is just a trick, a distraction. He would probably strangle me in the fits of passion, or ravage my body in some dark, unspeakable ways and leave me maimed and bleeding. Their kind is rumored to be...savage.

"Talysse," he repeats hoarsely, flicking his wet silver strands over his shoulders. His eyes are completely black now, fixed on me; calloused fingers crawl up the inside of my thigh, closer and closer to my entrance, leaving a trail of goosebumps and scorching need. My nipples peek between the cascade of wet hair, and his dark, predatory gaze sweeps over them before locking with mine. His knuckles brush over my soaked, swollen folds as he leans in.

I whimper.

Cymmetra, help me.

His kiss is feral, a mix of demand and despair. As if he's trying to claim me while knowing this might be our last moment. Aeidas drinks me and consumes me, his hand at the back of my neck, pulling me in, holding me captive. I let out a moan when his finger circles my slit and dives in, curled in a way that touches something inside me, awakens something primal and savage. He lets go for a second, letting me take a breath, before continuing his onslaught. My hands land on his chest, and I swear my intention was to push him away. Instead, my fingers stroke his velvet bronzed skin, exploring the hard swells of his muscles, then close around his neck and pull him down to the floor with me.

Oh, Elders, help me! The sweet weight of his body is crushing me, and his hot rugged length is pressed against my mound. Moaning shamelessly, I rub myself slowly and deliberately against him, feeling his hardness throbbing under the thin fabric between us, while his finger continues caressing me on the inside. Arching into him, I serve my flesh to his hungry mouth as his tongue circles a nipple and his hand cups and squeezes it possessively. My eyes roll into my skull as his fangs gently graze the tender area.

"So beautiful," he murmurs between licks, and I fist his silky hair, trying to draw him even closer. His finger withdraws from my entrance, and he pushes my knees apart.

"There's no way back if I take this off, Talysse," he whispers. "Are you sure you want this?"

"Mhm," I murmur between his brutal kisses in one final attempt to regain my sanity, "only one of us would make it out of the Trials alive, Aeidas." He freezes and looks at me with an intensity that makes me squirm. Elders, I don't want him to stop.

"There are many long hours until daylight, Talysse." His low voice holds a promise of unspeakable pleasures. My body is straining, pressing against his, seeking his touch. Oh, what a fool I am. Letting myself get seduced by the Unseelie Prince. "Let's pretend the Trials don't exist. Let us just be Aeidas and Talysse here. When the sun rises, I'll be the Heir to the Unseelie crown, and you will be the most powerful human mage I've ever met." His whisper against my ear makes me thrash in his arms, needing more of him. "But until then, let's do what we both desire. Nobody would know. What happens here is our secret." His body is tense over mine, and I know he won't touch me unless I demand it.

"Nobody would know," I repeat, tasting the words and liking them. "Tonight, we will be Talysse and Aeidas and live through this, and in the morning...we'll see."

If Atos breaks the floor of this blessed cavern and declares he'll toss me into his darkest hell pit afterward, I'd still say yes. Unwilling to waste more time, I simply pull on the annoying cloth, managing to loosen it. He lets out another warning rumble when his heavy cock is released, thick and hard, a bead of moisture glistening on its silky crown. Thick veins bulge on its sides, and I gasp, struggling to imagine how this would fit inside me.

"Have you...been with a human before?" I ask, arching up and presenting my dripping opening to him.

"No, but it will fit," he rumbles between licks and grazes. He presses my knees even wider, and I feel the stinging stretch at my entrance. His lips return to mine as he slowly glides in, letting me savor every thick inch of his magnificence.

Stretched to that delicious border between pleasure and pain, I crave more. My flesh clenches around him, desperate for friction, and I greedily grind myself, each vein of his cock sending ripples of pleasure from my core down to every single part of my body with every slow, deliberate plunge. His hand is protectively cupping my nape, his lips trailing gentle little kisses along my jaw and down my neck.

"Are you all right, Talysse? Are you ready?" he whispers, and I moan in response, wet and filled, ready to be ravaged. "Hold on to me then," he rasps a warning and unleashes himself.

His savage thrusts make us skid along the moss. Surely, there will be some scratches and bruises on my back later, but who cares? Sheathed inside me almost completely, he touches some secret spot with every brutal stroke, and I'm edging closer and closer to my release. My hollering gets louder, and he captures my lips, swallowing every sound.

Blissful white light blurs the world around me, and waves of all-consuming pleasure ripple from my core to the ends of my hair, curl my toes, and nearly make me black out. Clawing at his back, I hang onto him, my only anchor to this world, while the ripples of pleasure still echo inside me. Sucking my lower lip, he growls inside my mouth, and shoves himself with one final, savage thrust, and the hot spurts of his seed fill me while my insides clamp around his cock, pumping him dry.

Sweaty and heaving, we collapse in each other's arms, and the serenity of this tiny chapel claims us.

I do not believe in love vows; I've witnessed a change of heart and deception too often. But there are actions that bind two souls, and after this, in the eyes of Seuta, we belong to each other.

I'm the one who awakens first, taking in the music of the water and the insects and his calm breathing. Aeidas looks like an Elder who has lost his way and ended up in this dying world, peacefully asleep in my arms. His warrior's chest rises up and down, his beautiful features smoothened by sleep. The long strands of his platinum hair are strewn on the moss around his head like a shimmering halo. The lower part of his chiseled plane stomach is dusted with fine dark hair, which forms a perfectly shaped dark triangle between his strong thighs.

His thick cock is resting on his stomach, half-hard, and I cannot stop myself from taking a closer look. I lean in, and before shame or any other thought hinders me, my lips close around it. It stiffens immediately, and Aeidas, eyes still closed, responds with a soft thrust. I slide my lips up and down his length, savoring his taste and the sensation of him getting hard again under my caress.

Eagerly, I take him deeper into my mouth, and I can swear that this is the finest dish I've ever tasted. Slickness pools between my thighs, and I slip a finger between them, spreading my folds. Then I do the most daring thing ever: I pull his glistening, bulging shaft out of my mouth and straddle him in one swift motion. His eyes flutter open, and his glowing jade irises darken when he realizes what's happening. I've halfway impaled myself on his hardness, writhing at the completely new sensation. Steely fingers dig in the flesh of my hips as he holds me in place and forcefully sheaths himself into me.

"Do you like that, mm?" His voice is raw and dangerous; I glide up and down his length, shamelessly serving my breasts to his mouth. "Oh, you like it," he rumbles and picks up my pace. Aroused by my daring move, he slams inside me, the sounds of his flesh meeting mine echoing in the cavern.

"Oh, Talysse...you will be my undoing!" he breathes and angles his hips, sending me over the edge. "Let me see you."

Before I can collect myself, I'm on my knees and elbows, my ass and opening, still twitching with aftershocks, right before him. He impales me, looming over my back, his hands around my hips. My knees will be surely bloodied, a distant voice remarks, but it doesn't matter. His skilled fingers have found my clit, teasing it with every thrust. Pleasure takes us both at the same time, our lips murmuring each other's names like a sinful prayer to a deity only we worship.

"I have never experienced such pleasure, Talysse," he whispers when we roll on the soft moss, completely spent. He pulls me in, and I settle into the curve between his shoulders and his neck—a place I favor—and breathe in his scent. The scent of our love-making. Something causes me slight discomfort in this bliss. My bracelet is warm, stinging my skin as if punishing me for what I've just done.

And as if this is not enough, Aeidas gently tips my nose.

"Look, Talysse." He points at the moss around us. Tiny blue flowers sprout and grow at the altar of our passion as if Cymmetra herself is blessing us.

THE PRINCE

THE LAST SUNSET

I wish I had the power to reach up to the sky and slow the spheres above us, as there's nothing I want more right now than to stay in this magical place, holding Talysse. Time has stopped since we entered this serene place, and I'm afraid I'll tear this world apart when daylight comes, and we have to leave.

Our sanctuary.

Carefully, I rise to my elbow and watch her peacefully sleeping in my arms, trusting me with her life. The darkness inside me stirs and reminds me of what's expected of me, the ruthless prince who needs the crown to make this world better. Instead of doing this, I surrender to this weakness, which will be my undoing. Her perfectly shaped breasts rise and fall, her delicate fingers twitch in her sleep, and her pinkish scar appear endearing to me. And this odd Seelie bracelet on her arm, faintly shimmering in the dark—

Probably an item her parents have purchased from one of the traveling merchants who risk their lives poking in ancient ruins. The scent of her hair fills the air, a mix of cleanness and sun-bathed gardens, hyacinth, and the tempting promise of happiness. Of a future.

In another life, maybe, if this cursed world still stands.

They say Elder Seuta brings souls destined to be together to meet again in another cycle, and praying for this will give me hope for the rest of my days.

This is not what a throne heir is expected to do. And I feel deep in my heart what the man in me needs to do. My desire to protect her runs so deep, and it's constantly warring with my sense of duty. A clash that can drive even the strong-minded insane.

The shadows inside me spill out, ephemeral tendrils of raw Unseelie power. Being around her like this is not safe.

Being around her for the rest of these cursed Trials is not safe. Gently, I lift her head, place it on the soft moss, and rise to my feet. I throw my clothes on and, soundless as the shadows I'm made of, leave this Elders-kissed place.

I linger around the cavern, Shadowblade drawn, until the mists around turn golden-rose, and the distant beating of hoofs announces the arrival of the royal guards.

The dawn we were both dreading has arrived.

Only after I see her climbing the steps of the black carriage do I spur my horse and leave.

*

We're to spend the day before the final Trial in a rundown village not far away, a remnant of the days when here stood the magnificent summer residence of the Seelie Kings, a haunted wasteland now. The village is poorly protected, inhabited by humans who grow their meager crops around, too afraid to approach the sea and fish. It is one of the first ones that would fall when the nights stretch into weeks soon. Their mage is an old human, seeing his last summer probably. Something heavy hangs in my chest when we ride down the muddy streets, followed by the haunted eyes of starving children, too weak to run after us.

My parents would cheer if this place is wiped out. It's not contributing goods or food to the kingdom, and its magical crystals could be put to good use somewhere else. Yet they haven't seen the hopelessness in those people's eyes, the dimmed light in the gaze of the newborn a woman lifts to show me, too tired to cry.

Taking one of the gold rings off my finger, I discreetly slip it into the hand of the sad, thin woman with the baby. It's enough to buy her and her child a safe passage to a better place or get her throat slit by the townsfolk. This tiny mercy doesn't make my heart any lighter. S*elf-serving and tyrannical* Talysse has called us, and now I see the point behind her harsh words.

A stone ruin with a makeshift straw roof has been prepared for us, and the servants have done their best to make the place more accommodating with thick carpets, silk, and gold-rimmed cutlery.

"Watch Talysse Nightglimmer's chambers. No one is to enter it, understood?" My knight nods and salutes. Then I grab a bow and head into the Wastelands to find some eatable, not-Tainted game.

Walking the lifeless planes has never felt lonelier. I slay some Tainted wolves and cut through a small horde lingering in the shadows of a scorched orchard. Nothing brings me the peace I need. Flashbacks of what happened in the cave torment me, quicken my pulse, and weigh on my heart. Decision time will be soon upon me.

The five skinny rabbits I leave at the city well would barely keep a couple of families fed, and I vow to myself to find a way to ease these people's suffering later. The sun mercilessly rolls toward the horizon, red as freshly spilled blood, and black carriages thunder along the neglected streets.

Bathed in blood, the night of the final Trial has arrived.

And all I could do was curse the cruel gods who put us through all this.

TALYSSE

THE HORDE

The first thing that strikes me when I crack my eyes open is the devastating absence of Aeidas's warmth beside me.

Aeidas has left. Just like that.

And it hurts more than expected.

Did I really believe that he'd give in to whatever is between us and let me walk out of the Trials freely? He's a Fae, a prince. Would he turn his back on his duty because of a human?

Snorting at my naivety, I grab my clothes. The Candle is still there, and so is the Flint, safe in the pouch around my neck. The prince has kept to his odd code of honor.

Outside, the first rays of the sun gild the mists, and a black carriage is already waiting for me. My muscles ache in a tender, blissful way, and so are other parts of my body.

The road meanders between melancholic landscapes before reaching a sad little village. Tenebris appears like a capital compared to this. People here are clearly suffering, their long faces telling more than a thousand words, and anger simmers inside me.

This is what the Fae did to us: their greed, their neglect, their lust for more power, their elitism. Despite Aeidas's beautiful words and vows to end the Hex, how could

I even consider for a second that he's any different than his kind who caused all this?

My trembling hand rises to shield my eyes but the images of suffering linger, refusing to fade.

The nights are getting longer, and soon, the sun will set forever.

This will be one of the first places to be swarmed by Shadowfeeders and Tainted; that pale blonde girl who tried to give me a flower but got shooed away by the Fae soldiers would be torn into pieces or join their ranks, just like Tayna.

Tears of powerless rage wet my cheeks. The world might be dying, but I still need to win this. Maybe there's hope. Maybe Aeidas's documents are false. Maybe I'd be able to find us a safe island somewhere…

"One small step after the other, Talysse," Father's favorite saying echoes in my mind, just like back then when he was encouraging me to climb trees in the garden. "Only with small steps you'll make it to the top."

For a brief moment, I find myself longing for the simple comfort of my father's arms, his voice reminding me that I'm a survivor. But such comforts belong to another world—a world that no longer exists.

The house we're brought to spend the day and prepare for the last Trial looks like a richly dressed corpse. The Unseelie have done their best to make it more presentable but achieved the opposite. The hastily dragged luxurious furniture, silver cutlery, and golden-threaded fabrics only deepen the contrast between the lavish decadence of the court and the suffocating reality in the kingdom's outskirts.

Two tall Fae soldiers clad in black take me to the doors of my room.

"How many contestants have returned?" I ask, and to my surprise, the bearded one with the soft brown eyes answers.

"It's only you, the prince, and Galeoth, m'lady. Lord Galeoth is wounded, recovering in his room. Seems like the waves crushed him against the beach rocks, and the healers asked not to disturb him."

"Take me to him," I demand, but the soldier shakes his head.

"He's asleep, m'lady. We better let the potions do their work."

I weigh in on my options for a long moment. Sneaking out is out of the question—the stern face of the Fae confirms that. My heart heavy with dark premonitions, I straighten my doublet and enter my room.

This can't be good. If Gale survives this but cannot participate in the Trial, he'd have to face the winner, even if he's in a helpless condition. One way or the other, he'd be slaughtered. And so would be I, if I'm not smart about this.

One small step after the other, Talysse.

To get better chances at this, I need rest. So I throw myself on the hard bed, covered in silk sheets, but sleep is elusive. Sweet shudders run down my body when flashbacks of the past night haunt my mind, followed by the cold, terrifying reminder that these could be my last hours. Memories of my childhood home and the serene face of Tayna finally give me the peace I so desperately need. After hours of tossing and turning, a fitful sleep claims me.

A hard knock on the door startles me awake, and I look through the grid window, rubbing my eyes with the heel of my hand. The day is dying, its blood staining the Wastelands. The old village mage heads to the crumbling two-story house they use as a Beacon, supported by two young men. It's the perfect capture of this dying realm.

The guard with the kind brown eyes enters and leaves a tray loaded with fresh food at the corner of the bed, then leaves without saying a word. Fingers trembling, I pile sauce-dripping meat on a slice of bread and force myself to chew and swallow. The food tastes like ash, and my fingers tremble. Soon it will be all over.

Just after finishing my meal and splashing some water on my face, trumpets summon us outside.

It is time.

The first stars flicker through the weak Blessed Light spell covering the village. Mage Stargaze is already there, her appearance more alien than ever. She looks like a well-preserved corpse who was called back to life and brought some strange knowledge along from its trip to Atos's Underworld.

Aeidas stands there, too, his straight shoulders clad in his usual inky shirt, his Ancestor's Mark visible on his bare chest. Fierce longing pierces my heart when I see him, his silver hair flowing in the evening breeze, his thumbs tucked in his belt.

This cold-hearted Fae bastard. He's not even looking at me. His face looks haunted, his eyes—bloodshot, and his gaze is fixed on the court mage. Steps echo behind me, and—Elders be blessed—Gale appears, limping, but winks merrily as he sees me. He's a bit paler than usual but looks fit enough to fight.

"Remember what I told you back in Nighthaven, Talysse," he whispers as I walk by. No time to ponder over his cryptic words as Aernysse starts talking.

"Pride of Phyllesia, best of the best, welcome to the Final Trial. The Elders have chosen a wise way for you to prove your virtue and devotion. Deep in the Silverbriar Forest lies a forsaken temple built in honor of the union between Atos and Cymmetra. It was a holy ground once. Now, the woods are the playground of Shadowfeeders, Tainted Ones, and other foul creatures. Your goal is to cross the woods and make it to the temple alive. There you must light the sacred fire."

That cannot be that hard, right? Cross a forest, survive, and light some damn fire.

"To win, you'd need to light the fire with the Flint and the Candle of Azalyah." All eyes pin me now, making me shuffle uncomfortably. "And you should be the only one alive of all contestants. There could be only one winner," she continues, her voice rising to a morbid crescendo. "If another one makes it to the temple alive, they can challenge the owner of the objects or do whatever it takes to obtain them. By any means necessary. The king and queen and the grandest noble houses will be present at the temple to witness the final."

Just great. Gale and Aeidas will hunt me for the relics, then fight each other over them if they get me, and the last one standing will light this Elders-cursed fire under the applause of the whole Unseelie court. Or I'll find some clever way to walk out of this alive.

Resourceful, Myrtle called me. I had to be. Death has been breathing in my neck since that day at the gallows, and I've always managed to be one step ahead.

I have a lifelong experience in avoiding death. And I plan to put it to good use tonight.

"Head to your appointed carriages now," the old mage orders, her tone dropping to a raspy, tired whisper, "and make the Elders proud."

Walking past Gale, I pat him on the back, and he flashes me a sad smile. Aeidas is nowhere to be seen.

The ride is not as long as I expected. The heavy carriage rolls to a stop, and the door cracks open. Night air rushes in, along with the whistling of the wind among dead branches and the not-so-distant howling of some tainted creature. My feet sink into a layer of dead leaves and branches.

"We're here. The Silverbriar Woods," the guard announces, and the carriage departs. The sound of the wheels dies out in the distance, and the black mass of the forest looms ahead.

The air grows colder under the black, bony canopy of dead ancient trees. The gloom deepens, and the Shadowfeeders should not be far behind. The moonlight barely filters through the thick branches, but I decide to save my scarce arcane energy in case I have to fight and stumble further in the twilight.

Finding the ruins of an old temple in these dead woods, which stretch endlessly in all directions, seems like a daunting task.

The dry branches beneath my boots crack like bones, and night birds call from the wood depths like lost souls. This is a purgatory. There are whispers that the Elders themselves show Mage Aernysse what they desire to see in the Nightfall Trials in visions she receives while meditating over a gap in the floor, deep in the palace's fundaments. A fiery river runs below it, bringing the roaring voice of Atos himself, the heat and the vapors coming straight from the Underworld. Something that makes me very skeptical. For all I know, the Elders have left this world, dooming us all to a long, painful death.

The trees grow denser deeper into the woods, and I cast my weak light spell. The forest around changes and springs to life, the shadows around dancing. A smile stretches my lips when I notice that life slowly returns to it.

Crickets chirp, low bushes with waxy leaves sprout between the dead tree trunks, and fireflies swirl ahead.

Life.

Life always finds a way.

Many believe that fireflies are a good omen, so I follow them. This direction is as good as any. The heel of my boot kicks something solid. When I bend over to investigate, my fingers brush against the rough, jagged surface of cobblestones, still warm from the sunlight. Finally, a clue and a direction to follow. All roads lead to the temple, Friar

Ben used to say. Whatever lies ahead, at least I am on the way to...something.

My heels are hurting, and my eyes are tired from trying to pierce the gloom. The stars are pacing their ethereal roads, the moon is sliding toward the horizon, and the road swirls endlessly before me. The frog croaking I heard some time ago is getting louder. The road leads to a stone bridge arching over a black creek, its surface reflecting the starry sky. When I am about to set foot onto the bridge, the frogs' choir suddenly mutes, and the black water beneath ripples. Cold sweat rolls down my temples when a dark figure slowly rises from the murky creek.

A damp, musty scent clings to the air, the unmistakable odor of decay and rot permeating everything. I take a cautious step back when something rustles in the tall reed. The stalks of the reed part and a water hag steps out of the thicket, leaving slimy trails on the gravelly bank.

Atos's warty backside!

Water hags—one of the most ancient Fae. Created by Cymmetra to watch over the creatures in the rivers and creeks, it was believed they were dead when the Hex spread over the world. My curiosity wrestles with my fear and wins. They're known to be harmless, but what had the Taint done to this one? Arcane sparkles dance around my wrists as I'm preparing to hurl a spell and throw her back if needed.

The scarce moonlight reflects upon milky white eyes and wrinkly pale skin, strands of green hair draping her bony shoulders. No signs of Taint, just an old and tired Fae, who studies me, head cocked.

"So many in the forest tonight," she hisses through darkened teeth, "a Seelie, an Unseelie, and someone—" She takes another step toward me, and I slightly back up. "What are you?" she asks, sniffing the air through the dark slits at the spot where her nose should be. "Touched by Cymmetra? Why are you hiding what you are?" She takes another step, and chills run down my spine.

"I...I am a human," I mumble.

"A human." She cackles loudly, scaring the frogs who have resumed their concert in the reed. "Fine, keep your secrets...human," she says, pointing at my mother's bracelet.

"Can you," my mouth feels suddenly dry, "can you tell me where the old temple is?"

She stares at me for a while, considering. "And what will you give me in exchange?"

"I don't have much as you see." The lie, nearly visible, hangs between us. No way I'm giving her the Candle or the Flint.

"That's all right." She leans in closer, and the scent of swampy water and rotting algae hits me again. "A promise would suffice. Promise me you will not forget my help when the time comes, touched by Cymmetra."

Well, that was easy. I was thinking that I'd to part with my hair or even a limb, as the legends say.

"Promised." I nod solemnly.

"Follow the old road until you reach the ruins of the tower. An old inn it was, for the pilgrims." She points behind her back, her dark eyes clouded by memories. "Lots of ale and music spilled there in the old times before darkness came. Then you go right. A wider path leads through an orchard with white trees. The temple is beyond it." She cocks her head, watching me.

"Thank you," I mumble, and she glides back to the water. "Wait!" Damned be my curiosity. "How come you're not—"

"Corrupted?" Her black mouth stretches into a gruesome smile. "Weakened, I might be. Be there are forces in this world, older and more powerful than the Taint, dear human." She cackles again. "You, of all, should know that." She measures me up and down again. "I see you carry precious things. Use them well; these woods are swarming with dark ones."

So she knew about the artifacts and yet didn't try to take them from me. A warm, fuzzy feeling spreads in my chest. Maybe the world is not that dark and evil. "How do I use them?" I ask.

She looks at me for a while, and then her bony fingers, connected with membranes, disappear among the algae that cover her body like a robe. A curved dagger lands at my feet, its spotless steel reflecting the light of my spell.

"I hope you put it to better use than its former owner," she says and disappears in the reed, her mad cackle mixing with the croaking of the frogs.

"Thank you," I whisper, then pick up the dagger and wipe it off my pants. Well, that was one hell of a confusing encounter.

Weighing the dagger in my hand, I'm pondering over her words. Of course! Elders, this is so obvious! I scrape some dry leaves from the forest floor, take the magical Flint out of the pouch around my neck, and strike it against the steel. It takes me some attempts, but soon, blue sparks land into the pile of leaves I'm using as kindling. Just enough to light the Candle of Azalyah. Time to see if there's any truth to the rumor that it keeps Shadowfeeders at bay.

It's burning with an unnaturally bright blueish flame, a flame that does not falter in the night breeze. My weak spell dissipates in a shower of arcane sparkles. Raising the Candle, its blueish light scatters the shadows, revealing a surreal landscape where cold, shimmering colors dance eerily. I tuck the blade in my belt and step on the bridge.

"Beware of the dark ones, Princess. If you need safety, come back to me. My water is protected." Half of her face peeks out of the black water, her voice reaching me among the bubbles. Her milky, inhuman eyes follow me as I cross the bridge.

Walking deeper into the woods, following her directions, one thought doesn't leave me alone. She met two others tonight. It's obvious who the Unseelie was. But there was a Seelie, too? All Seelie died in the war or were mercilessly executed by Aeidas's family in the aftermath. Are there any survivors in this area? And which side would they be on?

*

My legs are burning when the ruins of the inn the hag has described appear like a tombstone among the briar. The outlines of the main hall, a large oak growing at its heart now, are still recognizable. The stables are reduced to a pile of charred beams. Brushing my fingers over the old stones, still holding the warmth of the day, I try to imagine how the place must have looked before—welcoming light, music and the smell of roast must have tempted the weary passengers. All gone now, all destroyed by the Hex.

The forest has grown unusually quiet. The crickets and night birds are silent, and even the wind has stopped.

This is not good. I strain my eyes, trying to pierce the darkness beyond the light bubble of the Candle, and freeze. There, behind the lonely doorframe—the only still recognizable piece of masonry standing—the shadows deepen and lengthen. Two eyes, glowing with dark iridescence like pinpricks in the fabric of the world, fixated on me.

A Shadowfeeder!

And if there is one, more will follow.

My feet are faster than my brain. I hold the Candle above my head as branches and thorns smack my face, pull my hair, and tear my clothes. Each wound makes me gasp, leaving a trail of blood behind that the Shadowfeeders and their thralls will surely find delicious.

The path is lost among the thick dead trees. There's only charred soil and branches beneath my boots, no signs of the cobbled road that was supposed to lead me to the temple. I dreaded arriving at the temple but right now, it's a far better option than what's behind me, catching up. The temple would be protected by a halo, as the royal family and selected nobles wouldn't want to miss the grand finale of the Trials.

The sound of running feet behind me grows louder—

By the Elders!

They are a legion. Dozens of Tainted Ones—creatures who used to be human or Fae, now turned by dark blood—are chasing me, trying to cut me off. A mass of darkness follows them, controlling them. It looks as if they're herding me in a certain direction or just toying with me, like a cat with its prey.

The water hag! She said her water is protected. But how to get back there?

I frantically look around while leaping over a thick branch on the forest floor. This part of the woods is unfamiliar. The dead trees are different, their thorny branches clawing at me.

My lungs burn, each breath turning into agony. Sharp pain stings my calves with every step. How long will I last?

Primal, chilling fear threatens to paralyze me as ragged breathing reverberates behind me, mixed with the uneven steps of heavy boots. It's the type of breathing you hear from an exhausted horse. I throw a quick look over my shoulder and—

Black, lidless eyes stare back from a rotting face. Uneven, sharp teeth with pieces of flesh between them snap. The Tainted One is so close it just needs to reach out its clawed hand to grab me. And so many behind it—

Then, suddenly, the ground beneath my feet disappears.

So this is how I die.

Falling and breaking my neck. A preferable option to being torn apart by Tainted Ones or joining their ranks as a mindless monster.

A trunk breaks my fall, knocking the air from my lungs. My elbow meets a rock, and I shriek in agony. The worst happens when I reach the bottom of the ravine and roll to a stop. My ankle gets caught in some roots and twists at a bad angle, and my forehead slams into something hard.

My cry of pain is cut short by unconsciousness.

*

Waking up, I stare straight into the eyes of Death.

By some mercy of the Elders, I am still clutching the Candle tight, its flame unfaltering. Seems like the Shadowfeeder cannot enter the light it casts, a meager protection, but protection anyway. I sense him pacing around, testing its defenses with hungry tendrils. I'm sprawled on the floor, blood from the open wound on my forehead trickling into my eyes. My ankle sends searing, pulsating waves of pain all the way up to my heart.

The Shadowfeeder's thralls have surrounded me in a tight circle; all of them look down at me with their empty eyes, drool dripping from their dark, broken teeth.

Will the light protect me against them too, or does it work only against their masters?

Lips trembling, I slowly reach for the water hag's dagger and curse through my teeth when I realize it's lost during my tumble down the slope.

Great. Everything I have to defend myself against a Shadowfeeder and its horde now is an ancient Candle and my weak magic. Panic claws through my bones, piercing me with icy needles. Their rotting, twisted faces sneer at me beyond the blueish flicker in my shaking hand. The stench strangles me, and their noises—breathing, hissing, jaws snapping, bones cracking, and growling—fill the thick putrid air.

Will it hurt?

Will they tear me limb by limb, or will they open my stomach and feast on my innards while I'm still conscious, feeling every single tear and pull? Or will they go for my throat like a predator? It's doubtful they'd show me this mercy. Tears well up in my eyes at the thought of Tayna.

The seven-foot-tall Shadowfeeder looms over the light bubble I'm cowering in; not a man and not a monster, something in between, a creature of pure hatred. It tilts its head, studying me, those terrifying eyes fixed on my bracelet with some odd interest. I try to scramble up but without success. My beaten body just refuses to oblige.

A large Tainted One enters the light circle, my only protection.

"Elders take you!" I hiss. So the light can hold the Shadowfeeders at bay, but not their thralls. Useful knowledge I'll take with me to Atos's halls. My fingers close around a rock. Not planning on going down without a fight.

The creature stalks me with uneven steps. It still wears the armor of the Unseelie court guard. Long, scarce strands of white hair sprouting from its rotting skin. Its jaw is hanging loose, and the blue magic light reveals its teeth and the black tongue inside it. It takes another step toward me, and its heavy, studded boots are just inches away from my face.

My rock hits it right in the forehead, but the creature doesn't even flinch.

What kind of horrible, twisted death are they planning for me?

Its heavy boot steps on my forearm, and this surprises me. I thought he'd have attacked the hand holding the Candle, but instead, his weight crushes my wrist where Mother's bracelet is. The thrall presses, my bracelet bending and cutting into my skin, drawing a tormented whimper.

The air grows colder, the darkness deepening. The trees seem to close in above me. The forest itself seems to pulse with malevolent energy, each heartbeat a countdown to my doom.

The thralls' breaths grow harsher, more ragged, their eyes widening in a mix of hunger and madness.

The Tainted One's boot presses down harder, and a sickening crack echoes through the night as bones give way. Pain explodes in my wrist, dulling all my senses, but with it comes a surge of adrenaline.

I refuse to die here.

I desperately search for my magic inside. Maybe a throwing spell or some clever illusion can help—

There is nothing inside me.

Only terror and the cold grin of death. That magical lake, which has saved me countless times, is gone.

With a soft click, my mother's bracelet breaks, releasing my aching wrist. It's the first time I am not wearing it since I was three years old. The heavy boot continues crushing my wrist, but the world—

The world around me changes.

Everything changes.

The shadows around me swirl and coalesce, and I realize with a jolt that the bracelet has been suppressing something—something powerful.

Summoning every ounce of strength, I focus on the Candle's flame, willing it to burn brighter. The light flares up, casting long shadows that stretch and twist. The thralls recoil, their empty eyes now changed.

Fear.

They fear me.

I use this moment of insecurity and seek once again my magical lake.

And gasp.

Instead of the tender, moonlight-kissed surface, I find a roaring lava lake of sheer power.

The air around me crackles with energy. A rush of arcane power courses through me, shaking me, transforming me. My magic, no longer suppressed, surges to life and spills free into the night forest. The pain in my wrist and ankle dulls. The shadows retreat, and I rise to my feet, the Candle held high.

Unfamiliar spells find their way to my lips. Blinding lightning bolts shoot from my fingers, tearing thralls apart. Some just, holy rage has taken over my body, and my eyes meet those of the Shadowfeeder. They narrow with suspicion.

If only I had a weapon...It takes just a blink, and I feel an unfamiliar weight in my right hand. I look down and see a blade of pure light shimmering like the sun's rays over the water on a bright summer day.

A mad smile curls my lips as I raise it and take a step toward the tall, shadowy form. The thralls that have surrounded me are reduced to smoking, ichor-leaking pieces of rotting flesh. It's just me and the darkness now.

The Shadowfeeder lets out a low growl.

And it takes a step back.

Suddenly, my body knows what to do. With a shriek that echoes over the quiet forest, I plunge the blade deep into its chest.

The Shadowfeeder snarls, its form dissolving into the gloom. The remaining thralls, their connection to the creature severed, collapse to the ground, lifeless. The forest grows still, the night breeze picking up the stench and sweeping it away.

I look at the blade in my hand and around the desolated clearing where dozens of torn Tainted Ones are lying, terrifying even now.

A night bird resumes its calls in the distance, and the crickets—their eternal song.

Life. Life always finds a way.

No idea what magic has been locked inside me and where it came from, but it found me at the right moment. Miraculously, my body is completely healed.

I grin in the twilight.

It's time to find that temple and end this.

THE PRINCE

LONG LIVE THE KING

The Elders have granted me an unfair advantage in the final Trial: it's not my first visit to the Silverbriar Woods. I have rummaged through the temple ruins, turned every stone in search of something I cannot point my finger on, and camped near the creek of that confused but friendly water hag. In fact, it is one of my favorite places in the Wastelands; it reminds me of how it used to be before the anger of the gods unleashed the Hex.

The dark inevitability of the future rises like a curse from the churned soil, swirling around my riding boots, mixing with my shadows. A blade delves deep into my heart, making each step slower and heavier. Flashes of the moments we shared with Talysse make me halt and lean against a trunk, rubbing my temples.

Cursed be the Trials, cursed be the cruel, heartless gods who demand this, and cursed be this whole dark, rotting world!

What needs to be done is clear. A swift and painless death by my hand is the best outcome for all of us. For the whole realm. The way to the crown goes over her dead body; it's as simple as that. No Unseelie will follow a king who shows mercy to a human. No Unseelie will bow to a king who hesitates to claim his victory and land the final blow to a weaker enemy.

Better get it over with fast. I will go to that temple and give them the spectacle they came for.

Yet I'm still praying for a miracle when something makes me stand still.

Blood.

A trail of it, leading to a steep ravine.

And a stench that's easy to recognize. Tainted Ones.

My rage solidifies, takes shape at my side, and the Shadowblade shimmers in my hand.

Leaping over the edge, I land softly on my feet and press my forearm to my nose. Elders! Over three dozen mutilated Tainted Ones lie around—torn apart by spells, burned or broken. Puddles of reeking ichor cover the forest floor, and their innards already attract the insects. They are lying in a circle around a tiny spot.

There's blood here, too, untainted one. Lots of it. Smeared over a sharp-edged rock, leaving a trail of thick droplets around. Seems like someone rolled down the edge of the ravine and landed here.

My fingers tremble, and I squeeze the hilt of the blade tighter. Traces of a fight, heavy footprints, and—

A cry of despair claws its way up my throat: Talysse's broken, bent bracelet in the dirt.

Elders, no—

I drop to my knees and rake shaking fingers through my hair, wailing like a wounded beast, like someone whose heart is being torn out.

I beat the ground with my fists until my knuckles are a torn, bloodied mess, crying her name, cursing and pleading with all gods until my voice breaks to a mad whisper. A void opens in my chest, raging and hungry, threatening to swallow me whole.

To the darkest hell pit with this world. My pain turns into fury, and I speak blasphemous, dark vows, promising Atos to descend to his halls and rip his throat out should he not release her.

I cradle my legs, sobbing, and try to clear my head.

Talysse's death was inevitable, but an end like this is the worst thing possible. Unbearable as it is, in my darkest moments, I've imagined her death at my hands—gentle, painless, sealed with a kiss, like laying a loved one to rest.

When I close my eyes, her face flashes before me, her soft skin and sweet lips, then clawed hands leave bloody marks over it, slashing it open. Was she torn apart by the horde or dragged away by a Shadowfeeder to be turned into one of them?

A pain so primal and visceral tears through my whole being that all I could do is howl like a beast.

Tears of rage blurring my vision, I check every single corpse, but alas. The only sign of her remains is the broken, deformed bracelet in my hand.

Nothing left of her. And the magical relics are gone too.

Galeoth.

It must be him; Talysse cannot cast such a powerful spell and kill that many. That fucking vulture robbed her and is probably on his way to the temple.

I grind my teeth so hard that the pain sobers me up.

Time to make him bleed. Time to make the world feel my pain.

*

There is a bleeding hole where my heart once was when I reach the halo of magic cupping the old temple. My parents, Aernysse Stargaze, and the most privileged families always attend the Trials' finale.

Crystal clusters and mages feed the magic protecting the ruins, and squads of heavily armed royal guards have enclosed the ruins in a circle. Royal guards, not Shadowblades, I note and smile darkly. My parents, unsure of the Trial outcome, want to prevent my loyal men from interfering and tipping the scales in my favor.

Heartless but understandable. To ignore the rules in favor of your only surviving son would mean weakness, and weakness equals a death sentence in the Unseelie court.

The ruins are circular, like an amphitheater. They surround the shrine where the holy fire has been burning for centuries. My steps echo ominously among the ruins, cutting short the whispers of the colorful crowd of courtiers: a blur of gold and diamonds, complex hairdos and vanity.

My parents sit on thrones of gilded wood just above the mosaic-covered floors, mage Aernysse standing behind them. Toppled statues and exquisitely carved pillars crowd the arena-like surface, lined up by armed to the teeth knights. With the halo crackling above my head and the dozens of torches burning, the light is blinding. A wave of gasps ripples the crowd when I turn to face them, not bothering to hide my darkness and the pain, twisting my features.

All I have to do is wait for Galeoth, kill him, and take what he stole from Talysse. Then the bloodied crown will be mine and my chance to avenge her and make this cursed world a better place.

The sound of steps draws my eyes to the entrance.

Grief must have made me lose my mind. Because it looks as if Elder Cymmetra herself has strolled in.

But no—

This cannot be—

Beautiful and terrifying as the goddess herself, Talysse stands before me.

More beautiful than anything in this cursed, rotting world.

And I am torn between dropping to my knees before her, worshipping her, and closing her in my arms, suffocating her with kisses.

Then reality gets me in its chokehold.

There are no more kisses for us.

No future.

I have to kill her.

I take a hesitant step toward her, as she does toward me, two lost souls trapped by the insidious threads of Seuta, light, and shadow dancing in the final moments of this world.

There's something oddly different about her, more visible now when we're closer. I refuse to accept the truth, though her perfect skin, her eyes glowing with immortal radiance, and her hair flowing in thick curls beneath her waist speak volumes.

Her wild, blinding magic, draping around her makes me pause.

The shrieks in the crowd and the clanking of weapons confirm my dreadful suspicion.

This is no human standing before me.

It is when she summons her Sunblade that I know it with certainty.

Talysse is one of them.

The archenemies we hunted into extinction. Those who refused to lay their weapons at our feet, prolonging the bloodbath of the war and triggering the Hex.

A Seelie.

And Seuta makes it worse—her ragged doublet and shirt display her neck and collarbone—the place where her burn scar once was. There, carved into her skin by the Elders, is her Ancestral Mark.

My knuckles turn white, and the Shadowblade slides into my palm.

"Stand back," I snarl to the knights who are closing their circle around us.

"Prince Aeidas," she says, and Atos take me, her smile makes my pulse quicken and my cock stir, "it's good to see you alive and well."

Even her voice sounds different now.

I open my mouth, my brain unable to produce a fitting response, when an agonizing howl makes me whip my head toward the audience. This was my mother's voice. Our eyes meet briefly when a spear bursts from her chest, coloring the

325

white gown she's wearing deep crimson. Next to her, my father's headless corpse slowly buckles its knees and collapses.

If Talysse—if that Seelie has something to do with this, I swear—

Death comes like a hurricane from the night sky, furious, unbidden, and unexpected. As if the cruel, cold stars shower us with blades, taking my people down one by one.

A legion of Seelie storms into the amphitheater, led by—

I raise my Shadowblade to skewer the damned traitor. When did this bastard sprout wings?

Do all the humans turn Seelie now?

Galeoth—fast and brutal, deals death among my court. He's wearing golden armor, and his powerful white wings carry him with an unfathomable speed. He's barking orders to his soldiers, who sow death among our ranks.

Unseelie blood splashes the ancient mosaics; pleas and shrieks echo through the woods.

I shout commands to the remaining soldiers, regrouping them. Transforming my blade into a spear, I manage to take many of them down. But more and more sweep in from the collapsed roof, death reincarnated as warriors with swift white wings.

The air is thick with the metallic scent of blood. I surrender to the battle fury and lose sight of Talysse, in the eye of the storm, unharmed by the Seelie. Of course, they won't harm her; they're her people. Her eyes are wide, her Sunblade up. She seems as confused as I was just a minute ago.

Galeoth's voice slices the cries and the hollering:

"Get the princess! Leave none alive!"

A princess, I note darkly. Yet she's not flying, so a half-blood then. Worth investigating later.

I stand amid the chaos, the few remaining Unseelie soldiers by my side, bracing for our last stand.

"Hold your ground!" I roar, my voice cutting through the din of battle. "Archers, now! Mages, on three, two, one!"

Hot blood trickles over us like warm summer rain. The archers manage to get many of them, and I'm grateful to whoever organized the defense of the final Trial. But the real breakthrough comes when the mages, including Aernysse, send a scorching volley of death, taking many of them down. The surviving knights greedily take this chance for vengeance, and brutally slaughter them, desecrating this holy place.

Slashing and stabbing, ripping off wings and slicing throats, I slowly make my way to Talysse.

And because the cursed gods cannot make it easier for me, Galeoth lands before me, his eyes blazing with fury. "Keep your filthy hands off her, Prince," he spits.

I respond with a low growl, raising my blade.

We clash, my Shadowblade shifting and morphing to counter each of his attacks. He wields his sword with grace and precision, but my endless training facing the threats of the Wastelands gives me the edge. I parry a strike aimed at my heart, the Shadowblade transforming into a shield at the last second.

"Is she a part of this?" I roar in his face. With a swift motion, it shifts back into a blade, and I drive it toward Galeoth, forcing him to retreat.

Around us, the battle rages. My soldiers fight bravely, outnumbered but not outmatched. The mages send blinding surges of lethal light to the skies, bringing more of them down, to the raised blades waiting to meet them. Drenched in blood and sweat, I feel like my heart has been ripped from my chest twice. I've lost Talysse once, only so that the cruel gods bring her back to me to be taken again. The ruins become a labyrinth of death, the thunder of spells, clanking of steel, and the cries of the wounded and dying echoing through the forest surrounding us. I catch glimpses of my men holding their own, their desperation fueling their ferocity.

Galeoth strikes again, his blade singing through the air. I block it, our swords locking. "Is she a part of this?" I insist, but the cursed Seelie responds with a cruel smile. Now his glamour is lifted, I can see him well. There's immortal radiance in his eyes, and his bronzed skin is glowing. His massive golden earrings, carved with runes, are missing. The realization nearly costs me my life as a sweep of his blade almost misses my shoulder.

"So you've figured out my trick, Prince," he mocks. "My people are skilled in creating illusions like this." He gestures toward Talysse, and a surge of fury makes me strike at him again, nearly breaking his defense. Now, it is my turn to smile. The prick might act all confident and arrogant, but I can clearly see his rapidly rising chest, the sweat trickling into his eyes, and his open mouth gasping for air. I'll finish him soon.

A dying Seelie plummets from above, nearly taking me down in his agony, but I quickly recover my balance, just to see Galeoth turning on his heel and leaping toward Talysse.

Never, never turn your back on a foe wielding a Shadowblade. His cursed wings are in the way of my blade, now shaped as a spear, so I get him in his lower back. Just ten feet away from the petrified and bloodied Talysse, he halts, and his knees give in.

A cruel smile dancing on my lips, I stride toward him, stepping over pools of blood and corpses. This bastard will pay for slaughtering my family. I must be a gruesome sight as soldiers—Seelie and Unseelie alike—quickly step out of my way. With his final strength, he yanks my blade out and takes to the night sky, barking orders to his remaining men.

And leaving Talysse behind.

My soldiers rally, cutting through the remaining enemies on the ground with renewed vigor. I turn, the Shadowblade back in my hand, transforming now into an ax, cleaving through the winged warriors that dare approach.

They are retreating, bidding us with a deadly volley of arrows from above. I leap toward Talysse, but she's unharmed.

The battle is over. The legion of Seelie Fae lies slaughtered among the ruins. I stand amidst the carnage and the scent of blood, breathing heavily, my body aching, but it's my heart that's hurting the most. The few soldiers that remain gather around me, their eyes filled with awe and respect.

The Shadowblade shifts back into a sword, its dark surface gleaming in the light of the spell above us.

Darkness pools at my feet. The gloom inside me is growing, tainting everything. The ruins have grown quiet again.

I look around, taking in all the bodies and the pools of blood, my parents among them, along with the best of our court. Then my eyes land on Talysse, the only Seelie still standing there, and something breaks inside me.

I cast a spell that sends Talysse flying. She lands on her back, her head hitting the floor. "Chain her tightly. Make sure she cannot summon that cursed blade. I need to know how a legion of Seelie entered our lands, as all these traitorous bastards should've been dead decades ago. And her too." I turn around and point at Aernysse Stargaze, standing bloodied and confused next to my dead parents. "She failed to notice that there were two Seelie right under her nose. In our court. Chain them both and drag them to the Pits."

The soldiers are all on their knees, their fists pressed to their chests.

"Long live the king," one shouts. "Long live the king!" The rest pick up, and soon, the ruins shake with their roar. I take in all the death around: the blood-soaked ancient tiles, the mutilated corpses, the sliced white wings of our enemies, and the severed heads, the smell of blood, steel, and magic in the air. My gaze follows the unconscious body of Talysse, being dragged away.

"What are your orders, Your Majesty?"

Death and ruins are such a befitting decorum for the beginning of my reign.

I straighten my shoulders and dismiss my blade.

The world is about to change.

"I declare this Trial over."

TALYSSE

THE PITS

The smell of old stone and mold hits me first, pulling me back to reality. Then come the distant sounds. Silence so thick and consuming it distorts reality, broken only by the occasional drip of water and the muffled voices of guards above. I'm lying on the cold, wet rock, its surface digging into my skin.

The dungeons in the Unseelie palace are legendary. Built to contain the rebellious archons—enormous creatures who helped the Elders shape the world but then rejected them and sought to destroy their creations. The archons are long dead, turned to stone and then to dust, but the walls designed to withstand their brutal strength still stand.

I crack an eye open, cautiously taking in my surroundings. A single sconce flickers beyond the rusted bars, casting dim light into my cell. I try to roll over and sit up, but chains pull tight, restricting my movements. With a grunt, I manage to sit, assessing my injuries.

My mouth is parched, but the scratches that once marred my skin are gone. No open wound on my forehead, and oddly, no headache either. I glance down at my torn shirt, expecting to see the pink scar that's marked me for years. But it's gone too, replaced by smooth skin threaded with strange purple lines, like—

"It's an Ancestral Mark, like Aeidas's," a voice interrupts my thoughts. Desmond steps into the light, his small eyes gleaming. "I brought you cookies. I'll fetch some water, too, but I couldn't carry everything at once." The rat busies himself, untying a bundle he's dragged along, while I stare at my skin, struggling to process his words.

"Desmond! What happened? I am so confused. There was a Shadowfeeder in the forest, and they broke my bracelet, then everything changed. I made it to the temple, but something horrible happened—"

"Here, Talysse, let me put it in your mouth—" Desmond interrupts, pushing a piece of cookie at me.

I part my lips to protest, but he takes this opportunity and stuffs the cookie in my mouth.

To get out of this mess, I need my strength. Even if it means being fed cookie crumbles by a rat in a dungeon from the dawn of time. This all looks like some mad dream. A part of me clings to the sweet delusion that Mother would walk into my room carrying hot pancakes, plant a kiss on my forehead, and ask me how the night was.

It passes quickly. Mother is dead. Tayna will have an uncertain fate, and—

"Aeidas?" I ask, chewing thoughtfully.

"He's busy arranging the funeral for his parents and his coronation."

A strangled sigh escapes me. The image of Aeidas's face, twisted with pure hatred as he casts that spell, flashes through my mind. It will haunt me forever.

"Did he ask about me?"

The rodent is suddenly too busy brushing cookie crumbs off his brocade jerkin, ignoring the question.

"And Galeoth—he has wings. He is a Seelie!"

"Oh, sweetheart," the rat covers his snout with disturbingly human-like paws, "you don't know?"

"That he's a Seelie posing as a human? Of course I don't—"

"That you are Seelie, too. And of royal blood, judging by your Mark. A descendant of the bloodline that triggered the Hex."

The brittle crust of denial shatters instantly, and the world spins around me. Everything I knew—about myself, my family, my past—is a lie.

Seelie Fae were hunted into extinction years ago.

My parents harbored two of the last ones.

There's no royal Seelie bloodline anymore. Their last royal family was slaughtered in the last war.

This cannot be.

And how...how was it possible to hide this?

Always hide your treasure in plain sight was one of my father's most beloved sayings. I can nearly see him sitting in the chair before the fire in his study, rubbing the large ruby ring with our family symbol. A phoenix. The same symbol carved above the fireplace and the entrance door.

Always hide your treasure in plain sight. Faint memories resurface. Mother's teary eyes when she grabs the tin pot with milk from the stove and takes a step toward me, murmuring some words that make me sleepy. The agonizing pain when hot milk spilled on me.

Her hurried hands washed me with cold water, removing my beloved necklace—the necklace I've been wearing since I was a babe, its colorful large beads carved with unknown symbols. Then she slipped the then-too-big bracelet above my elbow. Long days in the bed followed, her humming a song beside me, forcing me to drink gallons of bitter tea that made me tired...

This explains it all. The hatred burning in the prince's eyes, that raging magic burning inside me after the bracelet was destroyed. I squirm in the chains, trying to reach that bottomless fiery lake of power to cast a spell, but nothing happens.

"The chains are warded against magic," Desmond says, shoving another piece of cookie into my mouth. And I am too confused to resist, my mind too busy rearranging the details from my past.

Has all my life been a lie? Are my parents really my parents?

"How—" I start.

"You seem half-blood. No wings." He scurries down my back to check, then climbs back up. "That bracelet of yours was glamouring you. Your folks knew your true nature and were protecting you. My guess is a Seelie royal escaped the purging and got involved with humans. Halflings are rare—" he continues, assuming a lecturing tone, "human and Fae pregnancies have different durations, and babies rarely survive. Mothers rarely survive. A Fae female carries a baby for years, while humans need just nine months, so you see, things can get easily messy—"

"I know, Desmond," I interrupt, impatiently struggling against the chains. "But there should be answers somewhere. If I can get home, search my parents' house, there must be something."

Desmond's snout droops, and his usually lively tail hangs still.

"I am afraid that's not possible, Talysse. You know how Seelie are treated here."

The realization hits me like a blow. Surviving the Trials doesn't guarantee anything. I might be tortured and killed like the rest of the Seelie.

"What does he intend to do with me?" I finally ask. Desmond shifts nervously.

"I have to go. Someone will answer your question soon. Eat your cookies. You'll need your strength."

His tiny form slips through the cell bars, leaving me alone with my thoughts. But I don't need an answer. I know what happens to captured Seelie. Everyone knows the stories. Executed in the most horrific ways, forced to fight monsters or tossed to the Tainted Ones for sport.

I can't let it end like this. Not after everything—Tayna, Myrtle, my parents.

It can't all be for nothing.

I pull at the chains, twisting painfully, but it's futile. The Unseelie knew what they were doing. When all seems hopeless, you rest. You gather strength. And you wait for the right moment to strike.

Curling up on the cold, damp floor, I let my thoughts race, searching for any scrap of information, any detail I might have missed, that could lead me to freedom.

THE PRINCE

THE SCAFFOLD

I clutch the pieces of the broken bracelet that Talysse had been wearing for most of her life. The spell weaved into it was exquisite—powerful but refined, designed to conceal the identity of the bearer, the lines of the magical symbols carved with perfection. Skillfully crafted for deceit. Something the Seelie excel at.

The pale light of the wax candles makes my parents and my brother next to them appear as if they're in deep, serene sleep. Not butchered by traitors. The air in the crypt is heavy with the sweet scent of the piles of wilting flowers and the incense. My kin. Dead because I couldn't protect them. The powerful, cruel, and despotic king and his loyal, silent queen. My brother, the heir, poisoned, his murderer still out there, unpunished. The darkness festers inside me, gripping my heart, flowing through my veins, tainting my very essence. It grows more powerful each day, but I still remain loyal to my purpose. To my plan to end the Hex.

The bracelet pieces slip back into my pocket as I climb the steps, leaving behind the crypt and the remnants of my old life.

The too-kind prince, the Wildling, remains there, laid to rest among the dead. The dead he was too weak to protect.

From the carved crypt door emerges a king with a calloused heart who'd do whatever it takes to achieve his goal.

To protect his people.

In that, I shall never fail again.

My steps echo among the empty corridors, mingling with the howling of the mourners in the palace above. It's time for justice. And I'll deal with it in the swift, brutal way typical for my kind.

*

I have taken my time to plan the execution in the slightest detail. It will happen at the Traitor's Gate, where the light of the Halo is dimmed. Beyond the walls are the Wastelands and all the horrors dwelling in them.

I was receiving reports that the court was infiltrated by an unknown enemy, but even after days of torture, Aernysse Stargaze didn't break. She claimed she was innocent. Well, I happen to have a different opinion.

The halo has just wrapped the city in its tender golden light, and the cold stars flicker beyond it with mocking indifference.

The freshly cut planks of the wooden scaffold and the banks for the nobles surrounding it still trickle resin. The spectators are already in their seats. I have selected the attendees carefully. Only the cruelest schemers, the rebels, and traitors sit on the wooden benches, probably interpreting my invitation as a warning. Or as a sign of benevolence. They are enjoying their refreshments, oblivious to what's about to come, eagerly awaiting the bloody spectacle. I climb the rough-hewn wooden steps to the scaffold with my Shadowblades knights at my side. The murmurs muffle. We must be a gruesome sight. All of us clad in full black armor, our blades on display.

"Bring in the accused!" I rumble, and the guards drag the shackled mage to the scaffold. Gods, she's a pitiful sight. Bloodied and bruised, wearing a tattered hemp shirt, she's missing fingers and an eye and has to be carried to the scaffold. Older than any other Unseelie in this court, everyone can clearly see that life is leaving her. I'll grant her a quick death out of respect for all the years she served my family. A more merciful ruler would've exiled her for her negligence in missing two of our sworn enemies right under our noses. But this mistake has cost the life of the royal family. Her existence would still be a threat, and I don't plan on wasting my precious resources on watching the old witch and guessing what she's up to. I have enough enemies as it is.

"You are accused of neglecting your duties to keep our kingdom safe. You failed to detect the presence of two Seelie Fae in our court, one of them of royal blood. This failure brought the demise of my parents. For this, I sentence you to die." My voice is loud and clear, and the audience trembles in blood-thirsty anticipation.

One of my knights takes a pair of scissors and cuts her hair short; the snipping is the only sound echoing the tall city walls. Petrified, Aernysse is forced to her knees, and I stalk toward her, blade drawn.

"Mercy..." her bloodless lips mumble.

Mercy means weakness. Something that died with my parents in that temple deep in Silverbriar Woods. Numb, I raise my Shadowblade.

A swift swing and her head rolls down the scaffold to the front rows of benches, and a tall crimson beam spurts from her neck. Then, her body collapses on the planks with a thud, and the crowd explodes in loud cheering. One of the nobles in the front row lifts the severed head and spins her in some macabre dance, making me wince with disgust.

What a fine selection of spectators I've made. This is the worst of my court. The blackest souls, the heartless monsters, the unscrupulous opportunists.

The darkness beyond the city walls grows thicker. New refreshments are served. The chamberlain was ordered not to be savvy on the wine. The crowd is exchanging rude jokes, and a troupe of artists climbs the blood-soaked scaffold, one of them dressed as Aernysse, and performs a play of the mage's arrival in Atos's Underworld.

The audience is roaring with laughter, the wine flows like a river, and all of them look to the street leading to the palace for the next execution planned for tonight. They lick their lips, eager for the highlight of the night.

The cheer and the scent of blood have surely attracted Shadowfeeders and Tainted outside, but the halo and the tall walls keep them at bay.

The night is already pitch black, and I can hear grunts, wails and dragging steps on the other side of the city walls; and scratching on the gate. The guards on the parapet are getting nervous, shouting commands, and shooting at something below.

"Bring in the Seelie!" It's a struggle to maintain my impassive and imperious demeanor.

I avoid looking into Talysse's eyes when they bring her before me, but the sight of her tattered clothes and the bruises from the heavy shackles on her arms make me wince. She pales a little when she sees all the blood and Aernysse's lifeless body but straightens her shoulders and climbs the steps to her doom with dignity. Her Ancestral Mark across her collarbone is clearly on display—I narrow my eyes, memorizing every single detail of it. For a split second, our eyes lock.

"Talysse of No Name, you are accused of high treason, conspiring against the crown, resulting in the death of the royal family and many Unseelie casualties. I hereby sentence you to death." Even the wind, sweeping petals, and dry leaves along the night streets, has died out. The crowd holds its breath.

"I have a final wish, Aeidas," she speaks boldly, drawing a wave of protests and insults from the audience. Chicken bones and half eaten fruits aimed at her shower the scaffold. I ignore the disrespectful way she addressed me and nod, encouraging her to speak.

"I want to meet my end without chains," she says.

Oh, Talysse.

It's hard to swallow my chuckle. You're making it so easy for me. I stride toward her, the keys to her chains in my pocket. Leaning in, inhaling this maddening scent of hyacinth and sunshine one last time, I unlock the heavy padlock. The chains drop with a deafening rattle.

"Be ready, Talysse," I whisper in her ear, "be ready to run."

The crowd grows eerily quiet, all eyes following eagerly my moves. Everyone was murmuring that I was infatuated with her, that I wanted her for my concubine. Many have seen us together. The spectators leave their benches and creep closer to the scaffold, eager to see not only blood spill but a death sentence to an impossible love. They want to see my heart break.

I take a step back, taking in her inky hair braided in a crown, the curve of her neck, and the delicate, sharp tip of her ear peeking between the strands. My knights disperse among the crowd as I raise my blade.

The crowd is confused. Instead of looking at the kneeling Seelie before me, I look up to the sky.

Three...

Two...

One...

The bell of the temple of Heroy rings three times, marking midnight.

Then, just like that, the light of the Beacon flickers and dies.

The city plunges into darkness.

The first Shadowfeeders take care of the guards, and the gate swings wide open for the horde to enter. I smile darkly. I've just made the demons do my work.

While Tainted are ripping the audience at my feet to ribbons, I help Talysse up.

Her Sunblade appears immediately, and she looks at me with those cornflower petals eyes, unsure what to do.

"Run, Talysse. Take the Guardsmen's door." I point my blade at the low, inconspicuous gate away from the turmoil. "And make sure we never cross paths again." Dark threats drip from these words.

I must restrain myself, so overwhelming is the need to run after her. My body cannot bear being away from her. She runs, taking away with her the last remains of the man I was before, leaving a cold, callused shell behind.

I watch her hack her way to the Guardsmen's tower with that beautiful and terrifying blade of hers.

Elders, she's a sight to behold. Then, I turn on my heel and throw myself in the battle.

TALYSSE

ESCAPE

Death is constantly on the back of my mind since the day my parents died.

On that day when everything was lost, I stood for hours at the gallows, long after everyone left. My eyes were fixed on my parents' lifeless bodies, dangling in the wind like rag dolls. I have searched that magical pool inside me for any spells to bring them back to life; I prayed to all Elders, and I cried. Without any success, of course. I was a terrified child, not a necromancer. So, I just stood there and watched helplessly their faces change, turn dark, and the crows get cockier. One landed on my father's shoulder, and I chased it with a rock, but it returned with friends.

The vision of my own death crept into my young mind back then. When Friar Ben came to take me to the orphanage later that night, my first question was: "What happens to people when they die?"

He gave me the standard tale of Atos's Underworld that looks a lot like our world, but the good people are having good lives, and the bad ones are going to hell pits teeming with demons, but somehow, this story has never been satisfying for me.

Well, tonight, I am about to find out.

I step onto the scaffold, nearly slipping on the pools of blood of the Unseelie court mage. Her headless body, soaked in crimson and tossed aside like a broken toy, demonstrates what awaits me.

This is when the terror strikes, its sticky tentacles wrapping around my feet, nearly making me stumble. I have always had different scenarios about my own end, but I have never imagined that it would be by the hand of the man I feel so drawn to.

Yet the Elders, cruel as they are, seem to have other plans for me.

I struggle to realize what is happening when hordes of Tainted swarm the nobles around the scaffold.

"Talysse," the prince calls me back to my senses, "run, Talysse. Take the Guardsmen's door." He points at it, and I nod, still processing that turn of events.

When life gives you sour apples—

You bet I'll make some fine apple pie out of this second chance.

The mysterious blade that seems to appear when I need it slips into my hand, and I hop off the scaffold. The Tainted are busy pulling out the intestines of a courtier two feet away to notice me, and just like that, I make it to the small, inconspicuous door in one of the towers.

THE PRINCE

THE PROPHECY

Between two sword strikes I realize I'd rather face all the torments of Atos's hell pits and laugh at all the inventive torture methods of his demons than lose her again. Seelie or not.

Seelie or not, she's the light of my darkness, the moon of my night, and the thought of seeing her body, headless and limp like Aernysse's, is simply unbearable.

So, I gladly ripped my chest open, took my heart out, and placed it in her palms. Now, she's free to take it wherever she wishes.

For me, there's only one hope left, that we'd meet in another life, as Seuta promises to souls that are bound. Because after this bracelet cracked, so did the wall between us.

We're connected. We're mates, bound to search for each other and breathe for each other in all lifetimes. Too bad the cruel gods made us implacable enemies, and for that, I'll curse them to the end of my days.

I look around as if awakening from a dream. Hordes are ravaging the streets, killing everything in their path. Shadowfeeders spawn in the dark alleys.

It's time to wipe that stupid grin off my face and save my city.

The halo flickers above me and springs back to life, just as I ordered it, confusing the enemy and herding it into dark corners.

I bark orders to my knights, and we go hunting the dark ones.

*

The pavement is still slippery with blood, and mourning cries echo from each and every corner, but there is no time to lose.

My coronation is not a celebration. It's a funeral feast.

I enter the throne room, followed closely by my men. Mourning red silk sheets drape the black walls, the lights in the halls dimmed so the souls of the dead find their way to Atos's Underworld and not get lured back to our world by the light. The priests and priestesses, clad in gold and red, await me at the feet of Father's throne.

Chiron, the High Priest of the Five, nods at me solemnly when he sees me approach. My eyes are fixed on the tall, spired crown lying on a crimson pillow. Red is everywhere around me in these days. The priests wince when I loom over them, but Chiron greets me without faltering. He was Aernysse's enemy, and I've done him a great service tonight.

The holy people chant their prayers and throw more incense in the burners around.

I have no time for this nonsense.

I grab the crown from the pillow, my hands still smeared with Tainted blood. Without waiting for Chiron to finish the blessings, I place it over my head and immediately feel the weight of it. Forged by star metal, encrusted with crystals from the throne of Atos himself, it's loaded with memories of triumph and suffering. I climb the steps to the throne and sit down without hesitation.

"Chiron." The old priest startles, still mumbling prayers and blessings.

"Yes, my lord," he says, avoiding to look me in the eye.

"Can you read the Elders' tongue?"

He nods.

"Then tell me what this means." In my haste, I summon the Shadow blade as a dagger and quickly carve the symbols in the flesh of my forearm. An exact copy of how mine and Talysse's Ancestral Marks would look side by side. I know that the complete symbol on my shoulder stands for Unseelie—my people, and hers—for Seelie. But together with the symbol below, it didn't form a coherent phrase. It was the beginning of something about the Hex, but cut in half, and nobody could figure them out. But now they appear complete when the two marks are brought together.

"The Sacred tongue uses single symbols to convey complex meanings." The old Fae is studying my carved flesh, unbothered by the ruby drops dripping on the throne's armrests. This cursed chair had been washed in blood many times and had witnessed more than one royal head rolling down the steep carpeted stairs.

"I am not here for a lecture, priest," I growl, my impatience growing. Whatever secret our skins are about the reveal, I know it is of utter importance for my goal.

"This part says Unseelie." His crooked finger taps on my part of the Mark, something I know very well, and I pinch the bridge of my nose. Elders help me so that I don't slit his throat in my fury. "And this stands for Seelie," he concludes, and I am already raising my blade.

"Have you seen what happened to Aernysse?" I ask, and he pales. "Then be quick and tell me what the rest stands for. And make sure you tell the truth if you don't want to enter Atos's Underworld in pieces. Tiny pieces."

"When brought together, the last two symbols mean—forgive me, Your Majesty—the first one stands without a doubt about the end of the Hex, and the last one could be interpreted as a union." I glare at him, and his throat bobs under the parchment-like skin.

"Unseelie and Seelie are to end the Hex with a union—" he squeaks.

"What in the name of the Five means that? Does it mean I have to sign a trading agreement with the remaining Seelie? Because, like we've been shown in the last days, it seems to be more of them than we thought," I ask bitterly.

"Union can be interpreted as in matrimony, Your Majesty. And Unseelie and Seelie can refer to the royal bloodlines, not the whole kind."

"Matrimony like…marriage?" I ask, dumbfounded. I lack the sophisticated education of his kind, and if he's mistaken, I will crush every single bone in his body. Will make it heal and then do it again.

"Unseelie and Seelie…to end the Hex through union," Chiron stammers, his voice trembling. "A union by matrimony, Your Majesty, witnessed by the Five."

I shoot to my feet, my fingers closing around his throat.

"Are you sure of what you're telling me?" I rasp, lifting him. His feet dangle beneath his golden-red robes, and his slipper lands at the feet of the throne.

"I...I swear in my life, Your Majesty. Ask anyone proficient in the sacred tongue, and they'll confirm. It's clear as daylight."

I stagger back onto the throne, releasing the old priest, who rolls down in a mess of gold, crimson, and confusion.

The Hex can be lifted when the two royal bloodlines are united. By marriage.

My roaring laughter, so unfitting of all the death around, startles my knights, the priests, and all the courtiers who gathered to witness the ceremony. Surely, they think me mad.

But I don't care.

I have a bride to catch.

TALYSSE

EPILOGUE

The sound of the battle raging on the streets of Nighthaven muffles when the heavy oak door of the Guardsmen Tower closes behind my back. A single wax candle, placed on a rough table, bathes the room in warm light. Guards' rosters are drawn with chalk on the walls, and there's another door at the far end of the room. It's slightly ajar, and the shimmer of the halo filters through the gap. They've made the Beacon work again.

I quickly cross the room, massaging my numb wrists, feeling the weight of the past hours settle into my bones. I nearly stumble upon a backpack on the floor.

"For Talysse Nightglimmer," a note placed on top of it says.

I hurriedly rummage through its contents: bread and dried meat, cheese enough to last a week. When my fingers close around the Candle and the Flint, my lips tremble. And there's gold, lots of it, shiny Unseelie coins that can buy me and Tayna passage to wherever we wish. A hooded cloak of thin wool hangs on the door handle. As I pull the hood low over my face and lift the backpack, a sudden shuffle from the side pocket startles me.

"Can you please be more careful? My bones are very sensitive," a tiny voice complains.

"Desmond? Why are you here?"

"Someone has to keep you safe, Talysse. You're not an expert in traveling the Wastelands—" the rat declares, his paws smoothing his whiskers.

"Oh, and you are?"

"Aeidas took me on some of his expeditions, and he loved sharing his stories with me. They call him the Wildling, you know. He's changed, Talysse." His voice sounds troubled now. "And I'm not sure if I can stand by and watch this."

"Are you comfortable there?" I ask, opening the door and stepping into the night. The idea of having an experienced companion in the long nights ahead starts becoming appealing.

"As comfortable as it gets. So where are we going to?" Desmond positions himself comfortably in the backpack pocket.

"Home. To get my sister and find a safe place for us somewhere."

The night is quiet; the crickets have resumed their songs. No sign of Unseelie patrols or any Shadowfeeders, except for some Tainted corpses scattered in the field at the feet of the city walls.

"Fine. Let's go see if those cats are really the size of lynxes," the rodent agrees, and we head into the Wastelands.

The Halo of Nighthaven fades behind me. The stars chart their mysterious maps above us, guiding us to the unknown, and somewhere ahead, fireflies dance in the night.

End of Book 1
Talysse's adventure continues in Book 2 of The Elders' Hex Series: The Shadow and the Firefly

Printed in Great Britain
by Amazon